PRAFULLA MOHANTI

CHANGING VILLAGE, CHANGING LIFE

With drawings by the author

VIKING

VIKING
Published by the Penguin Group
27 Wrights Lane, London W8 5TZ, England
Viking Penguin Inc., 40 West 23rd Street, New York, New York 10010, USA
Penguin Books Australia Ltd, Ringwood, Victoria, Australia
Penguin Books Canada Ltd, 2801 John Street, Markham, Ontario, Canada L3R 1B4
Penguin Books (NZ) Ltd, 182–190 Wairau Road, Auckland 10, New Zealand
Penguin Books Ltd, Registered Offices: Harmondsworth, Middlesex, England

First published in Great Britain by Viking 1990

Printed in Great Britain by Butler & Tanner Ltd, Frome and London

Typeset in 11/13pt Lasercomp Old Style

A CIP catalogue record for this book is available from the British Library

ISBN 0-670-823058

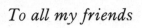

To all my friends

CONTENTS

ACKNOWLEDGMENTS

Kingsley Martin, who said that if I ever wrote a book about my village he would be the first to read it. Jim Richards, who encouraged me by accepting my article for the *Architectural Review* and appreciating my style. Reg Davis-Poynter, who commissioned me to write *My Village, My Life*. Tony Lacey, for asking me to write *Changing Village, Changing Life*. Asa Briggs, for reading the manuscript, and Derek Moore for typing it. Mark Hamilton, Ronald Blythe, Lailan Young, Robin Stringer, Duff Hart-Davis, Cecile Pineda, Denis Hart, Deshmanta Giri, Jadunath Prasad and Gyatri Das, Sk Matlub Ali, Bill Morton and Roy Malkin, among many friends who have provided me with moral support. Above all, the villagers of Nanpur whose love and co-operation have made this book possible.

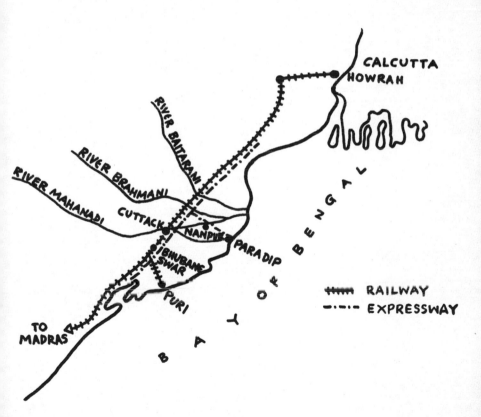

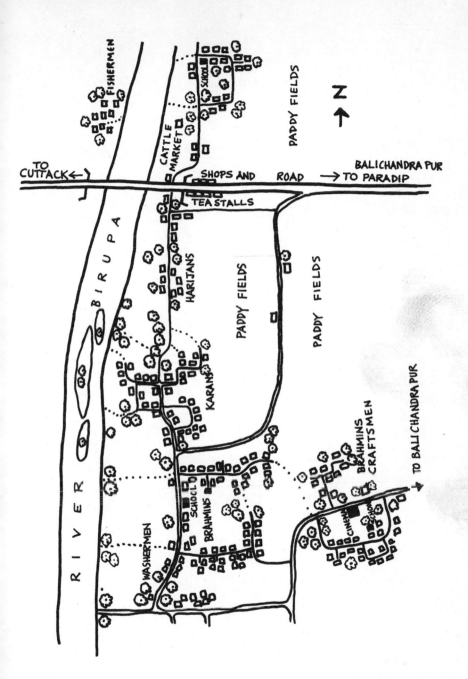

1

THE LECTURE

'THE sun was shining and the sky was blue. It was the morning of 15 August 1947. I was at school. We all gathered in the playground, sang "Bande Mataram", and hoisted the national flag in orange, white and green. The headmaster gave a speech and told us that we were now free from British rule. I did not understand what he meant. I had never seen an Englishman, or even a policeman, and I thought we were all free in the village.

'Freedom had a special meaning for me. I wanted the village to be free from poverty and suffering. Many of my childhood friends had died of cholera, typhoid and diphtheria, and some had been disfigured by smallpox. Terror swept through the village when the epidemic struck. It came spreading like the monsoon rain. I was so frightened that I had nightmares. The villagers worshipped Mahlia Budha, the village deity, for protection. I am lucky that I survived.

'This happened in my village of Nanpur. It is a Hindu village situated on the right bank of the river Birupa, in the Cuttack district of Orissa. The nearest town, Cuttack, is thirty miles away, on the railway line between Calcutta and Madras. There were no proper roads then, no electricity, no clean drinking water, no school, no doctor. The villagers did not know there were such places as hospitals. They had no clocks or watches and time was measured by looking at the sun. The day began with the sunrise and ended with the sunset. People lived, loved, dreamt, struggled, suffered, died.

Life continued after death. They were content. The villagers believed in God and karma and accepted life as it came. The village was self-contained, isolated. Occasionally an aeroplane flew overhead and the villagers came out of their homes to watch. I knew there was another world outside. I was curious to find out about it, but it did not mean anything to me. My village was my only real world. I belonged there.

'When I was twenty-one days old my parents held the name-giving ceremony. The astrologer engraved my *jatak* on a palm leaf, the Brahmin priest worshipped Satyanarayan to bless me, and the villagers were invited to a feast. I was named Prafulla Chandra Mohanti. Prafulla means happy and Chandra in Sanskrit is moon. Mohanti is a common family name for the Karan caste. My parents also gave me a nickname, Kuna, the little one. I was given my identity in the village.

'Nanpur was a beautiful village with mango groves, paddy fields and palm trees which swayed in the wind like dancers. In the distance there was a range of hills. The way the villagers moved, talked and formed groups was like a ballet. I did not have to look for beauty, it was there, everywhere. I watched the changing colours of the rice fields from vivid green to golden yellow, the sweet-scented flowers which opened out at night, the multi-coloured birds and the brilliant sunrises and sunsets. It was magic, and I felt at one with Nature.

'The river Birupa gave Nanpur its identity and played an important part in its life. In the monsoon the river overflowed, submerging the surrounding paddy fields. The villages stood like islands in a lake and the only way to go from one to the other was by boat. In the dry season the river bed dried up completely and provided me with a bed of clean sand on which I played with friends.

'When I was three years old my grandmother took me to the *chatashali*, held on a villager's verandah. The teacher blessed me by stroking my outstretched palm with his cane. Then he took my right hand and with a piece of clay chalk helped me to draw three circles on the mud floor – Brahma, Vishnu and Maheswar. Oriya script is round, and practising the circles helped me to develop good handwriting.

'The houses were built of mud walls and thatched roofs, with a central courtyard which was private and provided shelter from the sun. Local carpenters and craftsmen helped the villagers with the construction of their homes.

'Art was a part of daily life. The villagers decorated the floors and walls of their houses with rice paste for religious festivals and ceremonies. My mother was a good painter and I followed her instinctively. I became so good that I was invited by the other villagers to decorate their houses. Their appreciation encouraged me.

'There was no radio, cinema or television, but there was never a dull moment. Festivals brought life and colour, and the most popular was Holi. In the dry season travelling dancers, snake charmers and puppeteers came visiting and a wave of excitement went through the village when they arrived. Plays were performed in the open air. They started in the evening and continued until sunrise. The characters inspired me and I produced plays with my friends on the village path, using flowers and leaves for costumes, and ash and coloured powder for make-up. There were no ready-made materials and I had to improvise.

'When I was five years old I went to the primary school in the next village of Kusupur, two miles away and had to walk there everyday. There, I noticed that some children were not allowed to enter the classrooms but were given lessons separately on the verandah. That worried me: these children were my friends and I could not understand why we could not be in the classroom together. As I was a good student, some of them would come to my house for help in their studies. But my grandmother always warned me not to touch them. If by mistake I did so, she forced me to take a bath. On the other hand when the Brahmin priest came, he was invited inside the house and given his special mat to sit on.

'After matriculating from the high school, I decided to study science to become a doctor and enrolled at a college in Cuttack. There I stayed in a hostel, but I found it difficult to adjust to town life. The students came from all over Orissa and there was tension between the boys who came from villages and those from towns. The town boys called the village boys "Brown Rice" and the village boys retorted with "White Rice". Yet, the village boys soon imitated the town boys, discarding their village clothes and eating habits. They ate bread and biscuits, went to cinemas and restaurants, wore smartly tailored trousers, adopted the latest fashion in hair-style and spoke in English with their friends. They became ashamed of their village identity and tried to hide it. When their relatives from the villages visited them, they looked embarrassed and some even explained to their friends that they were servants.

'I did not find science interesting and spent most of my time painting and writing. As a result I did not do well in my exams and could not get a place in the medical school. I thought of going to Calcutta to study medicine but my aunts were vehemently opposed to the idea: for them Calcutta was a dark place which destroyed people. The villagers with no other choice went there to work, caught TB, VD, or both, and died.

'There was nobody to guide me in the choice of a career or tell me what opportunities there were. It was by chance that I saw an advertisement for a scholarship to study architecture in Bombay. Without knowing what an architect was, I applied and was accepted. That changed my life.

'Bombay is 1,300 miles from my village. The journey took three days by train. It was my first visit to a large city and I felt lost. It was also the first time I was able to see my village from a distance. I missed it and missed my mother, and when I went home during the holidays I usually stayed longer than the time allowed.

'The school of architecture was a Victorian Gothic building in the centre of the city. It had been established by the British and the method of education was Western. The training bore no relation to my village or culture. I learnt to design Western-style buildings – houses, flats, offices, hotels, theatres, cinemas – by referring to magazines imported from the West. I designed houses with Western-style bathrooms and furniture, but when I went back to the village I swam in the river and sat cross-legged on the mud floor.

'Most of my teachers had been educated in Britain and I was given the impression that British architecture was the best. Architects with British qualifications got better jobs and commissions. So soon after graduating as an architect, in 1960, I went to London for further qualifications and experience. I found the city noisy, polluted and lonely and came to the conclusion that my village, with its love, sunshine, blue skies and clean air, was a better place for living.

'In London for the first time I realized I was an Indian. When people asked me where I was from, I said, "India." I became conscious of my Indian identity, with my roots in my village, embedded in Indian village culture. In Nanpur I was the son of a Karan family; in Cuttack I was a boy from Nanpur; in Bombay I was a student from Orissa; and in London I was an architect from India. I was able to see India from a distance.

'My degree in architecture from Bombay University was not recognized by the Royal Institute of British Architects, so I decided to study town planning in Leeds. There I faced racial discrimination while searching for a place to live. Feeling alone and lonely, I decorated the walls of my rented room with village symbols to create a place in which I could feel secure. Gradually this became a means of self-expression. I was not receiving a grant, so I thought I would try selling some paintings to help pay towards my education. That is how I held my first exhibition as a painter at Leeds University, in the spring of 1964. The art critics wrote favourably and Leeds City Art Gallery bought a painting for its permanent collection. I was accepted as a painter. That gave me another identity.

'The study of town planning helped me to understand the problems of people relating to their environment. When I first arrived in London I lived in a leafy suburb and worked for a fashionable architect in the West End. Most of my friends were architects, planners, engineers, and I lived a life which had no relationship with my village or with the poor in England. In Leeds I saw families living in back-to-back houses without proper washing facilities and became aware of the problems of housing. The industrial landscape under the smoke-filled sky made me realize how beautiful my village was.

'As I travelled around England I saw how rapid industrialization had ruined the countryside. If the planners, politicians and administrators in India were not careful, the same thing could happen there. I came to the conclusion that since the majority of the population lived in villages, the village should be taken as the theme for India's development. Groups of villages should be developed as social, cultural and economic units under broad regional and national plans. These units exist in a natural way all over India. My aim was to plan and design them with imagination. Each unit would have a market place with a community centre containing a theatre, art gallery, school, library, advice centre and health clinic. Work would be provided in the villages with small-scale industries to help the communities and with a co-operative system for farming and crafts.

'I wrote a letter to the Government of India describing my ideas. I did not know who to send the letter to, so I addressed it to the President. He forwarded it to the Planning Commission and my letter got lost among all the other files. When I came to India in 1966 and tried to talk to planners, administrators and politicians I found only apathy. I saw people decaying in the streets and nobody seemed to care. Disappointed and disillusioned, I returned to London to work as an architect-planner for the Greater London Council.

'I thought that if I wrote about my village, people would be aware of its problems as well as its beauty. By chance I met a publisher in London who liked my idea, and commissioned me, so I wrote my first book, *My Village, My Life*. In it I analysed the village structure and helped the villagers to speak about their lives, their hopes and fears. The book was published in the autumn of 1973 and the critics said it was literature. I was delighted: a great achievement for a village boy who had taught himself to read and write in English! But when I offered the book to well-known Indian publishers they rejected it, saying it would not sell. If a book about an Indian village, written by an Indian writer, is not published by Indian publishers, why should others do it?

'When I am in London I forget about the dust, mosquitoes and the frustration of living in India. All that remains in my mind is a beautiful vision of glorious sunsets and loving friends. I long to return. As soon as I arrive in India, I come face to face with corruption, inefficiency, apathy, callousness. I feel suffocated.

'My village is changing. A straight road was built in the

mid-sixties to carry iron ore from the mines to the port of Paradip, forty miles away. It runs right through the village, dividing it into two. In 1974 the first bus came to the village connecting it with the rest of India. The road has brought noise, pollution and all the pressures of urbanization.

'Balichandrapur, the market place two miles away, has turned into a town without any plan or design. Nylon, stainless steel, plastic, fizzy drinks have reached the village. Electricity has come too but there are frequent power cuts. There is a cinema and a video hall, and the television set has become an accepted part of the dowry. Whisky and rum are sold openly in the market place and there is even prostitution. This is progress, I am told. Yet there is poverty and no clean drinking water or sanitation. Families have increased in size but food production has not kept pace. Floods and droughts occur regularly, causing suffering and malnutrition.

'Education has helped to break down caste barriers. The member of parliament for the village is a Harijan. There is now a middle English school, built by the villagers. It has been destroyed several times by cyclones and floods but rebuilt. There are 250 students, seven classes and three rooms. Two classes are held in each room and one class is held on the verandah. There are no proper blackboards or reading materials. When I visited the school, all the children said they wanted to do government jobs. I asked them what they had eaten that morning: out of thirty Harijan children, nearly all of them said, "Nothing." Their fathers work as day-labourers and earn ten rupees a day when work is available. I asked the teachers how they could teach hungry children. Their reply was, "We have not received our salary for the last three months."

'When I narrated my experience to a politician in the ruling party, he was sarcastic. "Our people learn to tell lies from childhood," he said. Ironically the school starts with a prayer in which the children acknowledge the presence of God in Nature. The children sing, "Why should I be afraid of telling the truth? Even if I die I must tell the truth. Oh

God, please teach me this, I need nothing else.''

'The villagers see education as the means of finding jobs as clerks in the town, sitting comfortably under a fan. Before Independence there were only three matriculates in the village and they all got jobs in the British administration. Now there are many highly educated young people sitting at home unemployed, doing nothing. Some have already left the village to find work in the cities. Their education makes them feel the village is an inferior place and they can no longer adjust to its life.

'In my childhood, village disputes were settled by five wise men. But now party politics have entered through the *grama panchayat* system which controls all aspects of village development. There are not only tensions but also allegations of corruption. Politicians come at election time, deliver speeches and make promises, but after the election they are rarely seen again.

'As I travel around India, I feel disturbed by the way it is changing. Changes are not necessarily development. I see the countryside being ruined in the name of progress. Villages are turning into towns, towns into cities, without any plan or design – a well here, a dam there, a road somewhere else – only to help the political party in power at election time. There does not seem to be any co-ordination between the various government agencies, and haphazard development is taking place everywhere. The government is imposing its projects on people, and there is no public participation. There is a Planning Commission in Delhi and there have been several five-year plans but there is no long-term national, regional or local plan for development. Nobody is thinking about what kind of India we want.

'The cities play an important role in their local regions as commercial centres. People are forced to leave their villages and go to towns with the hope of finding jobs. But the cities and towns lack the infrastructure to support their populations. They are overcrowded, noisy and polluted and unsuitable for human habitation. Unless there is a definite policy for development starting from the villages I can see the whole of India turning into a gigantic slum.

'Mahatma Gandhi said, "You people are seeing Delhi – this is not India. Go to the villages; that is India, therein lives the soul of India." Yet the Indian village does not exist in the consciousness of the politicians and administrators. India would be a different place if the Prime Minister lived in a village.'

As soon as I finished my talk at a university in Delhi, a young man got up and said, 'You are making a living by selling Indian poverty abroad.'

'You should remove poverty so that I won't have the opportunity to write about it,' I replied. 'But my writings are also about the beauty of village life and culture. Geographically a village in the north may be different from a village in the south, but the village way of life remains the same throughout India.'

Then questions were thrown at me from all corners of the room.

'How can you write about your village when you live in London?'

'What makes you think you can tell us how and where we should live?'

They were like arrows aimed to hurt. I wanted to leave, but controlled myself.

I looked at the audience carefully. There were about three hundred postgraduate students from all parts of India, healthy, neatly dressed, with bright eyes. They represented India's future.

'I am an artist, writer, architect and town planner and have travelled in many parts of the world. You think because I am based in London I have no right to express my views about India. But you forget that I'm an Indian and have my own vision of my village, India and the world. If I did not come here to remind you that the Indian village exists you would not think about it. The majority of the educated who decide on the destiny of our country are embarrassed by village India. For them the village represents poverty and ignorance, and if somehow it disappeared, India would acquire a respectable modern image.

'Whenever I talk to planners, politicians and administrators about the development of India, they complain that there are too many poor people living in villages. They do not stop to think that the villages have something to offer the modern man, and that villagers have as much right to live and share in the prosperity of our country as they themselves have. The government is in power because the villagers elected it. Eighty per cent of the population live in villages. From childhood we are made to think that our villages are inferior places to live in. The process of higher education and employment takes us away from the village.

'I do not know how many of you are from villages and go back regularly. I return to my village every year and the moment I leave it, I want to go back. Whatever I am today is because of my village. My village is part of me and wherever I go I carry it with me. My experience of the West has convinced me that if we could remove poverty and suffering, preserving the beauty and simplicity of life, the village would be an ideal place for living. It is only when we all feel proud of our roots that India can establish its identity in the world.'

It was past midnight when I returned to the guest-house where I was staying. It belonged to the government of Orissa and was less expensive than a hotel providing similar accommodation. All the state governments have guest-houses in Delhi for their visiting officials and politicians. Sometimes they also let rooms to private individuals belonging to their states, but at much higher rates. One night's rent is equivalent to a labourer's wage for two weeks in my village. I always feel guilty about staying in hotels and guest-houses because that money could be better spent in helping my village, but this time my friends did not have a room to spare.

I tried to sleep but the events of the evening kept coming back to my mind. I had come to Delhi after holding exhibitions in Bombay and Calcutta, and the images of those cities appeared before me, disturbing my peace.

Calcutta was a gigantic rubbish dump with people living there like rats. Outside an old, decaying hotel a little boy came up to me, stretching out his right hand, begging. He was about four, naked and holding a piece of bread in his left hand. There was a lovely smile on his face, which was like that of an old man, completely resigned. I stopped to find out who he was and how he got there. As I tried to talk to him, people gathered around us. I asked them if they knew the boy and they said sarcastically, 'He's a professional beggar.' The boy looked puzzled and took me to his parents, who had made a little tent around the corner in the next street. That was their home. They ignored me at first but when I talked to them in Bengali they seemed pleased and told me about themselves.

Their village was destroyed by flood. They had no food, no work, no home, so they came to Calcutta. There was nowhere to live so, like many other families, they ended up on the pavement in the city centre where some work is available. The father worked as a porter in the fruit market and the mother looked after the children. The boy was sent out to beg. 'We can't feed him, he must learn to look after himself,' they said.

When they found out that I was from Orissa, they told me about an old lady from Puri who lived a little way away. I went and talked to her. She was delighted when I spoke to her in Oriya and expressed her affection by touching my face with her wrinkled hands. Her husband had died when she was young. She came to Calcutta to cook for a relative, but he died. She had nobody and nowhere to go. She did not want to go back to her village. 'Who will look after me or give me food?' she said. 'They are all starving there.' She was happy in Calcutta where she had made friends, all living on the pavement.

My exhibition was held in a gallery in the centre of Calcutta. One evening a westernized Indian came, stood at the door of the gallery and exclaimed, 'Ultra-modern paintings! Who is the artist?' I introduced myself.

'Where are you from?'

'A village in Orissa.'

'If a village can produce such an artist, then we should all go and live in villages,' he said condescendingly.

He was the editor of an important English-language newspaper, and invited me to have lunch with him. When I arrived at the imposing-looking building, built during the British Raj, I saw people living on the pavement outside. A car was waiting to take us to a restaurant only a few yards away. During lunch he told me all about himself. He had been educated in England and had worked in London for several years, before returning to India to join the family business.

I asked him about the overcrowding in Calcutta and the people living in the slums and on the pavements.

'You get desensitized to poverty, otherwise it is impossible to survive in India,' he said.

In India, people get so used to poverty and suffering that they fail to notice it. I asked the director of an art gallery in Bombay if she knew the family living on the pavement outside. She looked surprised.

'Which family?' She must have seen them every day but had not noticed them. It was only when I pointed them out that she realized they were there.

I introduced myself to the family. When I told them I was a writer their immediate reply was, 'Please don't write about us. We live here, but nobody knows. If you write, people will know we exist. Then the authorities will drive us out.' They had left their village because of a drought.

In Delhi, I had gone to Chandni Chowk to collect some paintings from a framer. I had stacked them on the pavement and was waiting for a taxi. A young man came up to me and asked, 'Why have you put these paintings here?' He was in his twenties, thin and shabbily dressed.

'Why not?'

'This is my place.'

'How can the pavement be yours?'

'I sleep here.'

I looked around and saw several families preparing for the night. When I told the young man I was only waiting for a taxi the worried look on his face disappeared.

He had come to Delhi from a village in the north. His father, a tenant farmer, had died suddenly. As he was the eldest son, the responsibility of looking after his old mother and three young brothers and sisters fell on his shoulders. There was no regular work in his village so he had to come to Delhi. He worked as a porter during the day, but life was difficult he said, and he would like to go back to his village.

Many of the people I talked to in the cities, living in slums and on pavements, had come from villages. They were the victims of disasters like floods and drought. They had no land, no education, no money, no work, and had come to the cities to earn their living. As an old man told me, the whole world revolves around the stomach. The only place where they could live and bring up their children was in the slums.

I thought of a story my mother used to tell me, helping me to count as a child:

This little finger said, 'Mother, I'm hungry.'
The next finger said, 'Where can we get food?'
The middle finger said, 'We'll borrow.'
The first finger said, 'How can we pay it back?'
The big thumb said, 'We'll eat, drink, and leave the village.'

This very old story expresses the eternal sufferings of the villagers.

I once asked a boy in the village if he knew where India was. He said, 'In Delhi'. I wondered if he would ever know

Gandhi had said that Delhi is not India, and that the soul of India is in the villages.

Yet Mohandas Karamchand Gandhi, affectionately known as Mahatma, was born in a town, the son of a *diwan* to a princely state. He went to a high school which was modelled on an English public school. The medium of instruction was English and from his childhood he was brought up to be a sahib. He was sent by his family to study law in London and after qualifying as a barrister worked in South Africa. The main purpose of his return to India was a political one, to remove the British. All his actions relating to village development, like swaraj, *khadi* and spinning, were influenced by political ideology. He did not seem to have the vision of a modern India after the British had left. There was a vacuum when it came to looking into the future.

The British administrators were replaced by Indians who were more British than the British themselves. They came from well-to-do families, mainly from towns and cities, spoke English, imitating their previous masters, and dressed like Englishmen. They had nothing in common with poor Indians or those living in villages. The British exploited India for Britain, the brown sahibs exploited India for their families and friends. They despised the villagers and complained that there were too many of them.

The first Prime Minister, Pandit Jawaharlal Nehru, came from a wealthy Brahmin family. Educated at Harrow and Cambridge, his lifestyle was Western and very different from that of the ordinary Indian. His attempt to blend capitalism with socialism did not work. Although he introduced local development programmes he did not carry them through as an integrated policy. His idea of a *grama panchayat* brought party politics into the village, to its detriment. He was interested in industrializing India, and large-scale heavy industries were set up in remote areas. People were brought from villages to work there but this broke up families and communities.

Nehru's daughter, Indira Gandhi, became the Prime

Minister in 1966. She was an able politician and so popular that she was compared with Durga, the Goddess of Energy. She could have changed the face of India but her advisers lacked vision. She spent a lot of time trying to bring political stability and brought the cult of personality into Indian politics when she formed 'Indira Congress' – Congress (I). Her desire to help the villagers was also a political one. She knew the villagers' votes kept her in power. The buying of politicians became more open and corruption was accepted as a part of Indian life. She almost destroyed Indian democracy during the Emergency but the wisdom of the village voters preserved it by rejecting her at the 1977 election. Janata, the People's Party, was elected. The majority of the newly elected M Ps described their 'hobby' as 'the uplift of the rural poor' but their leaders quarrelled among themselves over the acquisition of power and about who should be the Prime Minister. After two years the villagers became disillusioned and voted Mrs Gandhi back.

After her assassination, her son, Rajiv Gandhi, became the Prime Minister by winning the election on the sympathy vote. Young people in the villages identified with him. They had high hopes and looked forward to a new India. But his talk of the twenty-first century and bringing computers to the village showed that he was out of touch with the real India.

One evening in Bombay, I was walking along the sea front when a young boy of about eight asked me for money. I ignored him. Suddenly he touched my feet and said, 'You are my father, give me money. I'm hungry.' His words went straight to my heart, he could have been my son. He told me that he and his mother had left their village because of drought. I remembered the teaching of King Ashoka in 261 BC: 'All men are my children. Just as, in regard to my own children, I desire that they may be provided by me with all kinds of welfare and happiness in this world and the next, that same I desire of all men.'

His words have been forgotten. Governments have come

and gone, yet the basic needs of life – food, clothes and shelter – are not available to the majority. But life in India continues because people have a strong desire to survive.

In the morning the birds sang and woke me up. The golden rays of the sun glittered on the leaves of a tree outside my window. It was full of red flowers, and green parrots danced from branch to branch. I felt optimistic about the future.

A professor from the university came to see me with his wife and a colleague who had been at the meeting the previous evening. He was enthusiastic about my talk and said how much he had liked it. They explained why the students had seemed so hostile. Most of them came from villages and wanted to succeed in life through education. That meant escaping from their roots, and my talk had made them feel guilty. The professor's colleague was from a village and wanted to go back, but there was no local university where he could teach, and no facilities for his children's education.

Talking about villages made me nostalgic for my own village. I wanted to go there as soon as possible.

2

THE JOURNEY

NANPUR is one thousand miles from Delhi. I could go
there by rail or by air. Indian Airlines have now introduced a daily flight to Bhubaneswar, the state capital, sixty
miles from the village. Previously, the journey was via Calcutta, with a change of aircraft. A little plane flew low like
a bird between Calcutta and Bhubaneswar and passengers
could enjoy the countryside spreading underneath: clusters
of trees, paddy fields, rivers and coastline. Going by plane is
quick, but it is expensive.

The first time I ever visited Delhi was in 1966 when I went
from London to talk to the Planning Commission about my
village development plans. Since then, I have made several
journeys for exhibitions and to visit friends. My mother and
myself were the first people from Nanpur to visit Delhi. I
had an exhibition of my paintings in 1970 and when I asked
my mother to come with me, she liked the idea. We went by
rickshaw to Dhanmandal, the nearest railway station, and
then by train to Cuttack. After a wait of twelve hours, we
caught an overnight express train which reached Calcutta at
six in the morning. Again we had to wait for twelve hours
before catching a train at six in the evening. We reached
New Delhi railway station at eleven o'clock the next
morning. Little has changed since then, except that there is
now a direct train from Cuttack to Delhi and the village is
connected by bus to Cuttack.

This time, I decided to travel to Nanpur by train, in second

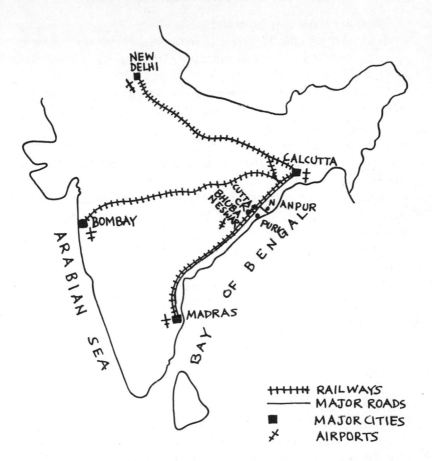

NEW
DELHI

CALCUTTA

CUTTA

BHUBA
NESWAR

NANPUR

BOMBAY

PURI

A
R
A
B
I
A
N

S
E
A

B
A
Y

O
F

B
E
N
G
A
L

MADRAS

+++++ RAILWAYS
——— MAJOR ROADS
■ MAJOR CITIES
✗ AIRPORTS

class. When I went to the railway station to buy my ticket I found a long queue waiting and when my turn came, the clerk behind the counter said no sleepers were available for several weeks. I explained my position and she suggested I went to the Tourist Office.

The Tourist Office was near by. I filled in a form stating my name, age, sex, train number, destination and the date of journey. When I handed over the reservation slip to the clerk she wanted to see my passport. I gave it to her.

'It is an Indian passport,' she exclaimed loudly.

'Yes.'

'You are not a foreign tourist.'

I paused a little, feeling embarrassed. How could I be a foreign tourist in my own country? 'I am based in London,' I said quietly.

'Take the form to the supervisor and get his signature. Only he can certify you as a foreign tourist.'

A middle-aged man was sitting alone at a table, keeping watch on all the counters. He was the supervisor. I explained my position to him. He was sympathetic and put his signature on my application.

When I returned to the counter I saw an Indian arguing with the clerk. He was from America and wanted to travel to Benares on a particular day.

'It is not what you want in India but what you can get,' the clerk replied abruptly.

The Indian demanded to see the supervisor.

'The trains are full and even the Prime Minister cannot help you.'

I paid for my ticket and the reservation charges. The clerk handed me two tickets, one for my journey and the other for the sleeper.

The train was due to leave at six the next morning. When I arrived at New Delhi station it was still dark. The city was silent and sleeping but the station was already crowded and busy. Streams of people went in and out. I negotiated with a coolie to carry my case and portfolio to the train. He asked me for the coach number. When I told him it was second class he did not approve. 'It's not very comfortable,' he said.

The train was leaving from a platform a long way away from the main entrance. We had to climb up a steep flight of steps and walk across an over-bridge to the opposite side of the station. The coolie knew exactly where the train was and pushed through the flow of incoming passengers. I followed him, admiring the way he walked straight, carrying the luggage on his head. He looked older and thinner than me but he was the stronger one. Reaching the platform, I helped him to unload the baggage and the coolie took them to the compartment and placed them carefully under the seat.

I sat down on the wooden bench near the window. The seat was hard and dusty and I wondered how I was going to spend the next thirty-six hours. I remembered the comment of the coolie.

The train left on time. Through the window I saw Delhi being left behind. The sun was struggling to shine through the grey sky, full of pollution. We passed through towns, cities, villages and the wheat fields of the fertile Ganges valley.

The coach was noisy and crowded. Groups of six passengers were accommodated in open compartments, three bunks on either side, and there were two-tier bunks all along the corridor. Whenever the train stopped beggars entered the coach – blind, lame or women with children in their arms. A blind man stood in the corridor singing a devotional song and then moved slowly among the passengers, collecting money. Vendors sold tea, coffee, fizzy drinks and snacks. Some of my fellow-passengers gossiped, played cards and shared food; the compartment had become a family.

The young man sitting opposite me was an engineering student and wanted to study in America. He asked for my advice. Soon, everybody knew that I lived in London and wanted my address so they could tell their friends.

Around four in the afternoon, I felt tired. The other passengers had come prepared with their bed rolls, but I did not have one. I asked the conductor if I could hire some bedding but he said it was not available to second-class passengers. I knew it would be impossible for me to sleep, so I requested him to move me to the air-conditioned sleeper. The conductor examined his chart and said it was full, but he had a few berths reserved for passengers getting on at the next station, and someone might not turn up. The young student told the conductor in Hindi, 'He's from London and not used to our trains. You help him and he'll help you.'

At the next station, an attendant came and carried my

luggage to the air-conditioned coach. It was reasonably clean, cool, with comfortable berths. The conductor had already arranged for the bed roll. He sat down beside me and made out the ticket. I gave him some money which was more than the fare and expected to receive the change. But he kept the whole amount, and I realized what the student had meant by 'help'.

The coach was totally different from the one I had just come from. Well-dressed men and women with children looked confident and gossiped among themselves. There was a government minister travelling in the next coach, I was told, and that was why the train was running on time. Two attendants guarded the coach and looked after the needs of the passengers. There was a pantry car from which I could order tea, coffee and simple meals. It was like being in a hotel with room service. The doors and windows were shut tight to prevent the heat and dust of India from getting in. I felt I was in an isolated capsule moving at speed.

When I got out of the train at Cuttack, I was overpowered by the heat. Kedar was waiting for me on the platform. He greeted me with a large smile on his round face and saying *namaskar* joining his hands as in prayer. Then, he took charge of everything and I just followed. He got a coolie to carry my bags to his car, parked in the forecourt of the station. He had recently bought a new Maruti car, the brainchild of Sanjay Gandhi, manufactured with Japanese collaboration. It was the symbol of Kedar's success.

Kedar is thirty-six and married to my brother's younger daughter. He owns a small pharmaceutical factory in Cuttack. When he decided to marry, twelve years ago, he had asked for a dowry of 10,000 rupees to start a business. The mediator who came with his proposal said that he would marry whoever paid the money first. My brother was anxious to get his daughter married so he paid the amount asked and the wedding took place. With the money as capital, Kedar was able to get a small loan from the government and start his business. During the last ten years he has worked hard and built up a profitable company, employing about twenty workers. His market is secure as he supplies medicines to government hospitals all over the state.

I asked him to take me to the bus station but he said he would drive me to Nanpur. The whole family was waiting for me in the village and he had been given the responsibility of taking me there. His words were like music to my ears. I was so exhausted by the train journey that I did not think I would have been able to endure the bus ride.

I have travelled to the village many times by bus and have always found the journey tiring. The overcrowded vehicles shake and rattle, and once a young girl sitting by my side was sick all over me. When the bus reached Nanpur I felt as if my joints were loose and my head was not a part of my body.

Kedar drove skilfully along the crowded streets of Cuttack avoiding the wandering cows, cycle rickshaws, cyclists and pedestrians. Cuttack is the main commercial centre of Orissa, with government offices, schools and colleges, a High Court and a teaching hospital. Several of my friends and relatives from the village work there and stay in rented accommodation with their families. Rents are high and most of them cannot afford self-contained flats or houses, so they share rooms and I have seen many families living together in crowded conditions. Cuttack has become a mini-Calcutta, with congested streets, open drains, mosquitoes, and piles of rubbish lying everywhere.

When we got on the main road to Nanpur I was horrified by the traffic. Huge overloaded lorries and buses with passengers hanging on to open doors came thundering towards us, blowing their horns loudly like trumpets. Had I been the driver, I would have stopped the car by the side of the road and run away. But Kedar did not seem to be disturbed. He wanted to drive fast but I asked him to slow down so that I could enjoy the scenery.

Moving along the bridge over the river Mahanadi, I saw a

beautiful range of hills to the west. They were the Eastern
Ghats, where the clouds from the Bay of Bengal collide,
producing the monsoon rain. Dark fumes from the chimneys
of a textile mill on the other side of the river filled the sky.
At the end of the bridge and along the river-bank was the
new industrial estate. A factory advertised its product, a
new fizzy drink called Campa-Cola, on a colourful hoarding.
Milkmen on cycles were on their way to Cuttack, balancing
large cans of adulterated milk.

Traffic moved at different speeds along the road. There
were pedestrians carrying bundles on their heads, cyclists,
bullock carts, motor-cycles – often with the whole family,
father, mother, and three small children – cars, jeeps, lorries
and buses. I saw crushed animals and overturned lorries and
buses. Accidents are regarded as a part of life. The fear
of smallpox and cholera has been replaced by the fear of
accidents. Before starting a journey by road, the villagers
worship the goddess Durga for protection.

We stopped at a shrine dedicated to the goddess, placed
under a banyan tree. A young man dressed in red sat near
by, with his red bicycle parked against the tree. A red flag
fluttered in the wind and was visible from a distance. The

young man brought some vermilion paste from the shrine
and put a spot on my forehead. Red is the colour of the
goddess Durga symbolizing life and energy. Passing buses
and lorries slowed down and dropped coins. Some also
stopped to receive the goddess's blessing. The young man
was in his twenties. He had bright clear eyes and his face was
filled with peace and contemplation. He pointed to the bend
in the road where there was a small bridge over a stream,
and told me he had seen many accidents there. He was from
a nearby village, the son of a Brahmin.

One day he was on his way to a friend's house, when he
watched helplessly as a bus turned over. Several people were
trapped and some old women and children died. He could
still hear the screams of the injured passengers. That night
he had a dream. The goddess Durga came to him and said,
'You must help these people. I am with you. Plant me
under the banyan tree near the bridge. I want to protect the
travellers.' The next day, he built the shrine. This was several
years ago.

I have seen many accidents on this spot. There is a sharp
bend in the road and drivers find it difficult to control their
vehicles. There are no signs warning the motorists of the
danger. Yet all along the road there are slogans in English
reminding the motorist to drive carefully. One reads, 'Better
to be Mr Late than Late Mr.' Since the erection of the shrine,
accidents have stopped on that spot. The young man has
now installed a red light on the shrine which shines during
the night and can be seen from a distance. Thousands of
vehicles pass every day, and from the donations he has
collected he is planning to build a school with a library and
reading room. It was his duty to provide a service to the
community, he said, and I was pleased he was using religion
for a constructive purpose. If the religious purpose of the
leaders of India was the removal of the caste system, poverty
and suffering, the country could be transformed.

A little further on, a man was walking on the side of the
road. He prostrated himself, got up, raised his hands to

pray, then prostrated himself again from the point where his outstretched hands had reached. He was on his way to the temple of Jagannath at Puri, following an ancient pilgrims' path. The journey was an act of penance for him. Since leaving his village ten days ago, he had covered only seven miles, and there were sixty more to go. He was about fifty but looked much older. His skin was tanned by the sun and the upper part of his thin body was bare.

Lorries and buses came from both directions and I was worried the man would be killed. He was not perturbed. 'If Lord Jagannath wants to take my life in this way, it is up to Him, but I would rather be crushed under the wheels of His chariot,' he said.

In the old days the devotees threw themselves under the wheels of Lord Jagannath's chariot in the belief that by dying that way, their souls went straight to heaven. He smiled in disbelief when I told him that large lorries in the West are called juggernauts, after Lord Jagannath.

The devotee was not in a hurry. He stopped when he felt tired and at sunset he left the road and went to the nearest village where people gave him food and shelter. He started his journey again at sunrise.

The road was built at the end of the nineteenth century by the British Raj. A terrible famine occurred in 1865–6, after a period of prolonged drought followed by severe floods. Food could not be brought in from other parts of India due to the lack of rail and road. As a result, people were forced to eat roots and some were even driven to eat corpses. Many turned into skeletons and thousands slowly starved to death. A commission was set up to investigate the causes of the famine. It estimated that a quarter of the population of Orissa had died and the local government representatives were blamed.

The famine put moral pressure on the British to build a railway connecting Calcutta with Madras. They also built a main road between the two cities, but there were no bridges over the large rivers and they had to be crossed by boat. Bridges were eventually built in the sixties, and for the first time it was possible to drive from Calcutta to Madras. The road followed the mud path leading to the temple of Lord Jagannath at Puri, one of the four main religious centres of India.

In my childhood the villagers walked along this road, called Jagannath Sadak, to Puri as it was considered a religious act to do so. But when I was four, my grandmother took me there by train. We walked twelve miles to the nearest railway station along a mud track, and crossed the two rivers on our way by boat. There were only two trains a day and missing one meant a wait of twelve hours for the next.

At Chandikhol, we left the main road and joined the expressway to Nanpur. The meeting of the Calcutta Madras road with the road to Paradip has made Chandikhol an important junction. Buses and lorries stop on the road and temporary stalls have sprung up to cater for the needs of the travellers. In twenty years a small flourishing town has developed, with tea stalls, restaurants, petrol-filling stations, a bank, a post office, tailors, hair-cutting saloons, a printing press, a high school and college, and a cinema. Yet the government regards Chandikhol as a bus stop, not a town, and has no plans for developing it. From time to time the police remove stallholders because they are encroaching on the highway, but they soon reappear.

All along the roads there are eating places where the motorists and lorry drivers stop to rest and have a meal. These eating places are called *dhabas* and are mostly kept by people from the Punjab. They are simple structures made of wood, bamboo and a thatched roof, and they stay open all night, like motorway cafés in the West. Wooden cots can be hired for the night and the food is clean and prepared to the customer's order. The owners are careful of their image because there is extreme competition.

Recently the government built a bus station, with permanent stalls for traders a short distance from the junction, and ordered the bus drivers to use it. But the stalls remained empty, and only government buses obeyed the order. The owners of private buses complained that by going to the bus stop they used more petrol. They continued to stop on the main road and the bus station was abandoned. It is difficult to enforce laws in India when public feeling is against them.

Everyone is eager to earn a few rupees and the Chandikhol junction has provided a source of income for many of the local unemployed. As the buses stop, vendors sell green coconuts, bananas and cucumbers. Little children go round, selling peanuts wrapped in newspaper. In the evening, the fishermen sell fish caught in the local rivers and ponds, and the farmers their fresh vegetables, all sitting by the roadside.

We left the junction and drove towards Nanpur. On both sides of the road were ponds, created by digging out the soil to build the twenty-foot-high embankment. Every year the floodwater brings the fish from the river, and they are left behind in the ponds when the water subsides. This provides a source of livelihood for the local fishermen. I have often watched them fish. Dark, slender bodies, carrying a bamboo net, move gracefully from one end of the pond to the other, enclosing the fish in a trap. Then, the fish are picked up, one by one, and put in a bamboo basket.

The main purpose of the road was to carry iron ore and minerals from the mines to the port. It took five years to build at an expenditure of twenty-two crores of rupees. The road was planned by a politician, the then Chief Minister of Orissa, and designed by the state government engineers, with assistance from the Central Road Research Institute of India. As the land was liable to flood, a high embankment was built to carry the road. No machinery was used and the entire construction was done by labourers. The road brought work to the local villagers and hope to the region. But the Chief Minister had no economic development plan for the locality, which is about two thousand square miles in area, with a population of several hundred thousand.

As soon as the road was complete, people started using it

as their path. There was no mud, very little dust, and it was dry and comfortable for the feet. Some villagers even dried rice on it. But no attempt was made to explain how to use it and a tremor of shock went through the countryside when the first accident occurred. A young boy walking to school was run over by a lorry. The driver hit and fled, the policy adopted by all lorry and bus drivers today. They know that if they stop they will be surrounded by an angry crowd, beaten up and that their vehicles will be set on fire. Later on, the drivers surrender to the police but somehow, through the process of law, manage to escape prosecution.

The first road accidents were not recorded because the government did not want to create a bad image for the road. Now, they are so common that it is impossible to keep track of them.

On both sides of the road patches of green rice fields spread out like a carpet over the brown parched land. We passed villages with mud huts, a single tree on a barren hilltop, a colourful market under a banyan tree, anthills high as temples, ponds filled with lilies and flowering weeds, cranes standing on one leg on the edge of the water, cattle grazing and farmers returning home with bundles of grain on their heads. A line of palm trees against a range of hills looked like a film set. A woman was drying rice on the side of the road and another was making flat cow-dung cakes for fuel.

The farmers were at work in the fields adjoining the ponds; ploughing with the help of bullocks, some lifting water manually, using a contraption made of bamboo and palm trunk. A group of women in bright saris was planting rice, squatting in a row and moving gracefully from one end of the muddy field to the other. They were all working hard, without any machine to help them. If only there was proper irrigation, I thought, they could have changed the whole area.

As we approached Nanpur, my childhood memories appeared fresh in my mind. Before the road, there were only fields and clusters of villages surrounded by mango groves and palm trees. I remembered going with my aunt to a festival at Chandikhol, walking along paddy fields and listening to her stories. Along the way we stopped under a banyan tree to eat the food we had carried with us. I admired the flowers, butterflies and birds. From my history book, I knew that there were Buddhist monasteries on top of the local hills and that the monks must have walked on those paths. Walking made me feel that I was a part of the soil.

When I was twelve years old I visited my father in the forest. He worked as a forester about 120 miles from the village and, to get there, I had to take a train and a bus. Just walking to the railway station with a friend took four hours. After that first time I walked many times to the railway station with my friends and on our way we would gossip, sing and tell stories to each other. Often I started out alone but after crossing the river by boat, I would meet up with other people going to the station. We talked, shared experiences, helped each other on our journey and became friends. We had a common purpose – to reach the station.

All that changed when a bus stopped on the road at Nanpur early one morning in 1975 on its way to Cuttack. The villagers were delighted that they could reach the town in two hours.

Now there are several buses to Cuttack, Puri, Bhubaneswar and even Calcutta. The villagers do not have to depend on the buses, they can travel on the lorries by paying a small fee to the drivers. They can even make several journeys to Cuttack in a day, choosing their own time.

3
MY FAMILY

FROM a distance Nanpur looks like a mass of trees. As we get nearer and cross over the ugly and badly maintained concrete bridge, I see the beautiful range of hills and the river, disappearing into the landscape. At the end of the bridge a sign says 'Nanpur' in English and Oriya, and there are a few stalls selling tea, snacks, pan and cigarettes right on the road. The road has given my village another identity, 'Nanpur on the Expressway'.

Oriya, the language of the village, is spoken by the thirty million people of Orissa. It is derived from Sanskrit and sounds similar to Bengali and Hindi, but the scripts are different. Very few people in the village can speak or understand English. There is a saying, 'When an Oriya is angry he speaks Hindi.'

As soon as my brother's grandchildren see me they begin to dance and sing '*Bilati oja, Bilati oja!*' Shamin, the four-year-old boy starts reciting, 'Baa, baa, black sheep, have you any wool? Yes sir, yes sir, three bags full.' He is not able to understand or pronounce the words properly but he has got the rhythm right. It sounds like, 'Baa, baa, bla hee, ha yu ee oo; yeh ar, yeh ar, tee ba fu.' Then his elder brother joins in and they perform a duet of English nursery rhymes, dancing and acting out the stories, moving their hands and shaking their heads. They only stop when I bring out a packet of sweets.

Several other children have followed the car and are standing on the verandah and in the courtyard. They are of all ages and it is difficult to tell who belongs to which family. I notice that many suffer from malnutrition, with bare feet and torn clothes. But their smiling faces express innocence and hope. They extend their hands and I distribute more sweets.

'Who are you?' I ask a little boy.

'He is the grandson of the astrologer,' the boy standing next to him says.

'My name is Manoj Nayak. I am running nine and studying in Class III.'

'What about you?' I point to his friend.

'He is the son of the milkman.'

'My name is Anil Behra. I am also running nine. We are classmates. We don't know any English or Hindi.'

'Why are you studying?'

'I want a job in the electricity department. I like my village, it is beautiful.'

The astrologer's grandson says, 'My grandfather is doing astrology, but my father works in the town. I'll be an astrologer like my grandfather. I'll prepare horoscopes, predict the future.'

'I don't want to keep cows,' Anil says strongly, 'I want a good job. I want to study B A and M A. I'll get married, have a car, and my wife will bring a television set for her dowry. I will build a big house in the village.'

'What is the caste system?'

'I don't know. We all play cricket together.'

'I bat.'

'I am a bowler.'

'My brother taught us to play cricket.'

'We have seen T V. We like it. We have also seen Oriya films in the cinema, but not Hindi; we cannot understand it.'

Three boys are standing together. I ask them their names and from their replies, I realize that one is a Harijan, one a Brahmin and the other a Karan. They are friends. They play

together at school but the Harijan boy is never invited to his
friends' homes.

I ask another boy, 'What is your name?'

'Anjan Kumar Jena. I'm ten and studying in Class IV.'

'Your father's name?'

'Kartik Jena.'

The astrologer's grandson says, 'He's a Harijan,' although
earlier he had told me he did not know about caste. I notice
that the children never talk about their caste directly. But
they know their place in village society.

Anjan's right hand is crippled.

'What happened?'

'When I was small I fell down and broke my arm. I cannot
do anything with my right hand. It has no strength. I eat,
write and do everything with my left hand.'

'Have you seen a doctor?'

'My father says he has no money. But my hand aches. I
have four brothers, two sisters, my parents and my grandmother, who is blind. In the morning I have a piece of *roti*
and a glass of raw tea with salt, no milk or sugar. My mother
makes the *rotis* and sometimes my share is about one and a
half pieces. At noon we eat boiled rice with some vegetables.
I like fried potatoes. I haven't eaten anything today. We
have a cow but it is not giving milk. My father works as a
labourer and gets about ten rupees a day. He works hard but
some days he gets only five rupees. I want to study and get
a job.'

'What is your name?' I ask a girl with a sad oval face.

'Kalpana. My parents call me "Kapi".'

'How old are you?'

'She's seven,' a boy standing near by says.

'Who are you?'

'I'm her brother.'

'Why are you replying for her?'

'She cannot speak properly.'

'Are you studying?' I ask the girl.

'No.'

'Why not?'

'I have no slate.'

'She's stupid,' says a little boy who is listening. He is well-fed with a round face.

'What is your name?'

'Abhay.'

'How old are you?'

'Six.'

'Are you going to school?'

'Yes.'

'Which Class?'

'One.'

'Are you a good student?'

'Yes,' he says confidently.

'Why are you studying?'

'I want to be a government officer.'

I can feel in the children a struggle to survive and do well in life. For them success means a good house, a car and a television set. Whether they come from a Harijan or high-caste family their ambitions are the same.

Kalpana was still standing with a look of resignation on her face. She is the daughter of a Harijan. Although her brothers go to school, her parents do not want to waste money on her education. She stays at home to look after her stepmother and her two small daughters. I ask her if she has ever drunk milk. 'Yes, when I was a child, from my mother.'

My relatives gather around me, all descendants from one man, three generations ago. My great-grandfather had three sons. My grandfather was the eldest and had two sons. My father was the elder and had two sons, my brother and myself. My brother has four sons; three of them are married, with children. In a hundred years, one man has been responsible for the creation of twenty-five family units, with at least 150 people. Similarly the village has grown. In 1961 the population of Nanpur was 2,000, with 350 households. Now there are 6,000 people and the number of family units has increased to 1,000.

The population of Nanpur has risen but the village area (530 acres) has remained the same, with a strict division between building land (29 acres) and farming land (348 acres). There is no planning authority or control but most villagers would not willingly build houses on paddy fields, as they are their source of food. As a result several families are sharing the same family house and there is overcrowding. But some villagers with money have started building homes on paddy fields.

People live in joint families. The parents, their sons and families, and any dependent relatives, live together sharing food cooked in the same kitchen. Other villagers are considered to be brothers and sisters, or uncles and aunts. A child belongs not only to his family but also to the whole village. I am the son of my parents but a brother and uncle to others. The whole village is like one large extended family sharing each other's joys and sorrows.

Although education is breaking down caste barriers in towns, caste is still the most important feature of the village. It defines a person's place and the work he or she is expected to do. One is born into a caste and this can never be changed. Caste can neither be bought with money nor acquired through education. In an arranged marriage system the bride and bridegroom must belong to the same caste. It is discussed openly and nobody feels offended.

Traditionally Hindus are divided into four castes – Brahmins, Kshatriyas, Vaishyas and Sudras. The Brahmins belong to the highest caste and only they can perform the ceremonies required by Hindu religion. Over the years there have been many sub-divisions and in my village people are known by their caste and according to the work they do. Caste gives a person his identity. In Nanpur there are Brahmins, Kshatriyas, Karans, astrologers, barbers, washermen and Harijans, formerly called 'Untouchables'. The Brahmins are not allowed to do manual work: they have to remain clean to attend to the gods.

The villagers are mainly farmers and craftsmen; each craft is the property of a particular caste and together the castes form the village community. They are all necessary for the running of a Hindu village. Castes operate as trade unions, looking after the interests of their members. For example, a barber's service is essential for the purification of the family at the death ceremony, and people from no other caste can perform that function. Even in towns, where the caste system is not rigid, it becomes important at the time of birth, death and marriage, when the necessary rituals must be performed by members of a particular caste.

Caste has survived over the centuries. The Moguls and the British Raj were not able to change the system. The Muslims tried to convert people with force but the Brahmins resisted and as long as people remained Hindus the caste system remained. People from the lower castes converted to Islam for gain – land, money and favours – and also as a reaction against the caste system. There are Muslim settlements around Nanpur made up of converted Hindus, mostly from the lower castes. But I do not know of any Brahmins who changed their religion and became Muslims.

There are no Christians in the area but missionaries come from Cuttack to distribute literature at Balichandrapur market. The birth of Christ and the birth of Krishna are so similar that the villagers are intrigued by the story of Baby Jesus. Hindus who converted to Christianity did so for money, land, education, jobs, wine and women. But Christians have been so influenced by Hindu religion that many observe the caste system. A Christian friend once told me that he was Brahmin by caste but Christian by religion.

Caste is related to culture. In the village the Karans have a refined taste. They are liberal in their approach and are the trend-setters. If a barber is good and cuts hair well he is called a '*karania* barber'. If a cake is delicately made and beautiful to look at then it is called a '*karania* cake'. But if

the cake is heavy and rough then it is called '*chasunia* cake', cake made by a farmer's wife.

The use of colour in clothes can give the wearer's caste away. The Karan and Brahmin women usually wear saris of pastel colours, whereas the women of the lower castes like bright-coloured saris. Karan women wear delicate jewellery, whereas women from the business communities wear heavy jewellery. But now the fashion is changing and television and cinema have a tremendous influence.

The Brahmins used to be the spiritual and religious leaders. They were the teachers and advisers to kings. They led austere lives and protected the Indian civilization of the sages, setting standards of simple living and high thinking for the rest to follow. But now they have become administrators, politicians, businessmen and even shopkeepers selling alcohol – the jobs associated with exploiting others. Many eat meat, drink alcohol and have become greedy and decadent. As a result, respect for them is decreasing.

My mother thought of the Brahmins as gods. When I was a child I was told by my mother to pay respect to them. They were the guardians of the moral standards of the village and should never be offended. A Brahmin's curse always came true, I was told. But my respect for the Brahmins disappeared when I went to school. In my class there were a number of Brahmin children who were not good students, and I did better than them in my studies. If the Brahmins believed they were superior and the villagers believed the same, why didn't they do better than me in their studies, I thought.

Sometimes my mother did not have enough money to pay for my school fees and she would call the family priest for help. He would take her gold bangles and lend her money at a high rate of interest. I also observed that when the priest performed religious ceremonies in the house, he was never satisfied with the fees offered by my mother, and often bargained. In this way he took money from different families and operated as a moneylender. Even at a young age I found this unethical. Taking money from clients and then lending it back at a high rate of interest seemed wrong to me.

Most of the villagers were poor and were forced to go to moneylenders. They were people from the business caste and had a bad reputation. The villagers needed their help but said nothing nice about them. So when I saw the Brahmin working as a moneylender I could not understand how he could do it.

When I was at school, I was asked by a Brahmin primary school teacher to help his son with his studies. The boy was one year younger than me and came to my house twice a week for coaching. I also helped others in the village because I wanted them to do well and lent them my books and notes. But when I asked the Brahmin boy and his father to help too, they made excuses – 'I'm tired', 'feeling sleepy', 'come tomorrow'. Once the boy's parents invited me for a midday meal in their house. I was served separately on the verandah while he and his father were served in another portion of the house. When we had finished eating, his mother removed the empty dishes used by him and his father but mine was left behind for a woman from the lower caste to clear. I felt humiliated and from that day, I did not accept any further invitations to eat in their house. The boy became an engineer and built a large house for himself in the village.

My family belongs to the Karan caste. They are progressive in their outlook, with reading and writing as their trade. People from my settlement usually work outside in towns as government officials or teachers. In other parts of India, we are called Kayasthas. At the worship of the goddess Durga, while the Vaishyas worship money and the Kshatriyas worship swords, the Karans worship books and pens.

Yet, neither my great-grandmother nor my grandmother could read or write. For a long time, my mother was not able to read or write either. While her brothers were sent to school, she was kept at home and taught cookery, needlework and how to manage a family. It was not considered necessary for women to be educated as their place was at home looking after the family. They learnt about life by listening to the readings from the epics and the Puranas, especially the *Mahabharata* and the *Ramayana*. A Brahmin came to the house to read the Puranas to my great-grandmother but she did not like depending on the priest. So she arranged for my mother to have lessons in reading and writing.

My father was keen that his daughter should be educated. He must have seen his senior officers sending their daughters to schools and colleges. There was no school in Nanpur but the villagers of Kusupur had built a girls' primary school. The headmistress went round the settlements persuading parents to send their daughters to her. A woman attendant was appointed to collect the girls from their homes and bring them back. My sister was sent to the school but when she reached puberty my grandmother would not allow her to continue her studies. 'She will become a *Kiristani*,' she grumbled.

My grandmother did not believe in women's emancipation although she controlled everybody in the house, including my grandfather and father. She once forced her husband to go through an elaborate purification ceremony when she found out that he had eaten with some Muslims in Cuttack. This ritual included drinking a mixture of cow dung and urine. My father was not allowed to take my mother with him to his place of work. She had to stay in the village to look after my grandmother.

In her spare time, my mother read the Puranas while the village women gathered around her to listen, discussing the various themes. She had a few Puranas, including the *Mahabharata* and the *Ramayana*, and she must have read them hundreds of times from the beginning to the end and then starting again.

The year before I was born the family house was destroyed by a fire. My father wanted to construct a new building with brick and cement but my grandmother objected. She did not like the idea of burning clay to make bricks. To her, earth was Vasudha, Mother Earth, and the Brahmin priest agreed with her. My father compromised with a timber structure supporting a corrugated-iron roof. The walls were made of mud, the timber was brought from the forest along the river during the monsoon, and several carpenters decorated the posts and joists with carvings. The house was built on a raised platform, with an outside verandah facing south and a small internal courtyard. In one corner stands the altar, containing the *tulashi* plant, so valuable for its medicinal properties that it is worshipped as a goddess.

My grandfather worked as the managing agent for a land-lord. He wanted to educate his son but there was no school in the village and my father walked six miles to the nearest primary school. He had to discontinue his studies at the age of twelve because there was no high school in the locality.

My brother was the eldest son, my parents expected a lot of him. My father tried to give him a good education and got him admitted to a school in the town where he was working. He even engaged tutors to coach him, but my brother was not interested in studying and did not complete his matricu-lation. My parents were disappointed. To help him settle down, they got him married but his wife died of typhoid only twenty days after the wedding. Without telling anybody he left home and joined the Royal Indian Air Force. It was during the Second World War. My mother was heartbroken and prayed to her gods for the war to end and her son to return.

After the war, my brother came back to the village and had nothing to do. He farmed a few acres of the family land for a year but was not successful. My father persuaded him to apply to the police service for a post of sub-inspector and he was accepted because of his service background. Soon afterwards, he married again. He is now retired and lives with his wife in the village.

He has four sons and two daughters, all grown-up. Apart from one son, they are all married. Eight years ago the eldest son, Satya, married a girl from Cuttack. He said he was in love with her.

'Does she love you?' I asked.

'Yes.'

'How do you know?'

'The way she looks at me.'

They had only looked at each other and they were in love.
They had met a few times in relatives' homes, surrounded
by friends, but had never talked to each other. There was an
exchange of emotions through their eyes which I had read
about only in novels.

Satya's parents had dreamt of selecting a bride with a
good dowry. But he was determined to marry the girl of his
choice and as it was a love marriage the question of dowry
did not arise.

My brother had wanted to educate his son, but although
Satya passed his matriculation, he was not interested in
higher studies. My brother was working in the steel town of
Rourkela as a police inspector and he arranged a job for him
in the factory. Satya refused: he regarded working there as
beneath his dignity and wanted a managerial post. Soon he
realized he did not have the necessary qualifications and tried
to get admission into a technical college to learn a skill. As
he was unable to get a place in Orissa, he went to Madras to
study automobile engineering. But in the end, the course
proved too difficult for him and he left without completing
it. Too ashamed to return to Rourkela, he went to the village
to help with the farming. Soon he found the village way of
life dull and longed for the excitement of the town. Until
then he had spent most of his life in towns.

After marriage, Satya had to look for work again. With
the high rate of unemployment it proved difficult for him to
get a job so he and his wife decided that she would train as
a pathologist. It is relatively easier for women to find jobs.
She studied for two years and now works as a laboratory
assistant in the Children's Hospital in Cuttack. They have
two small sons and live in a house two miles away from the
hospital.

Satya's wife works hard. She gets up early in the morning,

prepares the children for school and leaves home to reach the hospital by eight. Satya takes her on his motor-bike and brings her back at one. She then prepares the midday meal for the family and any guests. The children return shortly afterwards and they all eat together. After a short rest in the afternoon, life begins again with the television programmes. Although she is now privately preparing for her BA, which she thinks will help her in her career, she always helps the children with their homework.

Satya often sits at home staring at the sky. He has started several small businesses but none of them has been successful. He believes he is a failure.

Once he came with me to Delhi to find a job. The gallery where I had my exhibition wanted to employ him but, after a week, he left without telling me and returned to his family in Cuttack. Later he explained that he could not have managed on the salary: the cost of living in Delhi was so high it would have been impossible for him to save anything to send his wife, which was the only purpose of leaving home. He had enjoyed the opening of my exhibition, when there was plenty to eat and drink and he was introduced to the guests as my nephew, but he found Delhi hectic and impersonal and missed his family and friends. For him life in Cuttack was better. He had a comfortable bed there and a wife to look after him and provide him with meals. He decided to go back and do something in Cuttack to supplement his wife's income. So far he has not been successful. Without any social welfare scheme or unemployment benefit it is difficult for him and his wife to manage.

My brother's youngest son was a good student and did well in his exams. He now works as a sales representative for a large pharmaceutical company, but my brother would prefer to see him working as a government officer in Orissa. A government job is considered more prestigious than a company job, even though it may bring less money.

My brother decided to arrange his marriage while I was there. He looked for a suitable bride but none of the girls he saw was up to his expectations. Once the whole family travelled thirty miles to inspect a girl, but they returned home in the evening tired and disappointed. The girl had a squint and her educational qualifications had been exaggerated by the mediator. Educated boys want to marry educated girls these days.

Shortly after my return to London, I received a letter from my brother telling me that his son had found a girl for himself. Her family were anxious to get her married quickly and I was invited to attend the ceremony. My nephew was disappointed I was unable to be present at his wedding. He wrote me a letter saying that although he had known the girl, he fell in love with her only after my departure from India.

My brother's two daughters were not interested in studying and having careers. They are both married with children and busy looking after their families. One is married to Kedar and lives in Cuttack; the other, married to a college lecturer, lives in a nearby town.

Satya's wife was the first woman in my family to work outside the house to earn money. But now several girls from the village are working in towns as secretaries, receptionists, teachers and nurses. Once on the bus to Bhubaneswar a girl started talking to me, but although her face seemed familiar I could not remember her name. As the conversation progressed, I realized she was the daughter of one of my distant uncles in Nanpur, now working as a stenographer in a government department in Bhubaneswar. She is married to a journalist and her husband encourages her to work. But she finds life difficult as she has to commute sixty miles every day. Apart from doing her job she has the added responsibility of looking after her family and children. It would be easier for her if she could get accommodation in Bhubaneswar, but it is difficult to get government quarters without pulling strings. In spite of all her problems she likes working because she is independent. 'I don't want to be somebody's wife or daughter-in-law, I want to be myself,' she told me.

This is an attitude which is now being expressed more openly by educated girls. Although they are economically independent they are not emotionally free. They need husbands and families to gain respect in society.

Sita fell in love with one of her classmates while studying at the university in Bhubaneswar. She was twenty-two but looked younger. Her thin, sensitive, oval face was always filled with melancholy, as if she was crying inside. Her mother had died when she was very young and her father had married again, but Sita was looked after by her grandparents. She often came to our house to talk to my nephew about her studies. They were at college together. Sometimes she would ask me about the social services in England.

Sita was a good student and got a first-class Master's degree in sociology. She won a scholarship to study in Delhi for a year and the government of Orissa offered her a good job. When she returned to Bhubaneswar from Delhi she found that the attitude of her lover had changed. His parents were looking for a bride who would bring a large dowry. She knew that her father was against the dowry system and had spent the little money he had on her education.

One afternoon a car arrived in my settlement with a corpse. It was Sita's. Her grandfather was distraught. He walked from one end of the village to the other shouting, 'Her lover killed her!' Later, it was discovered that the previous day she had confronted her lover in Bhubaneswar about his marriage, threatening to commit suicide. He did not take her seriously and said he would marry whoever his parents chose for him. She had brought some tablets with her and she swallowed them in front of him. She collapsed and was taken to a relative's house. The men had gone to work and only the women were at home. Not knowing what to do, they panicked. Sita was crying out for help, pointing to her throat and eventually, the women managed to get her to the hospital, but she died soon afterwards. The police investigated and the boy told them that he loved Sita but was forced to agree to an arranged marriage.

Everyone in the village was distressed. It was such a waste of a beautiful life. Fortunately, tragedy was averted in another case.

When Neela was working in Cuttack as a health inspector she fell in love with a Brahmin boy and they wanted to marry. Both her parents were dead and her brother had brought her up and paid for her university education. Brahmins consider non-Brahmins as untouchable and nobody from our settlement had ever married a Brahmin before, so neither Neela's brother nor the boy's parents approved of the relationship. Neela became so unhappy that she took an overdose of sleeping pills. The next morning she was found unconscious and taken to hospital, where she later recovered. The incident confirmed to everyone that she really loved the boy and the wedding took place. But the Brahmin community did not accept her.

Once girls leave the village and go to towns for further education, they think the arranged marriage system is old-fashioned. It is easy for them to get jobs, and money gives them economic independence. The idea of romantic love is attractive but not encouraged by society. As a result the girls keep their relationships secret and when tensions arise, there is no one in the family to turn to for help.

My niece Radha kneels down and touches my feet to pay her respects. I ask her if she is happy.

'No. My brothers and sister have sons and I only have daughters. There must be something wrong with his genes. His sister has only produced girls.'

I am surprised by her scientific attitude to life which must be due to her regular visits to a gynaecologist in Cuttack. She did not conceive for three years after marriage and the members of her husband's family spread the rumour that she was barren. She was upset and told her mother who in turn came to me for help. It is not considered proper for wives to discuss these matters with their husbands.

I took my niece to a gynaecologist friend. I do not know what was discussed and what the treatment was, but a few months later Radha became pregnant. 'I was delighted that it was a healthy baby, but my husband's family was disappointed it was not a son,' she said.

Apart from consulting the gynaecologist, Radha worships gods and goddesses for a boy. The women of Nanpur worship Satyapir so that he will bless them with sons. My mother's first child was a daughter, then she had a son who died of diphtheria when he was two years old. Ten years passed and my mother could not conceive again. She became anxious and prayed to Satyapir. Soon my eldest brother was born. She dedicated him to the deity and named him Fakir Charan, after the wandering Muslim holy man. Satyapir is a Hindu-Muslim god; 'Satya' in Sanskrit means truth and 'pir' in Islam is saint. I believe that it was an attempt to bring Hindus and Muslims together through religion.

There is a poem in Oriya which says, 'What is the point of having a parrot as a pet if it does not chant the name of God? The house looks beautiful with a housewife, but what is the point of having a housewife if she does not have a son on her lap?' It is believed that a house is not a home without a child. Women are always blamed if they don't have children; nobody blames their husbands. Producing a child, particularly a son, elevates the status of the woman in the house: she is not only a wife but a mother.

When a child is born the first question asked is, 'Is it a boy or a girl?' If it is a girl she is accepted with disappointment. But if it is a boy the family celebrates with joy. Couples keep having children until a son is born. The plot on which the family house stands should never remain unoccupied. It is the responsibility of every male to ensure this. In my childhood people used to curse their enemies by saying, 'Let jackals howl on your family plot.'

A Brahmin in the village had six daughters before he could

accept family planning. Fortunately for him the seventh child was a son. The villagers do not like the idea of men having a vasectomy as they believe the operation makes them *napunsak*. Sanjay Gandhi's campaign during the Emergency, when men were forced to undergo vasectomies, gave the whole concept of family planning a bad name. Several men in the village say they have grown old, both mentally and physically, after their vasectomy. So women do not like their husbands to have the operation although there are financial incentives, and volunteer to be sterilized instead. Some complain of feeling unwell after sterilization but most suffer silently.

In case the wife or children die, there is always a hope for the man to marry again and have a son to continue the family name. The wife cannot marry again unless she is from a lower caste. In some cases wives have persuaded their husbands to have another wife so that a son can be born.

When I was studying in high school, I had a friend from a nearby village. He was the only son of a landowner. Our families used to visit each other and exchange presents. One year when I returned from spending the summer vacation with my father in the forest, I was told that my friend had died of typhoid. It was a great shock and his parents were completely shattered. His mother had conceived him after many years of marriage and it was now too late to have any more children. She tried to persuade her husband to marry again. He was unwilling but she made all the arrangements for the wedding. She selected the bride and forced him to go through the marriage ceremony. They were all excited when the new wife became pregnant, but a girl was born. Shortly afterwards the husband died.

After many years of marriage the village carpenter had no children. So he and his wife adopted his sister's son, but they soon realized it was not the same as having their own child. His wife told him she had promised her father-in-law the family name would continue and to his surprise, she announced to the whole village that she was getting her husband married again. A bride was selected by her from a poor family and on the honeymoon night she sent her reluctant husband to the new wife. Thereafter she decided which nights the husband should spend with her and which nights with the new wife. They both became pregnant. She gave birth to a son and the second wife had a daughter.

Children were always born at home. There were no hospitals or midwives and a Harijan woman came to help at the time of birth. But many women died. Becoming pregnant was like receiving a death sentence. Women gave birth squatting on the mud floor, holding on to a pole. No men were allowed into the room. A fire was lit to keep the mother and child warm. After the birth, the mother was not allowed to leave the room for seven days as she was considered impure. She was given herbal medicines including dry ginger mixed with honey and ghi to help her recover. Occasionally a little brandy was added. Shells were used to cut the umbilical cord and as spoons to feed the baby.

Now women from the better-off families go to Cuttack to have their babies delivered, either in hospital or in private nursing homes. Those who cannot afford the expense stay in the village and can have the help of a trained midwife, now attached to the health centre. There is no ambulance service and in complicated cases the mother is taken to the main hospital in Cuttack either by bus or taxi.

A few years ago I was shopping at Balichandrapur when I saw a small crowd. A woman from an interior village had been brought on a stretcher to the health centre. She had been having labour pains for five days and local remedies had no effect. At that time there was no midwife at the health centre and the doctor on duty was reluctant to take responsibility as surgery was essential. He advised taking her to hospital immediately. There was a feeling of despair as the family did not have any money for transport and medical treatment. The local shopkeepers got together, raised some money and sent her to Cuttack in a taxi. A son was born and the mother's life was saved.

Nothing has changed. Recently a woman from the washermen's settlement was giving birth at home. The baby's arm came out first but its body remained stuck. The women helping her were frightened and a relative took her to the health centre, four miles away. After several hours the doctor said he was unable to help and suggested taking her to another health centre. This involved a further journey of six miles in a cycle rickshaw. But the doctor there said she needed urgent surgery which could only be done in Cuttack.

The relative had no money to hire a vehicle, so he returned to the village for help. As the family was extremely poor, the villagers quickly donated some money and the woman was eventually taken to Cuttack Hospital in a state of collapse. An operation was carried out. The baby was already dead but by a miracle the mother survived.

Bunnu massages her six-month-old son with turmeric paste and castor oil while her father-in-law, my brother, narrates the story of the baby's birth.

As it was her first pregnancy, he took Bunnu regularly to Cuttack to be checked by a gynaecologist. Two weeks before the expected date of delivery they all moved to Cuttack – Bunnu, her husband, my brother and his wife. As soon as she complained of discomfort, she was taken to the hospital and admitted. There was a shortage of nursing staff so my brother, his wife and some other relatives stayed with Bunnu to look after her. The labour room was crowded as there were about five to ten relatives present for each expectant mother.

A doctor helped her to deliver. Everybody was so delighted that the baby was a boy that Bunnu was forgotten for a while. Nobody realized she was bleeding until a woman relative noticed a pool of blood on the floor. Bunnu was on the verge of collapse. There was no doctor to attend to her and my brother ran to the consultant's house near by. She telephoned the hospital and made arrangements for the treatment. Bunnu was given two pints of blood which had to be purchased from the blood bank.

Bunnu interrupts my brother by saying she cannot remember anything about the incident and that it is a wonderful feeling to be a mother.

My brother and his wife were disappointed that the baby had a dark skin. 'Nobody in our family is so dark,' my brother says. But to me the baby looks beautiful with a round smiling face and big bright eyes. At the age of six months he already knows that he is loved by everybody.

When I was a child, my mother prayed all the time. She offered herself completely to her gods. She had her personal gods which she kept in a box, wrapped in a piece of cloth. Every morning, after her bath, she sat on the floor performing her rituals. With the help of a little mirror she examined her hair, arranged it, and put a vermilion spot on her forehead and in the parting of her hair. Then she took out her gods, put them on a metal plate and washed them, taking a little of the water into her mouth. She decorated the gods with sandalwood paste, leaves of sacred basil, and yellow and white flowers – no red hibiscus, as red is the colour of the goddess Durga. Then a plate of bananas and molasses was offered. She took a little of the bananas and molasses and put them on the floor. Taking a little water in her right palm, which she moved in a circle, she lifted the plate and offered it to the gods. Then she bent down to pray. After that she read the *Bhagavadgita* and through the religious stories she learnt about life, art and music.

When my mother prayed, I prayed with her. I wanted to have my own gods so I bought some brass images of Radha and Krishna and worshipped them on my own, imitating my mother. I made a little wooden temple for them and painted it with bright colours. The gods were like my children. I woke them up in the morning, offered them food, and put them to bed at night. I got immense pleasure from serving them. I entertained them with lights and incense, celebrating all the festivals connected with Radha and Krishna.

When I left for Bombay to study architecture my mother looked after my gods as well as her own. As she grew older she was unable to perform the rituals herself and a Brahmin boy came every day to attend to them.

Now the collection of deities has increased. The other members of the family have added their gods and goddesses and my sister-in-law is responsible for looking after them. Like my mother, she spends a lot of her time performing all the rituals. In place of my little temple now stands a bigger one, where the gods are kept on a large wooden platform in a small room of their own. It is called *thakura ghara*. Among the gods is a photograph of Sai Baba, the holy man from South India with his Afro haircut. My brother and his wife are devotees and affectionately call him 'Baba'. He has followers from all over India and, according to his disciples, he performs miracles. He produces gold chains, fruit and holy ash from the empty air as if by magic and offers them to his devotees. In the beginning, my brother was sceptical about Sai Baba but his wife converted him. When he was ill and having problems with his job she persuaded him to visit Sai Baba. Reluctantly, he made the long journey with some friends. Devotees had come from all over India and it was a large gathering, but the holy man came and talked to him, giving him some *bibhuti*. He returned home feeling peaceful and happy. His problems were resolved and his illness subsided. Now he wears a chain round his neck with a photograph of the holy man in a locket.

Most of the villagers have their personal gods whom they worship daily. As the men are busy working they do not have time to perform the daily religious rituals and the responsibility falls on the women. Until recently the Harijan women had no time either as they went out to work in the fields. Now some young Harijan women are imitating their high-caste neighbours by not doing manual work and staying at home to look after their families, so they have the time to worship gods and goddesses. While the educated women from high castes are discarding some of their elaborate rituals as old-fashioned, the Harijan women are performing them with sincerity, in the belief that by being religious they can also prosper.

4

WOMEN

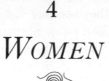

THE role of a woman in Nanpur is still that of a housewife and a mother. She has the responsibility of looking after the household and if she manages it well, bringing prosperity, she is compared to Laxmi, the Goddess of Wealth. If she destroys its unity, then she is called Kali or Chandi, the Goddesses of Destruction.

From childhood, girls are trained to become good housewives and to look after their husbands and their families. Women learn to make sacrifices for men, they cook food for them, clean their clothes and wash their dishes. It is not considered masculine for men to enter the kitchen, which is the most sacred place in the house. There is a strict division of labour: women look after the home while men go out to work and earn money for the family. Although this is breaking down, as educated women are beginning to go out to work, the responsibility of feeding the family remains with the mother. In the lower castes women are expected to go out to work, to supplement their husbands' income. They are more independent and often leave their husbands if there is tension. Divorces are accepted in lower castes but not in high castes as it is considered a disgrace.

Girls go through a special ceremony when they reach puberty. They are kept in a separate room for six days and not allowed to see a man's face. During that period the girls are considered impure and must not touch anything in the house. On the seventh day they take a bath, put on a new

sari and go to worship Lord Shiva. Rice pudding is distributed among the relatives and the village knows that the
girl is ready for marriage.

Getting a daughter married is a burden, but the villagers
believe that when God created men and women he created
partners for them. It is the responsibility of the parents to
search for the right one for their child. Everything depends
on the ability and willingness of the father to pay a dowry.
Although it is forbidden by law boys' parents openly demand
dowry – money, gold ornaments, a motor-cycle. Refriger-
ators and television sets have also been added to the list.
Money is most important as it is accepted that boys have to
give bribes to get jobs.

When my mother was married no dowry was demanded,
as my grandmother thought it more important to get a good
daughter-in-law. But now eligible grooms are treated like
items in an auction, and go to the highest bidder. In Orissa
an Indian administrative officer tops the list, closely followed
by engineers, doctors and bank officials. For a boy his job is
more important than his looks. But a girl must be beautiful,
a virgin and have a fair skin. Dark girls are considered ugly.

After marriage the bride leaves her parents' house and
goes to live with her husband's parents and family. This is
called *sashughara*. It is a very delicate situation for the girl
to adjust to, as the mother-in-law controls the running of the
family. Tension between the mother-in-law and the daughter-in-law is accepted as a fact of life but a clever wife
keeps her husband under her control. There is a saying that,
'Whoever sleeps beside you at night and whispers in your ear
is never wrong.' At the same time, men controlled by their
wives are often laughed at.

All girls know that one day they will go to *sashughara*, and
they are trained by their mothers, aunts and particularly
their sisters-in-law to be able to cope in their new sur-
roundings.

Now parents want their daughters to study, because educated boys want to marry educated girls who can work and

supplement their income. It is not easy to manage on one person's earnings.

There is almost no free mixing between boys and girls. A bride must be a virgin and if it is known that a girl has been mixing with boys it will be difficult for her to marry.

'I am married with two children, both boys – one is twelve and the other ten. My parents-in-law, my husband's two brothers and their families, live with us. Most of my time is spent in the kitchen, cooking for the family and the guests. We always have guests. Being a joint family we have lots of relatives and they like visiting us. It is difficult for me to cook on a wood fire, the smoke hurts my eyes, so I have asked my husband to bring a gas cooker from Cuttack. I have a small electric stove but I cannot depend on electricity. If it comes for five minutes it goes out for ten, the kitchen becomes dark and I can't see anything. One day I burnt my finger, but when I told my husband he got annoyed with me. He said I wanted to live in luxury and was not able to adjust to his village way of life. We have a kerosene stove as well but you have to push the pump and I haven't got the strength in my hands. My mother-in-law shouts at me instead of helping me. The house is only peaceful when she leaves and goes to visit her daughter.

'Recently my husband took her to the town where her daughter lives. Her daughter had given birth to a son and we had to spend money for the baby's delivery. But where would we get the money from? My husband works as a teacher and only gets about one thousand rupees a month. He takes it out on me and the children. When he went to see his sister he had to take money for a television set, part of the dowry still outstanding. On top of that there were the travelling and living expenses of himself and his mother for eight days. When I said we didn't have the money to give a TV as dowry, my sister-in-law cried. She said her parents-in-law kept rebuking her and wrote letter after letter telling us her sad stories. My mother-in-law started to cry that we didn't give enough to her daughter. So reluctantly, we agreed. The boy's parents wanted the TV in their village but I said to my mother-in-law, "Why should we send the TV to the village when our girl and her husband are staying in the town? Whatever we gave as dowry has been kept by the parents-in-law. If we have to give, then we should give to your daughter." But the boy's parents wanted to keep the dowry for their daughter's marriage.

'Visiting her daughter was an event for my mother-in-law. She was going there for the first time, and it was decided she should wear chappals. She didn't know how to wear them and kept putting the left one on the right foot and the right one on the left foot. I had to teach her how to wear them, and also how to wear undergarments. I said, "You are going to a modern household and they won't like you chewing pan or using tobacco as toothpaste." She said, "I'm not going to a stranger's house, I'm going to see my daughter and her husband. They will look after me." She practised for fifteen days before they were due to go. She wore the chappals wherever she went, but always had difficulty in putting them on properly. The children laughed. "Look, grandmother is wearing her chappals on the wrong feet!" I told them not to make fun of her. "She's an old woman," I said.

'My mother-in-law announced to all her friends that she was going to visit her daughter. "It's a new place and they have a different system. My son has bought me chappals, a new sari and undergarments" – and she showed them to everybody. When she came back from her visit she was full of praise. "My daughter has a dining table and a doormat to clean your feet, a water filter and a water tap. If you turn the tap the water comes." "Why didn't you stay there?" I asked. "How could I stay with my daughter?" she said.

'My sister-in-law is a lovely girl. She always helped me look after my children. We decided to educate her and she passed her Intermediate in arts. She was dark and not beautiful. We knew if we didn't get her married when she was young, it would be difficult to get a suitable bridegroom later on. So we looked for a groom and asked our friends to help us. In the end, a friend of my husband's brought a proposal. He said that the boy was not interested in seeing the girl, but I insisted that they should see each other. His father and brother came to see her and liked her, but I insisted the boy must see the girl as well.

'He came here during his summer holidays and when I saw him I started to cry. He was so handsome and fair. I knew he would want an equally beautiful bride. He greeted me and we sat down to talk. I thought I should warn him and said, "My sister-in-law is not as beautiful as you." "Beauty doesn't last, quality is important in life," he replied. "She must be a good girl, as she has been brought up by you." The mediator asked me to bring my sister-in-law into the room. I put a cup of coffee on a tray and asked her to serve the guest. But she started to cry. "Why are you crying?" I asked. "Girls have to go to the *sashughara* one day."

'My sister-in-law and I only stayed in the room for a minute. She put the tray on the table and we both left. The mediator came out and said, "Yes, the wedding will take place." I was so happy that I cried. People cry in pain and they also cry when they are happy. The boy asked me, "Sister, why are you crying?" But I started crying again. When I told my sister-in-law about the marriage she was silent. Then she said quietly, "Whatever you and my brother decide is all right by me." But before she had said she did not want to marry; she had seen the problems of married life.

'The boy's father had money, land, and had built a house of brick and cement. But he was very greedy. We spent ten thousand rupees on the agreement ceremony. We gave a gold chain, a gold ring, but nothing was to his liking. He demanded twenty thousand rupees in cash, gold ornaments for the bride, furniture, a table fan, an iron chest, a refrigerator, a television set and a motor-bike. We had to arrange for all this dowry to get the girl married. Nowadays even if you have money you can't get your daughters married, so we decided that whatever happened we would raise the money for the dowry. My husband had been saving regularly for his sister's wedding, but it was not enough. We got some more money from his Provident Fund and also borrowed from our relatives.

'My sister-in-law is happy. Her husband is a nice man. I was very worried at first. These days some brides commit suicide because of torment over the dowry. Parents say, "Others are getting so much dowry for their sons, why can't we get as much for ours who is equally qualified?" The dowry elevates a boy's status. We spent all that money on her wedding. Now she is pregnant and will come here for her delivery, and we will have to spend for that. But it is good, she can have some rest.

'We are building a new house. My brother-in-law works in Cuttack and says he cannot contribute more than two thousand rupees. His wife is very complicated. She keeps everything to herself. She had a daughter last year and again she's pregnant. She suffers from anaemia, she has no blood. So how can she get strength in her body? She can't have any medicines because of her pregnancy, but she is given milk and has a good diet. She complains that she has three daughters and I have sons. "It's better for you that I don't have any daughters, otherwise I wouldn't look after yours," I say. But I don't need any more children, sons or daughters. My only wish is to get my two sons established in life. Whether our children are sons or daughters, they are not going to look after us. We'll live alone in our old age.

'I see how the old people are being treated now. When the sons get married, they leave the village and stay in the towns with their up-to-date wives who are reluctant to come and live here. They say, "We won't go to a village, there's no road, no electricity, no cinema, no friends, no proper schools, our children will suffer, they won't get enough milk. We don't want to go and live in difficulties." Whether the girls are educated or uneducated, this is their attitude. If the father is ill in the village and sends a message to his son, his wife says, "You go and visit him first, then I will go with the children." Although nowadays daughters-in-law don't look after their mothers-in-law, I look after my husband's mother. I know I have to look after her.

'My eldest son is called Raja and the younger one Naba. Raja is very simple. He will eat anything you give him. If you hit him he won't cry. But Naba will react violently. He likes good food, meat, fish, eggs, but Raja doesn't make any fuss. He's satisfied with rice and dal. But he's not good at studies. He fails in mathematics and my husband punishes him. He's so afraid of his father that he forgets his studies.

'My husband says that the boys should always study as he did when he was a child. But what he doesn't realize is that when he was a child there wasn't a road and the village was isolated. He didn't know there was an outside world. Now the children of today know everything. They see television, cinema, so they want to eat well and dress well. If we are always telling our children about our wants and difficulties what will be their outlook? Once, we went to Cuttack to visit a relative. Their son had a small cycle and my sons wanted one. Naba pleaded with his father, "Papa, can't you buy a cycle for us?" My husband got angry with him and shouted. Naba was hurt, children are very sensitive. You have to explain to them, "Riding a cycle can cause accidents. You can have one when you grow up." Everyone has wishes and they don't cost money. Children don't understand our problems. They see other children wearing nice clothes and want them for themselves. They may not have good clothes for daily use, but at least they should have some nice clothes for special occasions, otherwise they feel unhappy.

'They don't tell their father, they tell the mother, "My friend has got beautiful clothes, we don't have any. His father earns the same as papa, but they have a clock, why can't we have one?" What can I say to that? When I discuss this with my husband he gets annoyed with me. He says I have got big eyes. I know I have suffered in my life but I don't want my children to suffer. I want my children to live well, eat well, dress well and remain healthy. What's the point of having money, it's not going to take me to heaven. My children are always pleading with me, "Give me this, give me that." Their father may be indifferent but a mother's heart cannot refuse to listen. Still, I'm helpless because I don't earn anything. I have no money to buy anything for my children.

'When Raja and Naba get older and go to college we'll have to spend more on them. If we had a girl we would have to spend at least three hundred rupees on a dress, and she would require three to four dresses to go to college. All the children are like that now. But how can you punish them? My husband is like a dictator, everybody must obey his orders. He says I'm not practical, as if he is the only one who is practical.

'There is a time for study and a time for play. If children study all the time, won't they get dull? As soon as their father arrives Raja gets frightened. He goes so quiet as if he has got no life in him. He won't eat anything while his father is in the room. But Naba is not frightened of his father. "I study well, so why should I be afraid of my father?" he says. Raja will sleep anywhere but Naba needs a clean bed. Still, their father wants them to be like him. He says that he had a simple life so everyone should lead simple lives. But we are not all the same. You like rice and dal, but I like fish curry and my children like goat meat.

'Naba is very smart. He looks after his clothes and is always acting. He studies well, speaks nicely, imitates others, is a good actor and dances all the time. But the school is not very good here. His friends are from uneducated families, so what can he learn from them? When he was about three he used to say, "Why is the bus not running on the train lines, and why is the train not running on the roads?" The other day he said, "When father had a bike he used to complain that his legs were tired, now he has got a scooter and still complains of tiredness in his legs. You sit on the scooter and it moves. Why should the legs ache?" He wants to know the reason behind everything. The other day he came and told me, "Why don't you work as a teacher? If you were a teacher you could go to school. You won't have to do all this work in the house. My wife will work. She won't be a housewife like you. When you grow old I'll keep a servant to look after you but I won't let you and father live together. Otherwise you will quarrel like our old grandfather and grandmother. You'll stay with me and father will stay with my brother."

'Naba will come to the kitchen and help me cook, cuddle me and then say to his brother, "Mother has cooked something nice, let us eat." He thinks he's the elder brother and that his elder brother is his younger brother. He loves his brother, they are always together. The villagers say they are like Rama and Laxman. If by chance his brother hasn't returned from school he'll get worried. "Where is my brother? Why hasn't he returned?" "Do you know my brother?" he will ask the children returning from the high school. "He is in Class VIII, have you seen him?" When his brother arrives he gets angry and says, "Where have you been? Why are you so late?" Then he will start embracing him. He fights with him but at the same time he is very fond of him.

'The other day I felt dizzy and fell down. I couldn't understand where I was. As I was recovering I heard Naba say to his brother, "Don't worry, mother is not dead. She is breathing. She has only fallen down. She's alive."

'At Cuttack in a relative's house he saw a wall clock and was intrigued by the sound it produced. So he asked me, "Why can't father get a wall clock like that?" He goes to school regularly. I think he will do well. He writes all the time and his right hand is getting bent by writing. But he's always hungry. He must be munching all the time and on holidays, he's particularly hungry.

'Once I asked my husband to buy a TV but he said, "If you get a TV then the children won't be interested in their studies," and he got annoyed at my suggestion. The neighbours on both sides have a TV so the children went and watched T V in their houses. They spent the whole of Sunday watching it. So I asked my husband again. He said he didn't have the money to buy it. I said, "You can sell my gold bangles." He kept quiet. The next week he went to Cuttack and got a television set. Although you can buy television sets in Balichandrapur, they're cheaper in Cuttack. The children are happy now. We watch the epics on Sunday mornings and in the afternoon we watch films. The children can't understand English but they can imagine the Hindi programmes.

'There's always tension in the house. My husband says I can't adjust to him and I don't know how to adjust. He doesn't say how I should adjust. I can't understand why he shouldn't adjust to me. He may like rice and dal but I want a change. If I have rice and dal today, the next day I want rice, dal and vegetables or sometimes a little fish curry or fried vegetables. If you eat rice and dal every day you lose your appetite. If I explain this to him, he will say I don't adjust to him.

'I'm not spending a lot. I don't go to the cinema or to the town. I stay at home and work like a slave. It's now two months since I asked my husband to buy a gas cylinder. He knows that my eyes water when I'm using firewood. I don't say these things to other people, I only blame my parents. They brought me up in a town in comfort and selected a husband for me who doesn't share my attitudes. I work twenty-four hours a day, don't you think I should want to go out a little?

'I would like to go to Cuttack and see my friends or go to a cinema. He goes to the school in the morning and comes home in the evening. He meets his friends, plays cards with them, but I struggle inside the house from morning to evening. I can't go anywhere on my own because I haven't got the money. Then he says, "Why don't you go out and work?" I reply, "Why didn't you tell me in the beginning, when I married you? Why after fourteen years of marriage? There are other teachers in your school, are their wives

working? I've seen them going out together, while I have to
stay at home.''

'Nobody enquires about my health. My mother-in-law
never speaks sweetly to me. She nags and it is impossible to
adjust with her. She always misunderstands and twists things
and her rule is like the British rule. If I don't complain about
my health and work all the time I'm a good daughter-in-law.
But if I fall ill and cannot work, after four or five days they
say, "Go to your father's house." She thought that when her
son married she would get a maidservant for herself. The day
I arrived, after the wedding, she made me drink the water
she had washed her feet in. After that I got all the worm
infections. But now my sister-in-law doesn't obey her.

'She used to say, "I have brought a Katki bride, she's from
the town and I have to be afraid of her." She always wants
her son and daughter-in-law to quarrel. The son is hers but
the daughter-in-law is an outsider. I said, "All right, get a
girl from the village and let's see how she will look after
you." My mother-in-law hasn't got the strength to fight with
my sister-in-law, who is a village girl. When she screams, the
whole house trembles, so my mother-in-law has to keep quiet,
she hasn't got the strength to fight with her. The other day,
I told her, "I treat you well because I come from an educated
family and I know how my father treated my mother." But
when I see her sad face I feel guilty. She's now an old woman,
how long is she going to live? I tell my sister-in-law not to
quarrel with her. I say, "She has sacrificed a lot to bring up
her sons, let us help them to live in peace. Will they live
for ever? Because we have our old parents-in-law we have
strength. We feel happy when we see them." But my sister-
in-law says I am supporting our mother-in-law. The drama
goes on. It's like the United Nations. You have to measure
a foot but walk an inch.'

According to Indian tradition women are goddesses, but in
fact they have always been under the control of men. Mrs
Gandhi changed this attitude and Indian women identified

themselves with her. If Mrs Gandhi could become a leader and control the men of India, women thought they could do the same.

A woman without a husband has no place in the village. It is considered a curse to become a widow. Widows are not allowed to take part in religious and social ceremonies as it is feared they may bring bad luck. After the husband's death a woman has to break her glass bangles and stop wearing the vermilion spot on her forehead. Often she is blamed for the death, but nobody blames a husband when his wife dies before him.

Rani is fifty-five, a widow and still beautiful. She has a contemplative oval face with very sad eyes which reflect all the suffering she has gone through in her life. Her husband died when she was thirty and the responsibility of looking after her six young children fell on her shoulders.

Her husband, Kanhu, was married before but his first wife committed suicide. A farmer working in the fields on the opposite side of the river saw her enter the water one day. He thought she was going to have a bath. But then, suddenly, she threw herself into the water and was carried away by the current. The whole village gathered on the bank of the river while the men searched for her in vain.

After her death Kanhu left the village to work in the forest. He was tall, thin and quite good-looking, although he had lost an eye when he was a child. When his friends asked him to marry again he refused to listen to them. 'Who would give me their daughter?' he said.

He lived alone until he was fifty, when he realized that he had no children to carry on the family name. He also needed a woman to look after him. He asked his friends to help him find a bride, but they suggested that he keep a mistress instead. It would have been possible for him to get a woman from a lower caste but he wanted to marry a girl from his own caste and have children by her. A relative introduced him to Rani's parents.

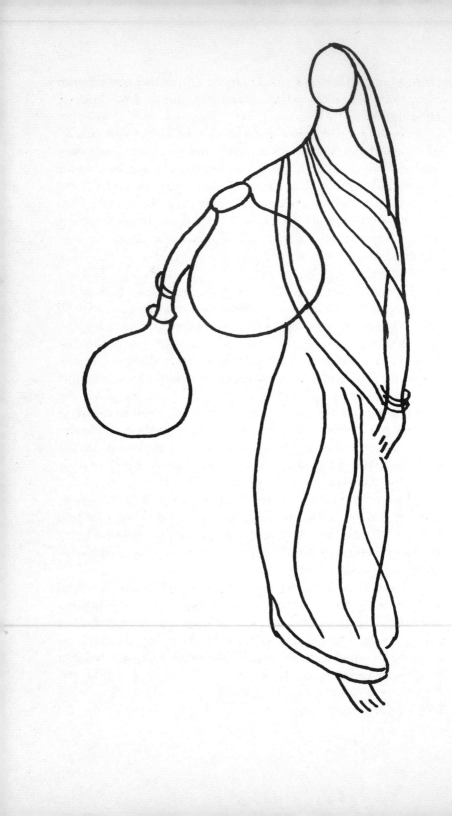

Rani was young and the villagers said that her husband was very lucky to have such a beautiful bride. On the honeymoon night Kanhu was so excited that he could not perform. The next night the same thing happened. He was worried. He thought he had a disease and consulted a friend, who suggested he saw the healer. But Kanhu did not believe in local remedies and said he wanted to see a doctor at Cuttack. He had lost his eye when he was a child because he had used some herbal ointment prepared by a healer. That memory was so strong that he was afraid of losing his virility.

Fortunately, he had a friend in town who worked in the electricity department and knew all the influential people. Among them was a young doctor, who had returned recently from London, and Kanhu and his friend decided to consult him. When it came to the fee his friend said, 'Don't worry, I'll look after that. I have helped the doctor's family so much. Whenever the electricity fails in their home I arrange for it to be repaired immediately. I'm sure he won't charge a fee.'

One evening they went to the doctor's house. The doctor listened to Kanhu's story, examined him and prescribed a series of medicines – vitamins, hormones and tranquillizers. They were expensive, but they worked. Rani became pregnant.

After that she became pregnant almost every year, and in ten years she had four sons and two daughters. The villagers thought it was a miracle. Kanhu's younger brother had been praying for children but could not have any. It was all God's *Leela*, the villagers said.

'My father died when I was very small. In our house there was my mother and several brothers and sisters. We had no land, only the family house. My mother did not have any money and worked as a part-time maidservant. Feeding us was a burden for her. She could not send any of us to school. My brothers could not read, so who cared about my going to school?

'When I reached puberty my mother was anxious to get

me married, but she had no money to pay for the dowry. All my friends were getting married, so I knew that one day I would also get married. But when this proposal came to marry an old man, I felt ashamed. My friends were marrying young and handsome boys and some of them made fun of me. I cried, but my mother said he was a good man and would look after me. He would also look after my young brothers and sisters and our problems would be solved. A young girl from our village had married a sixty-year-old man and was happy. My husband was younger than him, he was working and had money and land. It would be good for the family.

'After the marriage, when I looked at my husband's tired face with only one eye, I felt compassionate and kind and knew I would have to look after him. He was a very nice man. I never asked him for anything, for money or saris. He always gave them to me. He was very proud when our first son was born and gave a big feast to his friends and relatives at the name-giving ceremony. He named the little baby "Bhagwan". I was only seventeen and then, one after the other, I had six children – four sons and two daughters. My husband wanted to look after them and educate them. He said that when our children stood on their own feet our pains would be over. I was so busy looking after the family and children that I had no time to think. But there were some very happy days.

'Then suddenly my husband became ill. There was a growth in his stomach and I could feel it. I sold all my jewellery and arranged for him to have an operation in the hospital. He stayed there for three months. I spent all our savings on medicines and doctors, but he became thinner and thinner. One day the doctor told me there was no hope. Suddenly I felt the world had come to an end. But when I looked at the faces of my children I knew I had to live for them. I discussed the future with my husband and we decided to come to Nanpur to claim our portion of the ancestral property. Until then, his brother had been enjoying it all.

We came by train to the railway station and I arranged for a bullock cart to bring us here. When we arrived in the village, we found that his younger brother and his wife were occupying all the rooms in the family house. We spent two nights on the verandah until they reluctantly vacated two rooms for us.

'My old friends and relatives came to see me. They were helpful and gave me moral support. They looked after the children while I was nursing my husband. There was no food, so I sold some land. After a month my husband died. I had to sell some more land to pay for the cremation. I broke my bangles and removed the vermilion spot. It was a very distressing moment. I felt like committing suicide but again I knew I had to live for my children.

'It is difficult for a woman to survive alone in the village and I needed the support of a man. Several men came to see me under the pretext of helping me. I knew what they wanted just by looking at their eyes. They were married with wives and children whom I knew. I liked one of those men. He looked like my husband; he was the same age and had lost one of his eyes during his childhood when he had smallpox. He had money and land and was respected by all the villagers. I thought he would help me to settle the land dispute with my husband's brother. Some evenings he came to see me and stayed on for a while talking about his experiences.

'One night when the whole village was dark and silent, I heard a knock at the door. When I opened it I found him standing there. I asked him to come inside. I could not ask him to leave. I had thought I was too old to have a child and was horrified when I realized I was pregnant. Naranama, the washerwoman, told everyone in the village about it. She washes the sari after every monthly period. Some women came and asked if it was true. I said that I had a disease. Then after a month, they came to ask me again and I burst out crying. My friends said, "Don't worry, the world hasn't come to an end."

'I decided to have an abortion. It was a hard decision but

I knew it would be best for me. What would my children think when they grew up and knew about the child? If the child came into this world its life would really be difficult. I had six children and couldn't look after them properly. How could I look after an extra one? A friend brought a woman from the Untouchable settlement to me. She carried out abortions privately and wanted a lot of money. I didn't have enough. I tried to borrow from my relatives and friends but they were not prepared to lend it to me. Destroying an embryo was considered a great sin and they didn't want their money spent on that. I did not know what to do.

'My husband's brother was upset. He went and quarrelled with the man. "You have brought disgrace to the family," he told me. The man came to me and asked me to go and live with him and his wife. But how could I do that with my children in the same village? His wife supported him. "My husband is a virile man, not impotent, like some others in the village." Her remarks were pointed at my husband's brother.

'Six months passed. I still had no money to pay for the abortion. I was praying to God to help me. Then unexpectedly a relative came to my house. He asked me if I really wanted an abortion and he took me to Cuttack with him, where he had rented a house for me. I was not worried about it. That night two men came back with my relative. They were the doctors. I was given an injection and became unconscious. When I woke up it was early morning. I stayed in Cuttack for a week and returned home. The village women gathered around me and asked me what the doctor did. I felt like spitting in their faces. In the night the man came and knocked at the door. I did not open it.

'A widow's life is hard. Widows in the lower castes can get married again, but it is not done in our caste. I was not even allowed to leave the house or talk to a man: people would gossip that I was bringing shame to the family and the settlement. Nobody was prepared to help me. I had to help myself. I worked in relatives' homes and got some food and money. That's how I was able to feed my children. Now they have grown up and the two eldest sons are working in the town. One manages a small restaurant and the other works as a police constable. They are both married and have children. I am a grandmother.

'The next son was a tailor, he was a nice boy, very helpful. He was supporting the family because at that time his two elder brothers were unemployed. Suddenly one night he died of a snake bite. He had been sleeping on the verandah and woke up, saying something had bitten him. His elder brother was sleeping near him and when they both got up they found a snake. They killed it. The snake had bitten my son on the shoulder and after a while he felt unwell. He cried out, "Brother, help me, I'm going to die!" I did not know what to do. My feet could not move. The daughters got up and started to cry. Two boys from the village came to help. They went to the health centre but nobody was there. Then they went to a healer. He came to see my son and said, "Why did you kill the snake? I can't help you now. I could have done something if the snake was alive. Take him to the hospital in Cuttack." They put him on a motor-bike and carried him to hospital, but on the way he died. They brought him back to the village. His veins had burst and were oozing with blood. I felt my own life was bleeding. My husband had died on my lap and the village boys left my son on my lap. My pain was unbearable, but I had to live for my other children.

'I managed to get my two daughters married. I had no money for the dowry, so I couldn't get educated boys for them. The girls have left now, but two other girls have come – my daughters-in-law. They have children and we all live together.

'My youngest son did not study and just wandered about. Once, he went away with a lorry driver and only returned after two months. I was very worried about him. Sometimes without telling me, his brothers, or anybody in the village, he would go away to his uncle's house. I would start worrying. But now he is old enough to have some sense. He got a loan from the bank to start his own business and has started a small stall near the bridge, selling cigarettes, betel nuts and other things. People from our caste never succeed in business, but my son has a good business sense. He is not giving any money to me as he says he wants to save and have a proper shop in Balichandrapur.

'I am always busy in the house and there is no time to think about myself and my past. The past is gone, there is no point in thinking about it. My only worry now is about how my grandchildren will prosper in life and be able to stand on their own feet. It's all God's will. It is all written in their fate. But I will try to help them.'

In the old days women were so frightened of becoming widows that some even lived austere lives while they were married. They hoped that the God of Death would take pity on them and not make them widows. It is considered fortunate for women to die while their husbands are alive. They are decorated like brides and taken to the cremation ground. Other women take the bangles and rings from the dead woman and wear them, hoping that by doing so they will also die before their husbands.

In the lower castes, widows are allowed to remarry, but some do not because they think that if they do, it may be their fate to become widows again.

Naba is seventy, a widow, and has been supplying groceries to the village women for as long as I can remember. Women from the high castes are not allowed to go to the market place to do their shopping and Naba provides a service to them. They look forward to her weekly visits which give them an opportunity to sit together and gossip. Although her prices are a little high and the measures incorrect, she is popular and liked by the women. She often supplies goods on credit.

Naba belongs to the traders' caste and her husband died when she was sixteen. She never remarried, although widow marriage is allowed in her caste. She was afraid that if her second husband died she would be blamed again and held responsible, and would find it difficult to forgive herself.

She helped her brothers in their business and went to the market, keeping a record of the prices. She used to carry the groceries in a cane basket, but now that she's old and weak she finds it difficult to carry it on her head. But she still comes to the village once a week as she does not want to disappoint her customers.

'I used measures made of cane and bamboo, but now I use weights and a balance. My brother's son says that the old measures are illegal, but I still use them for measuring oil and groceries. I am used to them and find it difficult to use the new method. My customers don't mind, they know I'm not cheating them.

'I can only count up to twenty. When I'm selling I keep a count by drawing marks on the floor with a piece of chalk.

'My father arranged my marriage. I had never seen my husband before. It was not like these days when the boys and girls see each other before marriage. My *sashughara* was in a village six miles from here. My husband went to Calcutta ten days after our wedding and died there of cholera. He was only eighteen. I had no chance to see him properly. When the news of his death came my parents-in-law started crying. I was the first person they blamed. I was an outsider in the house and I had brought them bad luck. My mother-in-law said that her son had died because he had married me.

'My father knew it would be difficult for me to continue living there, so he brought me back to the village after twelve days of mourning. I have been here ever since. My parents wanted me to marry again but I refused. I was worried that if my husband died, it would prove that there was something wrong with my fate. My brothers and their children love me and I love them. I try to help them as much as I can, otherwise how can they manage?

'My brothers have educated their children. One son is working as a clerk in Bhubaneswar and the daughter has trained as a homeopath in Calcutta. She's married to a doctor

and they live in Cuttack. I wish my father had educated me.
My brothers' daughters are educated, have jobs and do not
depend on their men.'

A man can marry again if his wife dies and he has money
and land, but it is difficult for widows to remarry: not many
young men are willing to marry them. Although educated
widows can get jobs, become independent and escape from
the torment of their husband's family, the social stigma
remains. People gossip if they have friendships with other
men.

Champak married at the age of nineteen and became a
widow when she was twenty-two. Her husband was a small
businessman and died unexpectedly. She was pregnant at
the time and the shock of losing her husband was so great
that the baby was born prematurely. It was a boy and he
gave her a purpose in life.

Now she lives in Cuttack with her parents-in-law but she
comes to Nanpur from time to time to visit her parents.
Luckily she is educated and has a job, and this has helped
her to become independent. But the burden of widowhood is
still upon her.

'When my husband died suddenly I felt that my world
had come to an end. Then my son was born and I knew I
must look after him.

'At the time of my marriage, I had already completed my
studies but hadn't taken my BA exams. My parents were
eager to get me married and when they found a good bridegroom they did not want to delay the wedding. After my
husband's death I wanted to go back to college to complete
my degree but my parents-in-law would not allow me. I
would be unable to adjust to student life, they said, and who
would look after the baby? They really didn't want their
daughter-in-law to go out of their house and have the opportunity to meet other men. They were worried I would marry
again and bring disgrace to the family. I pleaded with my
father-in-law but he was adamant. Then I lost my temper. I

said, "I learnt from my parents to look after my reputation, not from you. If you keep me a prisoner in this house, do you think I won't lose my character if I want to? Am I not able to look after myself?" He looked stunned. I did not realize I could speak with such a strong voice.

'I worked hard and passed my BA. Then I completed my degree in education. I wanted to work so I could get away from my parents-in-law and their house, which was like a prison. I was not allowed to talk to any men, as if I was losing my chastity just by talking to them. I applied for a job to work as a teacher in a school in Bhubaneswar. I was called for an interview and one of my brothers took me there. I didn't know how to go alone by bus then, and was frightened I would get lost. My parents had given me a lot of moral support but they are simple and innocent people, and they didn't want to interfere with my parents-in-law.

'The interview went well and I got the job. I felt very happy when I got one hundred and seventy rupees for my ten days' salary. I gave it to my father-in-law. He said it was my fate. "If your husband was alive, would it have been necessary for you to work? He would have kept you in luxury." I wept.

'My parents-in-law are always worried that I might marry again and people would gossip, "The woman of that family ran away with a man." But I don't want to do that, I have my son to think of.

'In the house there are the strict rules of my parents-in-law and at school I am under the strict control of the head-teacher. Their words are like razor blades. They cut through me. I used to cry a lot. I never heard such rude words from anybody in my childhood. Everybody loved me in the village.

'My father-in-law is very mean. I usually read up to twelve at night but he grumbles, "Who is going to pay for the electricity?"

'My husband's younger brother and his family used to live with us. It was a joint family. One day, myself and my sister-in-law went to the cinema. My sister-in-law must see one film every week, otherwise the rice in her stomach would not digest. That evening we returned late and were eating our food when my father-in-law asked why we hadn't eaten before. My mother-in-law said we had gone to see a film. He retorted, "Why didn't they spend the night in the cinema hall?" My sister-in-law was so upset that she immediately left the table without finishing her food. Then she persuaded her husband to leave the house on the pretext of their children's education. Now they live separately in a rented house two miles away, out of the control of the parents-in-law.

'I have to travel twenty miles each way to the school. I don't like teaching there. The head-teacher is rude and vulgar. But what can I do? It is only because I am teaching that I am able to get away from the house and keep my sanity. The main gate of the house is locked at nine in the evening and after that nobody is allowed to go outside. Father-in-law locks the gate and keeps the key under his pillow.

'My mother-in-law says, "We got a bride for our son to look after us, not to do a job." She also says, "*Bohu*, are you in need of money? Why are you working?" I keep silent but sometimes I want to scream, "If you cared for me you wouldn't say such things. You are only worried about your prestige. If I had died, wouldn't you have got your son married again? After the tenth day of my death you would have got a new bride for your son, saying, 'How can he live alone? Who is going to look after him?' But what about me? Have you ever thought about how I feel?'"

Kanak is one of two sisters, thin, shy, and well-behaved. She was brought up in a large joint family with her father, grandfather, uncles, aunts and their children. The house was always full of people coming and going. The front door was never closed.

After her grandfather's death the property was divided between her father and her two uncles. The family house was

divided too, and her father got two rooms, in which they
lived.

Kanak and her sister, only a year younger, were sent to
school but were not really interested in their studies. They
left half-way through. When they reached puberty their
mother wanted to get them married, but there was no money
to pay the dowry. When the marriage season came and
neighbours and relatives brought proposals, the father
stayed in bed, pretending he had either a fever or a headache.
In this way ten years passed, and the girls remained unmarried.

The family had house gods, Radha and Krishna, and a
Brahmin boy came to perform the rituals. He was about
eighteen, an orphan and very good-looking. Kanak's mother
treated him like her own son and asked him to stay with
them. Other girls in the village had brothers and Kanak was
sad she did not have one. She accepted the Brahmin boy like
her own brother and looked after him. She made his bed and
prepared the mosquito nets at night. Soon they fell in love.
One evening when the rest of the family had gone to visit a
relative, Kanak stayed to look after the house.

It was a beautiful summer evening with a full moon. The
Brahmin boy showed Kanak a book of poems and told her
about the love between Radha and Krishna. Something
between them happened which was like a dream for Kanak.

After a month Kanak felt a change in her body, but
she could not understand what was happening. She was
apprehensive. Two more months passed and she still did not
understand. But her mother realized Kanak was pregnant
and told her husband. Together they questioned Kanak
about her condition but she remained silent. They knew there
had been an affair between Kanak and the Brahmin boy but
it was not possible to get them married because of caste
restrictions. They searched for a groom but large dowries
were demanded and Kanak's father was reluctant to give
any. In the end the marriage negotiation was finalized with
a boy from a nearby village. He was the only son of a widow,

a matriculate, handsome and intelligent. He realized that as Kanak's father had no sons he would get a portion of the property after his father-in-law's death.

The wedding took place in the village. It was a simple celebration. On the honeymoon night Kanak's husband found out that she was six months pregnant. Earlier that evening the barber's wife had also noticed her swollen stomach while dressing her, and told the villagers. The next day the boy took Kanak back to her parents.

'I couldn't have made her six months pregnant in one night,' he said.

It was a disgrace for the family and the village, but Kanak's father insisted that she had a disease which caused her stomach to swell.

The boy took Kanak back to his house and he and his mother looked after her. Because the villagers gossiped he moved with her to a town where they lived in a rented room. When she had her labour pains he took her to the hospital on his bicycle. She gave birth to a son.

Kanak's husband hired a rickshaw and brought her and the baby back to her parents' house. There was a sensation in the village: Kanak had produced an instant son! He presented mother and child before her father, demanding money and saying, 'You said it was a disease.'

That night the father committed suicide.

The boy took his wife back to his house but from then on, he did not treat her well. His mother was a kind woman and she sent the young woman and the baby back to live with her mother. Soon afterwards the child died.

The villagers said to Kanak's mother, 'Now get her married to someone else or to the Brahmin boy.' But he had run away and both the mother and the aunts were unwilling to part with her as they were concerned about her future.

After a while, the husband started visiting her. He would come, spend a couple of nights and leave. Kanak became pregnant again and had a son.

A year later Kanak's mother died and she was left alone.

Sometimes her younger sister, married to a teacher in the next village, came to console her.

Now Kanak has accepted her fate and knows she has to stand on her own feet and look after her son. When her husband comes to visit her, her uncles and aunts quarrel with him and drive him out.

'Oh God, please make me a boy in my next incarnation,' a little girl said in her prayers. It was my sister, nearly fifty years ago. Now the attitude to girls is changing, but it is a very slow process.

'I am sixteen. I shall be taking my school-leaving certificate exam this year. I'm a good student. I hope to get a first class.

'We're Kandayats. My grandfather was a farmer, but my father works as a clerk in the cotton mills near Cuttack. He stays there and comes home during the holidays. My grandfather is dead and I live in the village with my mother, grandmother, a young brother and sister. We love our grandmother. In the evening she tells us all kinds of stories describing her childhood and married life. In those days the women wore veils down to their knees and stayed inside their homes. They spoke softly and rarely looked at a man's face. They wore heavy silver jewellery. They all seem so strange to me now. She also tells us folk tales about a demoness who kidnapped little children, and about a brother and sister, Tuan and Tuin, both orphans and poor, and how they tricked the tiger. We don't have such stories in our school-books.

'I have no boys as friends, all my friends are girls. We play together. I used to like swimming in the river but now my mother doesn't allow me to go there. I felt terrible when I reached puberty. Suddenly I was treated as a woman. Everybody in the village knew what had happened to me. I was kept in a room for six days and when I came out it was like leaving prison. I felt ashamed. People's attitude towards me changed. Now I am not allowed to go out alone, talk to boys or mix with them. My grandmother says I'm ready for

athed regularly in lukewarm water. Kohl is put on its eyes
to keep them clean and on the forehead as protection from
evil spirits, and *nazar* eyes. The child is breast-fed and when
it is nine months old, *annaprasanna* takes place. It is given
rice pudding to eat and, from then on, solid food.

At the age of one, children have their heads shaved, but
some boys retain their side-curls, which are dedicated to a
god. Later, these side-curls are cut off and presented to the
god. Garlands of garlic are also worn to protect them from
evil influences. Now polio and TB vaccinations are given at
the health centre.

Breast-feeding is usual. If the mother has not got enough
milk of her own, other women with young children volunteer.
Some children go on drinking their mother's milk until the
age of three or four. Nowadays, most educated women are
concerned about their figures and do not like breast-feeding
their children. Bottles and tins of baby food are on sale in
the market place in Balichandrapur.

Children are considered as divine and rarely punished.
They play everywhere and without many ready-made toys
they make up their own games. Younger children are looked
after by their older brothers and sisters. In the evenings
they used to gather round their grandparents to listen to
traditional folk tales, but this art is rapidly disappearing, as
television dominates that time of the day. Sadly, the inti-
macy of a grandmother's lap cannot be replaced by the
television set.

When they are about three years old the children are taken
to a *chatashali* and a plate of rice and fruit is offered to the
teacher. He initiates them into the world of learning. They
are taught to read, count and sing poems. They are also told
stories to form their character. But the villagers believe that
everything has already been determined by the planets at
the time of birth.

I asked Dharani Naik the astrologer whether the villagers
believed in astrology.

marriage and my mother is teaching me to cook. She says if
I don't cook well my mother-in-law will blame her for not
bringing me up properly. But I don't want to marry now. I
want to complete my studies, get a job and stand on my own
feet. Indira Gandhi was a woman and she became the Prime
Minister. Why can't other girls be like her? Of course, everything depends on fate. But should people leave everything
to fate? We have to try. I told my father, "Papa, don't think
of me as your daughter, I'm your son." My parents had
wanted a son, but I was born. I was the first child so they
were disappointed. My mother dressed me in trousers and
shirt and pretended I was a boy. Then my brother was born,
and she bought frocks for me.

'I like wearing saris, but it's difficult to walk in them. They
get dirty when I walk to school. It's also difficult to take
part in sports when you are wearing a sari. Fashion is changing and the girls are now wearing north Indian clothes. One
of my uncles taught me and two of my friends to ride a bike
but my grandmother does not allow it. In Cuttack I saw
several women riding bicycles, so why shouldn't the girls in
the village do the same?

'Most of my friends are not interested in studies. For them
attending school is a luxury. They are always concerned
about how to dress well, using modern make-up. Sometimes
we go to Balichandrapur to get lipstick and nail polish
without telling my grandmother.

'My mother is always busy. She spends most of her time
in the kitchen, cooking. She has no time to sit down and
relax. Some evenings and on Sundays I help her in the
kitchen. I also look after my brother and sister. The youngest
one is only four and she's very naughty. She uses my lipstick
and nail polish when I go to school. But I like my brother
and sister and I know they love me.

'The school is from ten to four. There are only two women
teachers, the others are all men. In my class out of twenty-
five students there are ten girls and fifteen boys. The boys
often tease us by drawing figures of monkeys but we know

that we study better than them. The boys spend a lot of time playing, while the girls are more sincere in studies. Of course some of them gossip a lot.

'My mother tells me that her grandmother did not allow her to go to school. She has studied only to Class V. But I want to study. Somehow I'll get my MA. My father wants to educate me and I know he loves me a lot. I want to work and help him. Maybe I'll get married. I'll marry whoever my father chooses, I know I can depend on him.'

5

RELIGION

WHEN a child is twenty-one days old the n ceremony takes place. The astrologer draw a piece of palm leaf, indicating the position of t the time of birth. The villagers are invited to a fea Brahmin priest worships Satyanarayan to bless with long life and prosperity. A long discussion ta over the selection of a suitable name for the chil past, names of gods and goddesses were chosen as t an opportunity to utter the sacred names every da times ugly names were chosen so that the God o would not be attracted. Now, exotic names are bein and educated parents sometimes make up names or g from works of literature.

According to custom, the child's maternal uncle attend the name-giving ceremony with presents for the Usually something made of gold is offered, a necklac pair of bracelets. If it is a boy the family is delighted. I the first child and a girl the villagers say the Godde Wealth has come to the house. But if the second chi also a girl she is accepted with disappointment. Girls considered a liability, they have to be fed, clothed, educa and given a dowry at marriage.

While the mother is busy looking after the house, grandparents and other female relatives look after the bal It is constantly kissed, cuddled and made a fuss of. It massaged with turmeric paste mixed with mustard oil ar

'Yes, they do. They have believed in it for centuries and they'll go on doing so. Everybody believes in it. Astrology will continue for ever.

'When a child is born I prepare its *jatak* indicating the position of the planets and stars at the time of birth. It takes me one whole day and for this I get ten rupees. I'm in the process of making one now. I have only engraved the lines and the letters on the palm leaf, but haven't put any black in yet. I make the black by burning the leaves of beans.

'I have made most of the *jataks* in this village and some in the surrounding villages. The villagers consult me for everything at every stage in their lives. They ask me if the planets are favourable, what are the auspicious days, and what are the right times for starting journeys. Parents come to me to get their children's *jataks* analysed.

'For weddings I compare the *jataks* of the bride and bridegroom to find out their compatibility. There are ten categories. This is called *dasa melak*. If the *jataks* tally well the union is called *raj jotak*, union of kings. Then only can the marriage take place. But if the *jataks* are like cobras, which is called *naga nadi*, the couple should not marry. If they do, they will quarrel and one of them will definitely die.

'A month ago a father came and showed me his daughter's *jatak* and the *jatak* of the proposed groom. He was anxious to get his daughter married and he thought he had found a suitable husband for her. When I analysed the *jataks* though, I found it was *naga nadi*, they would be like cobras to each other. I told him that the marriage should not take place. He was disappointed. But how can there be a marriage when there is *naga nadi*? It has never happened before. When I say "No", the marriage cannot take place.

'Your star is Leo. For the last thirteen months you have been having a bad time, with physical and mental pain. But from next month onwards things will change. Your planets are favourable and it will be good for you. People will welcome you wherever you go. You will have prosperity for the next thirteen months. Everything is written here in this

book, the *Panjika*. Astrology is a science, not black magic.'

He opened the book. 'It is in Oriya, not in English.' A villager listening to us said, '*Abadhan* knows a lot. His forecasts are always correct.'

I asked him about the future of Nanpur.

'Eight years ago you asked me the same question and I said it will turn into a town. It has now become a town. We have cinema, television, tea stalls, restaurants and people are drinking whisky and brandy. What else do you want? Nanpur, its name, starts with "N", so the sign of the village is Scorpio. It looks good for the village for the next thirteen months. India's sign is Sagittarius. Sani is its birth planet and is not good for India. Orissa is Taurus and has *Sani sapta*, when Saturn is angry. There will be a lot of fighting and tension inside the state; no friendliness or compatibility between people. Rajiv Gandhi's name starts with "R", so his sign is Libra. That is good for him and he will enjoy his life like a king.

'When I analysed my wife's horoscope I discovered there was a crucial moment at the age of fifty-two. I could not see any life after that. Two months after her fifty-first birthday she became ill. I consulted *baidyas* and doctors and they said she wouldn't live. After a month she died. I have studied my own *jatak* and I have life up to eighty-seven years. God has given me a long life.

'I'm eighty, I'm weak but I'm not blind. I have never used spectacles. When I was about forty I had some trouble with my eyes. The letters looked blurred. I did not take any notice of it and went on reading, writing and making *jataks*. I can write in the light of the oil lamp at night. I am glad I did not use spectacles when I was forty. If I had done so I would have become dependent on them. I made these *jataks*. Look how intricate they are.

'I have two sons. The eldest is forty and married with six children. He has studied up to Class IX and is doing a part-time government job. I have trained him to look after my *jezmans*. He knows astrology and can prepare *jataks* and take part in religious ceremonies. The youngest son is not interested in anything. I tried but failed. He wanders around doing nothing.

'We all live together, it's a large family. My daughter-in-law looks after me. When I had strength in my body I looked after the family. I ran two *chatashalis*, teaching children to read, write and count. Now I have no strength. I don't get proper food to eat so how will the strength come?'

There are six settlements in Nanpur and each one is mainly inhabited by a particular caste. My settlement belongs to the

Karans and comprises twenty-five houses clustered together on high ground and surrounded by mango groves and palm trees. Apart from the Karans there are two houses of barbers, one of an astrologer and one of a milkman. The Karans are all related to each other on the male side, so no marriage within the settlement can take place. All the houses are single-storey and planned in a traditional way, with inner courtyards, outside verandahs and small kitchen gardens at the back with a cow shed and the altar for the *tulashi* plant. Until recently the houses were built with mud walls and thatched roofs. Now permanent structures of brick and cement, totally out of character with the environment, have become signs of prosperity.

In the middle of the settlement stands the small temple of Gopinath, the beloved Hindu god, Krishna. In the past, Gopinath was kept and worshipped in an old thatched cottage but it was destroyed in a fire. Some villagers got together and constructed a brick building. Every spring Gopinath is carried in a palanquin with his consort Radha through the village, with a procession of musicians and dancers. That is the time of Holi when the villagers throw coloured water and powder on each other and even on animals, as an expression of love.

A narrow mud path winds through the settlement, leading to Mahlia Budha, the village god. As I walk along it I see houses with hedges of different kinds of cactus, cows tethered and at specific places, electricity poles made of concrete. When they were erected in the late sixties they looked ugly to me but now, set against a few badly designed brick structures, they do not seem so shocking. Television aerials have added a new dimension to the village landscape. Attached to bamboo poles on a few thatched roofs, they express the villagers' readiness to accept the space age and modern technology.

My relatives come out of their houses to talk to me and some accompany me to Mahlia Budha. Although the villagers have lost faith in politicians and planners their belief in God has become stronger. For them He is everywhere, in a man, in a tree or in a stone.

Every village has its local god, its protector. In Nanpur Mahlia Budha is a piece of stone in the shape of a *shiva lingam*, the phallic symbol of Shiva, the God of Creation, covered with vermilion paste and red hibiscus flowers. He sits under the ancient *varuna* tree in the western corner of the village, close to the river-bank. Kanhai Barik, the village barber, is his attendant. Before starting his daily work, Kanhai takes a bath in the river, puts on a fresh dhoti and attends to the deity, a ritual his forefathers have been performing for many years. This consists of washing Mahlia Budha with turmeric water, decorating him and offering food given by the villagers. Clay elephants and horses are presented during special ceremonies. It is believed that Mahlia Budha rides them during the night and goes from place to place protecting the village.

Mahlia Budha was given to the village by the barber's great-great-great-grandmother many generations ago. So it is only the barber's family who have the right to attend to the deity. According to the legend, there was once a terrible famine caused by floods and drought. The barber's great-great-great-grandmother had no food to feed her family and went round the villages begging. She carried a piece of stone in a basket to attract sympathy. The stone was her personal god. One evening as she was crossing the flooded river her basket fell into the water and she lost the stone. She went home distressed, did not eat anything and went to sleep. That night, a figure appeared in her dreams and told her, 'If you go to the river in the morning you will find me where you dropped me.' So at dawn she rushed there. The flood had subsided and the stone was lying on the sand. She was delighted. Over the years she grew older and weaker and the stone became larger and heavier. She was not able to carry it around so she offered it to the village. The village did not have its own god then, and the villagers planted the stone under a tree, appointing her family as the attendants.

Mahlia Budha soon became famous for protecting the village from epidemics such as cholera and smallpox. He spoke through a medium, chosen by the village elders. On the day of the ceremony the medium was prepared for the occasion. He had to fast for two days and take a vow not to touch meat or alcohol. The village musicians gathered. The smell of incense and the loud beating of drums accompanied by the sound of wind instruments created an atmosphere of spiritual excitement. Eventually the medium came running, charged with energy. He took the cane of the god from the village elder and demanded to know why he had been called. The elder told him they were frightened of cholera or smallpox. The medium usually replied that a number of goddesses had come to the village – three, five or seven sisters – and would not leave until they had taken a life. 'Give them drinks made of cottage cheese and molasses to pacify them.' Then, he visited the patients and blessed them. Soon afterwards he fell on the ground before the god and became normal again.

In my childhood I watched many such annual events and they produced a feeling of devotion and fear in me. It was only when I went to England and Mahlia Budha started appearing in my paintings that I accepted him as a friend.

The last time I saw the medium at work was in 1979. He was called to decide whether there was a place for another god in the village. A group of young children had placed a piece of small oval stone on the village path and started worshipping it as a part of their play. They performed the rituals by bathing the stone in turmeric water, anointing it with vermilion paste, decorating it with flowers, and offering molasses as food. The daily worship continued for a few days but stopped when there was a quarrel among the children. Then suddenly one of the children, a boy of seven, became hysterical and started rolling in the dust of the village path. His mother began to cry and the villagers gathered around him as they thought he was possessed by an evil spirit. A healer was called to cure him. He chanted mantras and sprinkled water over the boy, who started to mutter, 'I am the new god. I lie neglected on the village path. I must be worshipped with fruits and flowers.'

A bunch of ripe bananas was brought but he rejected it, saying the bunch was polluted. The young son of the family which had supplied the fruit had taken one from the bunch and eaten it, making the bananas unsuitable for offering to the god. The boy was called. He was so frightened that he immediately confessed he had stolen a banana. This confirmed for the villagers that the spirit of the new god was in the boy. A new bunch of bananas was brought, a Brahmin priest performed the ceremony and the boy recovered. His mother was delighted and took him home. The other children followed, but the boy only smiled at them. The word went round that a new god had arrived in the village.

Before worshipping the new god seriously the villagers decided to find out from Mahlia Budha who the god was and where he came from. A ceremony was performed. It attracted people from the surrounding villages and there was a feeling of excitement that a new god had arrived. The medium was prepared, musicians beat drums loudly, and the crowd started chanting for the medium to appear. Nothing happened. Kanhai Barik said that Mahlia Budha was sulking. It was not possible to keep up the momentum for a long period and the crowd began to chant in spasms. Suddenly the medium came running, his thin body radiating power. He danced and trembled, holding Mahlia Budha's cane. The village elder asked him about the new god.

'There's a place for many gods in this village.'

'Where shall we put him? Shall we build a temple?'

'Leave him where he is, by the village path.'

The medium fell to the ground and became normal again. I went forward to talk to him. He smiled and said he could not remember anything. After a few days a part of the village caught fire unexpectedly and the barber's house was burnt down. Kanhai said, 'Mahlia Budha is angry. The villagers should not have worshipped the new god.'

A few years earlier the villagers had planned to build a temple for Mahlia Budha, but the medium had opposed it. 'Don't build a prison for me. I like fresh air, the sun and the sky. I want to be free to move around.' The pile of bricks the villagers had specially prepared to build the temple still remains unused. Nobody has the courage to touch it.

One morning the medium's son announced that he was Mahlia Budha. His father protested and they started fighting. When the villagers arranged the next function, neither the father nor the son received the power to appear as the medium. 'The medium and his son have both gone mad,' Kanhai said. 'They drink alcohol and eat meat.'

Although smallpox and cholera are now under control, the power of Mahlia Budha, who was worshipped for his ability to cure the diseases, has not diminished.

Kanhai is seventy-two and lives in my settlement in a mud house which he has recently built with the help of his clients. He and his wife perform a valuable service for the villagers, attending to their religious and social ceremonies. He is paid an annual sum by each family for whom he works as a barber. He also acts as the village messenger, carrying news between families, and has a marvellous power of narration. His wife attends to the village women; she cuts and polishes their nails and decorates their feet. Apart from cutting hair, Kanhai knows the traditional methods of healing bone problems through massage.

'My forefathers used to attend to Mahlia Budha and now I am doing the same. He's my Master. What else have I got? I have neither crops nor crafts. I have no land or education. My life revolves around the Old Man. Whenever I am in difficulties I pray to Him and He listens. When my son was five months old he had a strange illness. For eighteen days he just remained with his mouth open. I didn't have the money to take him to hospital. There was a doctor in Balichandrapur but we didn't have the money to go to him. I consulted a homeopath I knew. I had cut his and his children's hair and I knew he would take an interest in my son. He was sympathetic and gave me medicines. He did not charge.

'I gave the pills to my son and prayed to Mahlia Budha. After taking the medicines he urinated a lot. We were worried, so I went to the homeopath again and told him what had happened. He said he had already given the most powerful medicine and refused to give anything else. He told me it was now God's will. When I got home and told my wife, she started to cry. I consoled her. "Whatever is written in our fate will happen. We can't do anything."

'The evening came. Wherever I looked it was dark. It was *Krushnapakshya*. Around ten in the evening my son choked with a cough and went cold. I touched him. He was like a piece of wood, without any life. I put my finger in his eye but he did not blink. I knew he was dead. After a few minutes I went to a neighbour. He realized what had happened and his family started crying in sympathy. He told me to wait until the morning but I did not want to keep a dead child in the house. My wife was hysterical, holding the baby in her lap.

'I sat on the verandah wondering what to do. Suddenly I heard a voice say, "Stop!" I thought to myself, "Was it the Divine Voice?" When I went to the house and touched my son the clamminess had gone, I could feel life in his skin. I put my finger on his pulse and could feel it beat slowly. Then I put my ear to his chest. The heartbeat was faint. After a few moments, he coughed a couple of times and started to move and play. Then he got hold of his mother's breast and drank her milk. He got better.

'Had it not been for the Old Man's voice, ordering me to wait, I would have buried my child on the bank of the river. I have complete faith in Mahlia Budha. I have dedicated my son to His service. He has been looking after my son all along. You remember my son had an abscess inside his thigh which had gone septic? He was only twenty-one and the date for his marriage was fixed. One morning he got up and complained about the pain in his thigh. When I looked at it, it was swollen and red. I fomented it but the thigh got bigger. We were all worried. I prayed to Mahlia Budha. "You saved him when he was five months old, You will have to save him now. He's my only son and your slave. He is your attendant. Who will take care of you if he dies?"

'That afternoon you arrived in the village unexpectedly and took him to the hospital at Cuttack. Mahlia Budha sent you, otherwise where could I have got the money to pay for the operation?

'All the villagers have tremendous faith in Him and people from other villages also come here to worship Him. After my death, my son will attend to Him. I have finished all my work. I have got my son married, and when Mahlia Budha calls me, I'll go. There is no strength in my body any more and my joints ache. I used to walk forty miles a day. Now if I walk a couple of miles I get tired. Even walking to the market is difficult.

'My son can read and write, but only in Oriya. He was not interested in studying. From childhood he was only interested in Mahlia Budha and spent a lot of his time making arrangements for His *puja*. I have taught him to cut hair. He is good and reliable and can attend to the villagers. I have been training him to take over from me. It's not necessary for me to blow my own trumpet. You know him, he's a good boy.

'I'm glad that I did not send him to high school. Look what happened to my cousin's son. His father sent him to school and spent a lot of money. He even got a tuition master to coach him. But the boy only passed his matriculation in the third division and at the second attempt. His father didn't train him to be a barber, so he's good for nothing now. He cannot get a job, nor work as a barber. My cousin died suddenly and his wife works in people's houses to get food for the children.

'The caste system is good. I shall never run down my caste because I know that the Brahmins and Karans belong to the higher castes. Do you think a Harijan will run down his caste? For him his caste is good. If my son did not become a barber, who will cut your hair? You can't cut it yourself. And what will happen at the rituals of birth and death? If our community didn't attend to you, you would remain impure. Of course the caste system creates differences, but it has been like this since the beginning. Even if you try, you cannot break it. Now people are forcibly trying to break it down. It's not good.

'In my childhood I used to walk everywhere. I only bought a bicycle five years ago, and that was for my son. It was second-hand, new bicycles cost a lot of money and I couldn't afford one. Now people are going by bus or lorry. They have become lazy. They waste a lot of time drinking tea and gossiping. Electricity has come, but how many people can afford it? Maybe some people can, but I can't.

'After many years of hard work I was able to build a thatched cottage for my son and myself. I got bamboo and straw from my clients. Whatever I get I spend. I have no money to buy a television set. But I have seen *Ramayana* on TV. Some evenings I go and sit in a friend's house to watch TV, but the programmes are in English or Hindi and I can't understand them. Anyway, most days there are power cuts. I have never been to a cinema. Many people say to me, "Let's go and see a film." But I get so tired in the evening that I fall asleep.

'I don't think this village is prospering. It's going down slowly. Most people don't have enough to eat and nobody's thinking about the poor. The country's also going down. Everybody is suffering.'

Sridhar is thirty, married, and Kanhai Barik's only son. He has been trained by his father to take over from him and attend to Mahlia Budha and the villagers. To supplement his income he has started a hairdressing saloon at Kusupur.

'Mahlia Budha listens to me. If I have problems and I am worried about something I pray to Him before going to sleep.

He comes to me during the night and consoles me. Do you remember when you took me to hospital? I was in terrible pain. I did not know what was wrong with me. During the night, before going to sleep, I got angry with Mahlia Budha and scolded Him. So He came to me in the disguise of an old Brahmin and put His hand on my head and told me, "Why are you so worried? You'll get better soon." I woke up and found myself in the hospital bed. The next day I had the operation. The surgeon said there was an abscess inside my thigh which had almost gone septic. After a week I felt better and came to the village to organize the annual festival for Mahlia Budha. For twenty-four hours musicians from surrounding villages came to Nanpur to chant the name of God. This festival has been going on every year for ten years.

'For the festival we collect money from the villagers. I also go to Cuttack, Bhubaneswar, Calcutta and Rourkela to get money from the villagers who are working there. They all give something because they have tremendous respect for Mahlia Budha. We get ten groups of singers and they have to be fed and looked after. The singing must go on continuously for twenty-four hours. Next year we plan to do it for seventy-two hours, so it will be expensive.

'We are all poor in the village and Mahlia Budha is the only one who helps us. The politicians come and go. At election time they make promises but after the election you don't see them. The same thing happens with government officers. They go about in their cars in the towns but have you ever seen the District Collector come to our village to ask us how we are? He gets his salary and stays in his luxury house in the town. But Mahlia Budha is in this village. He has got no roof over Him; He suffers the cold, the rain, the cyclone, and He's here all the time to help us. For the last month I have been going round collecting money. Two or three other people in the village are helping me.

'I am devoted to Mahlia Budha. Those who speak against Him suffer. Ten years ago there was a police officer in Balichandrapur who said that the medium was pretending and threatened to arrest him. Somehow the medium got to know about this. The police officer and two constables were on their way to the village to attend the ceremony when the medium said, "How dare they come to arrest me." He sent a villager with a message to bring the police officer to him, but the police officer was so frightened that he fled with his constables. A few days later he was transferred. He was accused of murdering the son of a washerwoman who was working for a trader at Balichandrapur. The trader complained that the boy had stolen his wrist-watch and the police arrested him and beat him to death. In the night the body was wrapped in a jute bag and dumped in the river and the next day it was found floating in the water. But in the meantime the police officer and the constables had disappeared.'

'Have you seen Mahlia Budha?'

'Sometimes I see Him in my dreams. But my father sees Him regularly in his dreams. We pray to Him every day. When I have problems I talk to Him.

'I only stay in the village to attend to Mahlia Budha. Whenever I arranged work outside the village something always happened and I couldn't go. Once I went to Rourkela and got a job in a saloon, but when I returned to the friend's house where I was staying, I had diarrhoea and started vomiting. I fell down and couldn't get up. My friend took me to hospital where I was given four saline injections. I got better. But I was unhappy that I was away from my parents. I kept seeing Mahlia Budha in my dreams, so I returned to the village. Recently I went to Bhubaneswar as I wanted to work as a barber for the police force but couldn't get the job. Mahlia Budha didn't want it. I cannot stay away from Him.

'Two years ago I got married. My father arranged it. I only saw my wife properly after my marriage. I always obey my parents, whatever they say is all right for me. My father did not demand a dowry and the girl's parents didn't give any. All he wanted was a good housewife. She's not only my wife but my parents' daughter-in-law. If they are happy with her, I am happy.

'Now I have got a small saloon and I get ten to fifteen rupees a day from it. In the name of Mahlia Budha, I am doing my work. I work from seven till eleven in the morning before the villagers have their bath. They all have their bath by midday. I charge two rupees for a haircut and fifty paisa for shaving. My customers are all villagers so I can't charge more. There are eight haircutting saloons at Balichandrapur competing with each other. If I went to a town I could earn fifty rupees a day but I want to stay here where I can earn ten to fifteen. All my clients are from the higher castes. I do not cut the hair of Harijans. I have to remain pure because I attend to Mahlia Budha.'

Arjun Satpathy is a Brahmin. He starts the day by having a bath in the river and praying to the sun.

'God is *jyoti*. What you call in English "electric current". The light is burning and its beams are spreading all over. If there's an electric lamp over there, its light comes here. Like that, God is light. Without God there is only darkness. That divine light is in everybody, everywhere. It is in you, asking me questions, and it's in me, giving you the answers.'

'If there is God in everybody, is God also in the Harijan?'

'Yes.'

'If there is God in the Harijan, how can he be untouchable?'

'God has made him untouchable. He has also made the caste system. God has created the difference, we are not all equal. It's like the twenty-two steps leading to the altar of Lord Jagannath. There are the top steps, the middle steps and the lower steps, and together they are twenty-two.'

'So on which step are you?'

'We are the top because we are the Brahmins.'

'What about the Harijans?'

'At the bottom.'

'Can they ever rise?'

'If they work correctly they can.'

'What kind of work?'

'If they keep clean, worship God and become pious, then they can rise in their next life, but not in this life. They are born Harijans because of their actions in previous lives. My forefathers and myself must have done good work in our past lives and that is why I am born a Brahmin. I'm doing good work in this life so that my soul will mingle with God and I won't return to this earth.'

'What is good work?'

'To believe in God, to respect Brahmins, parents, elders, strangers, be kind and hospitable, give alms to beggars, plant trees, dig wells.'

'Can a Harijan become a Brahmin?'

'It will take him hundreds of years and he has to go through a process of purification. It is only in a future life that he may become a Brahmin. According to the old system we weren't supposed to go inside the untouchable settlement or to touch them. But our government has now made them Harijans, and since then if we tell them anything, they start a case against us. The government gives them support, they get land, jobs, we get nothing.

'In my childhood food and clothes were cheap and easily available. There was no scarcity or adulteration. Wherever I went people respected me, but now they're respecting money and power. The politicians and the government officers are respected more than Brahmins. Through a Brahmin, people can reach God, but through the politicians and government officers they get money and jobs. Our values are getting lost. I'm glad that I'm at the last stage of my life, so I'm not worried. But I feel concerned about the future of my children. I have two daughters and one son, he's the youngest. My daughters were good students, and after matriculation I sent them to nurses' training. I didn't have any money to give them higher education. One daughter has completed her training and is now working as a nurse, she's like a son to me, supporting me. Nursing is *seva*, service to

God. It is the noblest of professions. A nurse looks after the
sick and gives them hope and comfort.

'The girls are working, so I won't have any difficulty in
getting husbands for them. But I have no money to pay for
the dowry.

'I am sending my son to a Sanskrit school. I want him to
study the Vedas and become a good Brahmin. My time is
over. There is no energy in my body any more. We are always
in need and I don't get proper food. Milk and ghi are like
dream products.

'Now I am an old man, most of my friends have gone, one
by one, and I am left alone. I try to do my religious work.
My job is to attend to the gods and perform religious rituals
for the villagers. I don't farm or work as a labourer. I have
to remain clean for my gods.

'Last year I fell ill. I had fever and was bedridden. My wife
and children had lost all hope but one night I had a dream.
In it, I was taken to the King of Death, Jama, by his two
attendants. He was sitting on a throne. When he saw me he
asked his attendants, "Why have you brought him here? It's
not his time yet," and he was angry with them. So they
brought me back. The next day I got better.

'Once you are born death is certain, whether you think
about it or not. I think the village is dying. Gradually it
is becoming a town. Now there is a cinema, a video hall,
electricity, a road; buses are running to Cuttack and Calcutta.
In my childhood there were no cars and we walked everywhere. I got to the railway station by walking through mud
and water, but now we catch a bus or lorry and in two hours
we are in Cuttack.

'Yet people are starving. Go round and see those children,
how undernourished they are. A boy who is about fifteen
looks as if he is ten. Children are not growing, they are all
getting smaller and smaller. You can't blame their parents,
they have no food and no job. So everybody goes without
food.'

'What do you think of Indira Gandhi's assassination?'

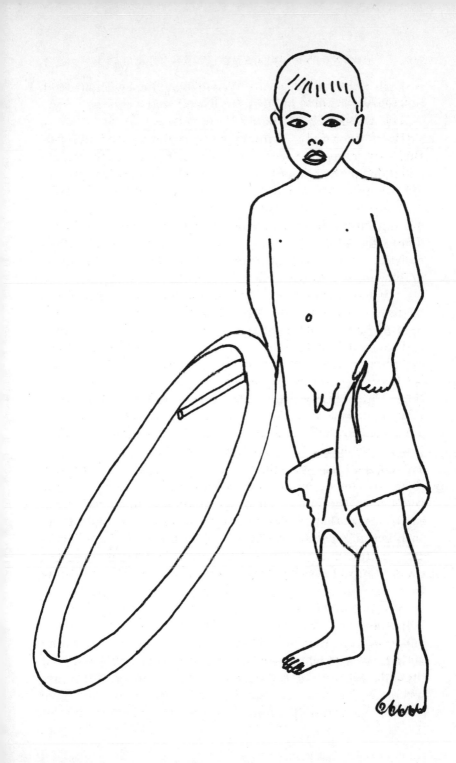

'Delhi is a long way away. We are dying here without food. So if they get killed in Delhi, it doesn't matter to us.'

'What about Rajiv Gandhi?'

'His mother was a Brahmin, she was clever, she had sense. But this young boy seems misguided. He wants to bring a telephone to the village, but who shall I talk to on the phone? My communication with God is only through my prayers.'

Jagannath, an incarnation of Vishnu, who is also Krishna, dominates village culture. Although there are Buddhist monuments on top of the nearby hills, there are no Buddhists in the village. Buddhist philosophy has been totally absorbed by Hinduism and the villagers practise non-violence and meditation in their daily lives.

The villagers are Vaishnavites, but they also worship Shiva and *shakti*. Shiva is the God of Creation and *shakti* is female energy, the Mother Goddess. She is also Durga, the Goddess of Creation and Protection, and Kali, the Goddess of Destruction. The goddesses Mangala and Chandi are Durga and Kali's respective incarnations. Their worship forms an important part of village life. In the autumn festival of Dusserah, images of Durga are made and worshipped. On Tuesdays women worship the goddess Mangala to protect their husbands and children. They make the images of the goddess on the village path by building a small mound of earth surrounded by a rectangular ditch, and decorate them with vermilion paste and red hibiscus flowers. The villagers are frightened of the destructive aspect of the goddess but the worship of Krishna fills their hearts with love and joy. In the evenings, groups of men sit together singing *kirtans* accompanied by drums and cymbals.

In the sixteenth century Sri Chaitanya walked with his followers from Bengal to Puri singing *kirtans* and preaching divine love and fellowship between men. They believed that the only way to reach God was to be His lover. There are several Vaishnava families in the village and they give mantras and initiate young people into the worship of

Vishnu. Everybody has a guru who whispers the sacred name
of Vishnu into their ear. Without initiation the soul will not
rest in peace after death. Chaitanya did not believe in the
caste system but now the Vaishnavites have formed a caste
of their own.

My guru who initiated me as a Vishnu worshipper came
regularly to our house to tell us stories about Vishnu. Now
his son is a guru. He is fifty and lives with his family in the
village.

'Krishna is transcendental bliss. Mourning is prohibited,
separation is to be celebrated. By remembering Krishna I
get happiness and joy. *Atma* doesn't die, it mingles with
Krishna.

'I ask myself, "Who am I?" I am made up of mind,
intelligence and ego. Life is the spark of Vishnu who is also
Sri Krishna. There's nothing superior to him.

'There are two types of energy – material and spiritual.
Material energy consists of land and water, spiritual energy
consists of mind and soul.

'Misconception of self is the cause of conflict. Real self is
atma and all lives are the creation of Krishna. We are all
born of Brahma. When we die we'll go to Brahma.

'We are Vaishnavas. We don't eat meat and fish, or drink
alcohol. *Tilak* and saffron robes are our symbols. We wear
necklaces made of the stems of the *tulashi* plant. We hand
down our knowledge to disciples without changing it.

'I am the *dasa* of Krishna, the servant of Krishna. We
have an eternal relationship with Krishna. If we forget the
love of Krishna we suffer. Krishna is light. If we concentrate
on light, there is light. When we look away there is darkness.
Remembrance of Krishna is important and we remember
him through *kirtans*, chanting *Hare nam*, the name of Hari –
"*Hare Krishna, Hare Krishna, Krishna Krishna, Hare, Hare.*"
If we remember Krishna we continue to have a relationship
with Krishna. If we remember our parents and friends,

whether dead or alive, we continue to have a relationship with them.'

There are ten families of Brahmins living in my village. They live together in one settlement. It is clean, with neatly kept houses, and surrounded by coconut trees. The coconut is the fruit which is offered to the gods and it is sold by the Brahmins to supplement their incomes. Non-Brahmins are not supposed to grow it in their gardens. If they do their sons will die, say the Brahmins.

Ten years ago an uncle of mine planted some coconut trees in his garden. When his wife objected he said it was only superstition. But when the trees were about to flower he became nervous and ill. He thought he was going to die because he had broken the rule. He consulted a doctor, who examined him thoroughly and said there was nothing wrong with him, but he still felt unwell. It was only when he saw the coconuts on the trees and the family was able to offer the fruit to Gopinath and Mahlia Budha that he felt better. Now several non-Brahmin families in the village have planted coconut trees.

The Brahmins work for about ten surrounding villages. Each family has its Brahmin to perform the religious rituals for them. It is only the Brahmins who are allowed to carry out the ceremonies required by the Hindu religion. The Brahmins wish their clients well because they know that their own financial well-being depends on the prosperity of their clients. In my childhood the Brahmins in my settlement only looked after gods and goddesses and performed social and religious ceremonies, but now several of them are working in towns as clerks and factory workers.

Niranjan Satpathy is the youngest of five brothers. His father was Gopinath's priest in our settlement. He sent his sons to school but they also helped him in his religious work. He did not have enough money to educate all of them so the two oldest sons went to Calcutta to work in a factory and sent money home. They worked for the Dunlop Rubber

Company and nobody in the village knew what type of work they did. Still, they were able to educate their three younger brothers. One was not able to pass his matriculation and went to Rourkela to work in the steel factory; the next brother got his Master's degree in Oriya literature and works as a lecturer in a government college, away from the village; Niranjan passed his matriculation in the third division, so the family decided it was not a good investment to send him to college for further education.

'In my childhood I had aspirations for higher education, but my dreams failed when I got a third class in the matriculation examination. I felt so ashamed that I could not show my face to my brothers. It was that dreadful English grammar which was the hindrance. I did not do well in English, that is why I got a third class. It was easier to find jobs in those days and I got a post as a clerk in the Land Settlement office. I worked there for three years but did not find it profitable. So I returned to the village to manage the household. I told my parents that I wanted to farm. They were not very keen in the beginning but my other brothers persuaded them to agree. Now I have put my ideas into practice.

'We have five acres of land and I grow rice, wheat, lentils, potatoes and ground nuts. My forefathers did not farm so I do not have any experience of farming. I am not supposed to work in the fields so I have to employ labourers and depend on them. That creates problems. Although I can't farm myself I have experience in getting work done, which I acquired while working for the Land Settlement. If I had some capital I could start a business dealing with farming equipment, manure and pesticides. I could make a little profit and help the public. But I cannot prosper because I have no money to invest. My parents and brothers are happy because they think I am doing well with my farming. I am making a profit, otherwise there wouldn't be any incentive for me to work. All my brothers work outside the village, so they don't help me. Whatever I get from the land is mine. I don't get much ready cash and the money I earn I spend on my family. I have my old parents, a wife, a daughter and a son. I want to educate my children so that they can do well in their lives. I want my son to be well-educated.

'I like village life and I think my village is beautiful. I want it to prosper. I advise the farmers to use manures and pesticides. I try to improve the minds of bad people. I tell the unemployed not to be ashamed of manual work. There are so many unemployed and I would like to help them. I am not in a position to do so because I have no work for them, but I can help labourers.

'I accept farming as a business. I could not earn my living as a Brahmin, performing religious rituals. I thought it was like begging, so I tried to do something more respectable, like a clerical job. But I found there was no money in it and it meant staying away from the village. My business has failed this year because of the drought. The gods are always against us.

'The life of Brahmins was very simple before. They managed with simple food, a pair of dhotis and a chaddar, and were always busy with their gods and religious acitivities. Now they have given in to temptation. They want to dress well, eat meat, drink alcohol, go to cinema, and even visit prostitutes. Whatever they see in the market they want to buy. Now on the television screen they see luxury goods being advertised and naturally they want them. So they need money and more money and as a result their way of life has changed. You see Brahmins as politicians, businessmen and bureaucrats. Some are even selling alcohol and meat. Now there's no difference between the Brahmins and the other castes, even the Harijans. Their lives are no longer pure, so they are not respected as before.'

Niranjan's brother, Dhira, works in the steel factory in Rourkela. When he went to work there he found to his horror that he had to mix with all kinds of people on the factory floor, including Harijans and Muslims. He was an insignificant part of a large factory and lost importance among the molten steel. He felt miserable.

A new wing was being built and one day the manager needed the services of a Brahmin for the inauguration ceremony. The educated Brahmins working for the company had forgotten how to perform religious rituals. Dhira volunteered. He felt important again in his role as a priest. Even the manager paid respect to him and he noticed that everybody at the gathering wanted his blessing. The plate near the altar, which he had been using for the ceremony, soon became filled with money, donations from the guests. From that day he was considered as special on the factory floor and was called Dhira Nana, brother Dhira. He became the family priest of the manager. Now his colleagues come to him for help if they want some favours from the manager. 'People will always require a Brahmin for their rituals,' Dhira says.

He visits the village three to four times a year and stays for a few days. Sometimes he comes specially to conduct marriage ceremonies. Last time I saw him was at the wedding of one of the girls in the village. He looked impressive in his ceremonial clothes and was even telling the Brahmins from the bridegroom's side how to perform the marriage ceremony correctly.

'When I'm in Rourkela I still feel that I am part of a machine. It's a big place and very few people know who I am. But when I come to the village everybody knows me and respects me. In the town I am one of many, here I am special. When I retire I'll come and live in the village.'

Raghu Mishra is one of the oldest surviving members of the Brahmin community. Although his body is frail his mind is clear and his voice strong.

'The Raja of Alamgiri wanted some Brahmins for religious rituals. So he brought our forefathers from Puri and settled them here with land and houses. That was hundreds of years ago, nobody knows exactly when. We don't have a history book tracing the family tree. I can only go back five generations.

'I was the eldest son so the responsibility of looking after the family fell on my shoulders. We were two brothers and two sisters. My father could not read or write, and he remembered the Sanskrit verses by listening to his uncle. When I was eight years old my father taught me the mantras to worship the gods. When I was nine I went through the thread ceremony, initiating me as a Brahmin. I knew I was a Brahmin because wherever I went people respected me. That was the custom.

'There was no school in our village or the surrounding villages. An astrologer was running the village *chatashali* in Kusupur and my father sent me there. I learnt to read, write and count. The primary school was at Kotpada on the other side of the river. It was a morning school and started at 6.30. Some boys from our village went there, but I couldn't go as I was helping my father. They walked eight miles every day. The high schools were at Barachana and Cuttack.

'The students and teachers were sincere, in those days. The teachers taught well, but now they're not interested in their students. Although my grandchildren are going to school they are also getting private coaching in the evening. I have to pay the fees. If the teaching in the school is adequate, why should it be necessary to have extra coaching? These days, the teachers are only interested in money, not teaching. The students are not sincere either. Their minds are not on education. There are lots of distractions now – cinema, television, video – and they even have strikes. They demand to copy in the examination hall. Do you call that education?

'I got married when I was twelve and my wife was ten. I had never seen her before. When they were young, our parents, who were friends, had promised to get their children married to each other. In those days people used to marry very young. If the girl was more than ten years old nobody was willing to accept her as a bride. Similarly the boys

got married before they were sixteen. Child marriage was a
custom in Brahmin families. Now girls are getting married
at twenty or twenty-five. I don't know what to say, whether
it's good or bad. Now my son says that we are in the modern
age and that child marriage is bad. If I say that child marriage is good, who is going to listen to me? He is sending
his nineteen-year-old daughter to the college. If I ask him,
"When are you getting her married?" he keeps silent and
ignores me.

'After my marriage, my wife stayed with her parents until
she reached puberty. Then there was another ceremony and
she came to live in our house. I was almost sixteen. I learned
about the husband and wife relationship from my friends.
They were married and had learned from their friends. One
of them had a palm leaf manuscript of *Kama Sutra* showing
the drawings of man-woman play. We used to look at it
secretly. Now there are many books on the subject in the
bookshop at Balichandrapur.

'The girls learnt from their mothers, aunts and sisters-in-
law. Women used to be very shy, wearing a veil. It was only
after giving birth to her first child that my wife showed her
face to the village. Now girls go round everywhere staring at
men.

'I was frightened of my father. I never spoke directly to
him. I always stood at a distance and looked at the ground
while talking to him. Then we were afraid to go near our
superiors, let along talk to them. There was a lot of respect
for old relatives. Now the children do not obey their parents
and answer them back.

'Times are changing. In those days there was a very good
relationship between brothers. Now they quarrel and fight
over property. The sweet relationship between husband and
wife is going. The modern age is influencing them and they
are aware of family life in the Western countries where there's
a lot of divorce. The educated ones are trying to imitate the
West. A relative got his son married but the bride left a week
after the wedding to live with her parents and she hasn't

come back. That was five years ago. Sometimes I discuss the past with my wife and reflect on the changes, but the relationships in our family are good. We all live together with my son and his family. Just as I looked after my parents when they were old, my son is now looking after us in our old age. But there are no good feelings between neighbours any more and they quarrel. In my youth if somebody was in difficulties the others got together and helped. Now everybody keeps to their own problems, which they cannot solve.

'If there were disputes people used to go to Gopi Patuari for help. He was the village elder. He would call two or three old people from the other villages and hold a *nisapo*. They would listen to both parties and come to a decision which was final and always obeyed. Nobody went to the courts of law. Now the government has introduced the *grama pan-chayat* system to look after village affairs by elected members. They are real crooks. Instead of helping the villagers they create differences between them. They work as mediators between the politicians, the government officers and the villagers. If we go to them with our disputes they will take some money from you, some money from me and promise to settle the matter, but they'd stay in their homes comfortably doing nothing, and we go on quarrelling.

'Party politics have divided the village and ruined its atmosphere. Even families are divided. In my day there was only one party, Congress, which brought Independence. Now there are so many – Janata, Socialist, Communist, Indira Congress. If the wife votes for Congress the husband supports Janata and there is a fight. After Mrs Gandhi's assassination, the women voted for Congress (I) and the men voted for the Opposition.

'The assassination of Indira Gandhi was a disgrace for India. To kill a woman is a great sin, our *shastras* say that. Women are like goddesses, and children and old people are like gods. They have to be respected and protected.

'There was no polling booth in our village and we used to

walk ten miles to Barachana to vote. Now we have a polling booth in the village primary school. It's a good thing which the government has done so that our women can vote and don't have to walk long distances.

'Politicians do a lot of canvassing. They come at election time and distribute money and favours to get votes. The Congress party has dug a well in the washermen's settlement.

'In my childhood there was rule by the landlord. The landlord for this area was Magu Sahu. He was a terror. If somebody was not able to pay rent he sent his *piadas* to collect the debt. They would come holding bamboo sticks and sit on the verandah demanding the money. If they were not paid there was a fine. On default the land was auctioned; one, two, three – gone. Property worth thousands would go for a hundred. People had to obey the orders of the landlord, there was no other way. That was during the British rule. When the village watchman came the villagers stayed inside their houses. He was employed by the police and he reported births, deaths and other incidents. Now there is a police station at Balichandrapur. People are going to the police for little things and asking them to arrest their enemies. In my youth it was considered against the prestige of the village to report to the police station. There was no burglary. People were busy working, there were no roads and the communication system was bad. Now thieves are coming from Cuttack and Calcutta by car, attacking the villagers with bombs, looting and disappearing. The police are ineffective.

'I don't think the British government was good. It not only sucked our blood, it sucked our bones and flesh as well. They imposed taxes on everything, even salt. It's good to be independent so that we can raise our heads and walk freely with dignity. But now our government is following the tricks of the British. There is so much tax, even for cutting hair and washing clothes. Soon they will impose tax on breathing and free speech.

'We have got electricity, but what's the point, there's always a power cut. Before, we had oil lamps which we could

control. Now we have no control over electricity. It comes
and goes, it has a mind of its own, it's whimsical.

'Things were cheap in my day. People grew vegetables in
their gardens. Gold and rice were cheap. A market was held
twice a week at Balichandrapur and the farmers from the
surrounding villages came to sell their produce. Now Balichandrapur and Kusupur have turned into daily markets and
everything is dear. Crops grew like magic, the soil was fertile.
But the farmers have ruined it by adding too many dangerous
manures and fertilizers. The rice these days has no taste.

'People from different castes did their jobs according to
the caste system and earned their livelihood. The Brahmins
performed religious rituals, the washermen washed clothes,
the barber cut hair. Now the Brahmins have become traders
and the barber goes to the town to work as a clerk. For me,
religion is doing one's job with sincerity. These days people
are not dedicated.

'In every village there was a *bhagabat toongi*, a room where
every evening the *Bhagabat* was read by a Brahmin and the
villagers gathered to listen. We had one in our village. Every
evening the reading went on for two to three hours. Now the
villagers are not interested in the *Bhagabat*. The old people
still listen but the young ones are only interested in cinema
and television.

'In the past there were many fasts and festivals. They are
still being performed but there's no devotion any more. The
Brahmins of my childhood did not eat meat or fish, their
lifestyle was simple and they wanted to remain pure. If they
touched a Sudra by chance, they took a bath in the river.
Now they are wearing shirts and trousers, shoes and neckties,
eating chicken, drinking alcohol, and the people have stopped
respecting them. We worshipped Mahlia Budha for curing
smallpox and cholera, and the medium protected the village.
But these days, he doesn't get the same kind of divine spirit
he used to. People say he drinks alcohol and eats mutton.'

A ten-year-old Brahmin boy used to come to our house every

day to attend to my mother's deities. He performed the rituals so delicately that it was a pleasure to watch him. Although he was paid very little money, he carried them out with great dedication. I remember a conversation we had.

'Who taught you to worship?'

'My father.'

'Do you know who God is?'

'Krishna.'

'When did you know you were a Brahmin?'

'When I was a child. At school I was told I was a Brahmin boy. I had my thread ceremony last year.'

'Do you know anything about the caste system?'

'No.'

'Do you go to school?'

'Yes.'

'Do you have any Harijan friends?'

'Yes.'

'Do you play with them?'

'No.'

'Why not?'

'My sacred thread would be polluted.'

'Who told you that?'

'My father.'

'What do you think of it?'

'I feel sad.'

'Do you feel sad because your sacred thread would be polluted?'

'No, I feel sad because I cannot play with my friends.'

'What will you do in the future?'

'Worship gods.'

That was nearly twenty years ago. Now he is married with a young daughter and works as a lorry driver.

'I started as a cleaner. Now I'm a driver. I wanted to do something to earn money. There was no money in doing religious rituals and I knew it would be difficult for me to support my family.

'I was not a good student. I failed my primary school

exams several times and had to give up studying. I had a
Harijan friend who helped his father in the fields. When I
told my father that I wanted to work as a farm labourer
he became angry. He said, "We are Brahmins, we are not
expected to work for others or do manual work. If you work
in the fields, what will the villagers think of me?"

'I used to watch the lorries running along the expressway
and that gave me the idea of becoming a driver. Driving a
vehicle seemed exciting to me. I used to think how lucky the
drivers were, going from place to place: if I could drive like
them I could also travel and see places. The drivers seemed
to have lots of money. When they stopped at a tea stall near
the bridge they spent without thinking. One day I plucked
up my courage and asked a lorry driver if he would teach me
to drive. He laughed. I felt small. He said it was hard work
and not suitable for a Brahmin boy and I was too young and
soft to work as a driver. He told me he had started as a
cleaner and it had taken many years to become a driver.

'A businessman in Balichandrapur had bought a bus and,
without asking my father, I went to him and asked if I could
work as a cleaner. He was surprised. He knew my father and
said he would talk to him. When my father found out I
wanted to be a driver he was very annoyed at first, but he
finally agreed.

'I had never done any cleaning work before. My mother,
aunts and sisters did all the household cleaning. In the beginning I didn't like cleaning the bus. Then I told myself the
bus was like my god. I cleaned it with the same kind of
devotion I used while attending to my deities and I started
enjoying my job. The bus was so clean that everybody
admired it. The owner was pleased and asked the driver to
teach me to drive. I was worried at first. I felt the bus was
controlling me. He showed me how to change gear, put the
brake on, reverse, and in a month I was able to drive,
although I had not taken the driving test. One day, while
coming from Cuttack, the driver asked me to drive. He sat
beside me, which gave me confidence. I had only driven

about a mile when I saw the police stopping vehicles and checking them. I was so nervous that I braked suddenly. The luggage from the top of the bus fell down and the passengers started to scream. A policeman came running towards us and a passenger complained to him that it was my fault. He asked me for my papers and I had none. The policeman kept me and the driver waiting for an hour and the passengers became angry. We paid some money to the policeman and he let us go. From that day I became careful.

'I decided to get my driving licence. I practised for another month and took the test, but the instructor failed me. I took the test again and again I failed. I was disheartened but I knew I was a good driver. A friend in Balichandrapur said the inspector wanted money, and that if I gave him some he would pass me. So I gave him two hundred rupees and passed my test. Had I paid the money before, I could have got my certificate without taking the test at all, but my father always told me not to be dishonest. These days, drivers pay money and get their licences but they cannot drive properly and there are so many accidents.

'I'm a careful driver. I drove the bus for a year but there was not much money. Now I drive a lorry from the mines to the port. The road has helped me: if there was no road I wouldn't have become a driver.

'I would like to drive an aeroplane. A month ago I took a family to Bhubaneswar airport by taxi. They were going to Delhi. It was wonderful to see the aeroplane land and take off like a bird. I would like to fly and be free, and see the world outside this village.'

'Prafulla *bhai, namaskar.*' Bharat greets me. I am surprised. This is the first time a Brahmin has paid respect to me in the village.

It is the custom for the non-Brahmins to pay respect to the Brahmins, young or old, by saying *'namaskar'.* They then respond by saying, *'ayusman hua,'* 'I bless you with long life.' It is unthinkable for a Brahmin to pay respect to a non-

Brahmin. But Bharat is six years younger than me, educated, and he is a reader in political science in a government college. So his attitude has changed.

Brahmin priests come to the house with sandalwood paste and leaves of sacred basil and bless the villagers. The villagers pay their respects and give a *dakshina*, either in money or uncooked food. The villagers believe that if they do this their souls will go to heaven when they die.

Respect for Brahmins is mixed with fear. There is a strong belief that a Brahmin's curse always comes true. Several stories in the epics describe this. The curses are like missiles, once they are uttered they have a destructive power of their own, so the villagers would never knowingly displease a Brahmin.

When I was about ten years old, I had a beautiful hand-made bell-metal bowl which I used for eating my cereals. One morning while serving my breakfast my mother said it was missing. I was very upset and tried to find out what had happened to it. A friend told me he had seen one of my cousins, a boy one year younger than me, going to a family in the Brahmin settlement. He said they were pawnbrokers. I knew the son of that family who was a classmate of mine. When I went to his house he was not there but to my delight, his mother brought out my bell-metal bowl. She said I could take it with me and bring the money later, but suddenly her husband came out to the verandah and said I should bring the money first. I ran back to my mother and got the money from her.

When I returned, the Brahmin boy was there with his father. I offered them the money and asked for the bowl but they said they knew nothing about it. I was shocked and angry. 'You a Brahmin and telling me a lie!' Without thinking I slapped the Brahmin boy on the face. I immediately realized what I had done. The Brahmin boy cried out and two other Brahmins came hurrying from their houses. The boy's father cursed me, 'You'll have leprosy and your hand will fall off.' I stood there feeling I had committed a sin. I came home and told my mother what had happened. She spat on me for protection but said I shouldn't have hit the boy.

Fortunately, the Brahmin boy had not gone through his thread ceremony and was not recognized as a full Brahmin. His family did not complain because they did not want to be involved in a case of theft. As my mother did not want to embarrass my cousin's family, the incident was never discussed again, but I was frightened by the curse. I went on praying to my gods and anxiously examining my body for several years to see if there were patches of leprosy. It was only after I passed matriculation in the first division and wrote good essays that my fears went.

Sudhakar is a Brahmin and a Tantric. He is sixty-five, slight, with light brown skin. His greying crew-cut hair stands up like a brush and his bright eyes radiate peace and contentment. He sits on the mud floor of a small room surrounded by images of Durga and Kali and speaks gently, giving confidence to people.

'Man is a part of this Universe and our body is a part of this soil. Our blood is also the water which surrounds us. The air we breathe is a part of the atmosphere. We are a part of Nature, a part of this world. When we die we'll become a part of this soil and mingle with Nature.

'When my son was small he suffered from meningitis. He was lying unconscious on the floor with his tiny head twisted and my father's heart was filled with pathos. A part of me was suffering and I prayed to God, "Oh God, if you want to take him, take him away quickly. Don't let him linger."

'My father, my younger brother, my wife and myself were sitting around him. He had a very high fever and his body was like fire. There was no doctor in the village and there was a feeling of gloom in all of us.

'It was a dark night. The owl hooted on the mango tree and the jackals started to howl. A tremor of fear went through my body. Then a cool breeze started to blow from the south, and suddenly I heard a knock on the door. When I opened it a holy man entered. He was wearing saffron robes. He said, "I have come to treat your son." He took my straw prayer mat, put it beside my son, sat down and started moving his hands over my son's body from head to foot. We could not ask him anything and stood like pieces of stone. We were speechless.

'He told us of a simple remedy, the stem of green grass with black pepper. He crushed them and gave the juice to my son. He gently stroked my son for about ten minutes, sitting in a position of great concentration. Then he got up and started to leave. My brother plucked up courage and asked him, "Where have you come from?" "Nasik," he replied. I prostrated myself on the floor, holding his feet. "Don't go, please stay," I cried out. "It's not necessary for me to stay any longer," he said and started to leave. We followed him. He walked on without talking to us and we walked behind. After about a mile we reached a mango grove. There, the holy man suddenly disappeared. We looked around and couldn't find him, and returned home sad. After a few minutes my son spoke, "Mother, I'm thirsty." Then gradually the fever subsided and he got better.

'There's a plum tree outside my house. Everybody in the village says a spirit lives in it. Some say they have seen it at night, a woman dressed in a white sari. Every night before going to bed we leave some rice, dal and curry on a plate for the spirit. We try to keep it contented and the spirit does not do any harm to anybody.

'Once a friend and his wife came to stay with us. Suddenly one evening the wife became ill and started muttering incoherently. Some villagers gathered and said she was possessed by the spirit who lives in the plum tree. I knew the mantras to remove the spirit from her body and arranged a ceremony. As I chanted the mantras my friend's wife started to cry, "Help me, I'm leaving. I'm a Brahmin widow. My husband died when I was young. A man working in Calcutta came to our house. He was the brother of a woman relative. He tempted me and I ran away with him. We stayed together and I became pregnant. I was about to deliver my child when he asked me to return to the village, where my parents would look after me. I agreed. We came by train and walked from the railway station. It was raining and the rivers were flooded. We crossed the first river by boat and when we arrived at the second one it was midnight and the boatman had gone. We took shelter under a tree. Then I went to the river to wash my feet and the young man came with me. As I was washing he pushed me and I drowned. I had longed to be a mother. I'm angry with him. I want to drink his blood."

'The possessed woman fell down and became unconscious. A few minutes later she recovered. All the men in the village were worried that the spirit would enter their women. So we all decided to have a ceremony. We chanted the name of Krishna for twenty-four hours, saying, *"Hare Rama, Hare Krishna, Krishna, Krishna, Hare, Hare,"* and the spirit left the tree. There's no fear any more.

'There are ghosts and witches in the village. The witches come out at night in faint moonlight. They are usually young women with unfulfilled desires, crying for children.'

As a child I was told there were a number of women in the village who were witches. They walked on their heads and went together to the cremation ground. They were all childless and mothers thought it was dangerous to show their young children to them. For protection they put kohl on their babies' eyes and garlands of garlic round their necks. The villagers believed that each and every person had the power to destroy someone just by looking at him. Healthy babies were not shown to strangers in case they cast envious eyes on them. It was unlucky to say that somebody looked well, or to appreciate beauty openly. My mother always spat on me when somebody said I was looking better.

It was also believed ghosts came out at night. They liked living in trees and were often seen sitting on one and spreading their legs to another. Some places were famous for their ghosts and I was so frightened that I never went near them.

When I returned home alone from school at night, I would close my eyes and run while my blood went cold.

When my father gave me a torch I took it with me to look for ghosts. As I switched it on some birds nesting on a tree were startled and made a noise. I felt sad that I had disturbed their peace. Now, with electricity, the illusion of ghosts is going.

Other creatures would also come out at night: bats flew from tree to tree stealing fruit, frogs filled the village air with their croaking, jackals howled at regular intervals all through the night. But now there is a constant humming from the traffic on the road destroying this natural music.

6

THE HARIJANS

NOBODY knows when the Harijans came to live in Nanpur. They are basket weavers and fishermen, and until recently the land on which their houses stood did not belong to them. It always belonged to their high-caste neighbours. They were considered untouchable until Mahatma Gandhi named them Harijans, Children of God. Although the Indian Constitution does not formally recognize caste, the Harijans receive special favours from the government. A certain number of places are reserved for them in colleges, government departments and even in Parliament. For example, the M P from my constituency must be a Harijan and the menial jobs in government departments, like sweeping, are always done by Harijans. No other caste is allowed to compete. Preferential treatment is also given to Harijan children at the time of selection for seats in colleges and for getting jobs. If there are two children of equal ability in a competitive exam, the Harijan child gets the scholarship. In professions like medicine and engineering, jobs are offered first to Harijans who can obtain a certain percentage of marks. They don't actually have to be good doctors or engineers.

All this has created resentment. The Brahmins think the Harijans are becoming the new Brahmins. In the past the king gave their caste land, money and favours but now the government – the new king – is giving those favours to the Harijans. But the Brahmins no longer want to remain priests:

they want to become government officers, doctors, engineers, businessmen and politicians and to have a better standard of living.

People still talk about Hari Malik, the Harijan who entered the temple with the help of the police. He lives in the Harijan settlement at Balichandrapur. Hari is forty, well-built, and was wearing a clean pair of white trousers and a short-sleeved white shirt when I went to see him. He invited me in and offered me a cup of tea, which was brought to me by his wife.

After completing his matriculation from the village high school at Balichandrapur, Hari went to work in Calcutta. He has two daughters and a son and is determined to educate them. His wife and children stay at home as he cannot afford to take them to Calcutta with him. There, he rents a room and shares it with two of his friends. He tries to save as much money as he can to send home and returns to the village about six times a year, mostly at festivals.

In Balichandrapur there is a famous temple dedicated to Lord Shiva where pilgrims from the nearby villages come to worship. During one of his visits home Hari sent his nine-year-old daughter there with a bowl of milk and a plate of bananas to be offered to the deity. It was his expression of thanks, as he had got a promotion in his office. Working in Calcutta he had forgotten that Harijans were still not allowed to enter the temple.

Brahmin priests accept coconuts and bananas from Harijans, but not milk, butter or cheese, and so the priest refused the offering. The daughter returned home and told her father what had happened. Until then the Harijans of his settlement had obeyed the rules of the community, made and dominated by the Brahmins and high castes. But Hari Malik was determined to exercise his rights. He went to the temple and talked to the Brahmin, who was sarcastic.

'You know you are not allowed to enter the temple. It is a sin. It has never happened before and will never happen in this village.'

Hari knew that according to the Indian Constitution

everybody was equal and had the right to enter any temple, so the next day, he wrote letters to the Chief Minister, the District Collector and the Superintendent of Police, describing his experience. A week later, the police came and escorted him to the temple. The Brahmins, the high-caste Hindus and other villagers gathered outside and watched silently. When he came in front of the deity he prostrated himself and prayed from a distance, but he did not have the courage to go near to the altar and touch the god. When he came out people asked him, 'Did you touch the god?' 'No,' he replied. 'You took all that trouble to go inside the temple and came out without touching Him?' 'Something inside my mind stopped me.'

Immediately after the police left, the Brahmins and the high-caste Hindus purified the temple by burning ghi and performing ceremonies.

A few days later, one of Hari's relatives was chopping down some leaves from a palm tree when he was bitten by a cobra and died. The villagers said that this was a sign that the deity was angry, as the cobra was the attendant to Lord Shiva. From that day the Harijans stopped going near the temple. But Hari still believes the government let him down. Had an antidote for snake venom been available in the health centre, his relative need not have died.

Most of the Harijans do not have their own well for drinking water. They get it from rivers, canals and ponds, and sometimes from high-caste Hindus, but they are not allowed to take the water from the well themselves. It must first be drawn by a high-caste Hindu who then gives it to the Harijans as an act of charity.

Until recently the Harijans in Nanpur did not have a well in their settlement. They got their water from the river. In the monsoon, when the water was muddy, they would purify it by sprinkling salt. Although they wanted a well, they did not have the money to get one.

A young Harijan boy came to me for help. There was a

government scheme to dig tube-wells, he said. To find out more about it I went to see the engineer-in-charge and discovered he had been a student in Cuttack at the same time as myself. He had qualified as a civil engineer and now worked as a senior officer for the Orissa government, in charge of public health. He had a comfortable office, a chauffeur-driven car, and spacious government quarters where he lived with his wife and daughter. His son was at boarding-school. He described everything he had achieved in life, including a house in Bhubaneswar which he had built with his own money. He said I was welcome to stay there whenever I visited. He was eager to help me and when I asked him about the well he summoned his assistant to bring the file. He looked at it carefully and said, 'Thirteen tube-wells have been dug by the government in your village.'

I was surprised. I had seen only one tube-well near the primary school, and its water was salty and not suitable for drinking. He insisted that according to his file there were thirteen. His attitude confirmed my belief that there is always a difference between the official record and the truth. But it is very rare for a villager to have access to government records or the opportunity to check whether they are true.

When I asked the villagers about the tube-wells I was told that some years ago a few tube-wells were dug, but their water had been salty and brown and that nobody had liked it. The wells were not maintained and the children played with them. Soon they were broken piece by piece and dismantled.

The digging of a well is always a political issue during an election campaign. The politicians promise the villagers that their party will dig wells, particularly in the Harijan settlements. But after the election nothing happens. During the last election when politicians came to canvass for Congress, the Harijans bargained: first the wells and then the votes. The digging of an open well started with the help of the Harijans, but before the work was finished the election was over and the contractor left. The well remained incomplete,

without any fence around it. One dark night while looking for her cow, an old woman from the Harijan settlement fell into it. Luckily she was rescued, but the next day the Harijans took a petition to the local development officer and after several months of investigation a concrete fence was built around the well.

From the back of my house Sidhia's mud hut in the Harijan settlement is clearly visible. He is always busy working and there is a worried look on his wrinkled face. As he cannot afford to buy proper clothes he wraps a piece of torn cloth round his waist. The upper part of his undernourished body remains bare.

Once I gave him a dhoti and a shirt after he had done some work for me but instead of wearing them himself, he gave them to his eldest son. 'I don't need them,' he said.

'I have nothing and my forefathers had nothing: there is nothing for me to leave behind for my children. My father built my present house. The plot of land on which it stands did not belong to me until recently, although my father and my forefathers lived there. Every year the floods came and destroyed our settlement. We considered the landlord as our master. In return for the land we gave him free labour and a portion of the vegetables and fruits we grew in the garden. Sometimes he would come with his son and pick the fruit from the trees. We said nothing.

'One day, the politicians came and told us, "You have lived on this land for so many years, the land is yours. Register a case against your landlord." I said, "How can I start a case against him? I know this land is his. How can it suddenly become mine? When I have problems I go to him for help. We live in the same village and we see each other every day. You are here now but after one hour you will be gone and it will be difficult for me to see you. How can we get their land in our name? It is not good."

'They explained. "The government has made a law giving

the ownership of the land to the tenants. But you will have to give some compensation."

'"Where can I get the money from? Land is so expensive."

'"You will have to pay only fifteen or twenty rupees."

'It was ridiculous, I thought, because land costs much more. It was immoral, so I said, "No."

'The next day my landlord came and told me that the people in his settlement had decided to give the land to us free. "If we wanted to remove you we would have done it a long time ago." Now the land is registered in my name.

'I don't know where my forefathers came from, but we have been living here for generations. I was born here, my father and grandfather were born here, and now my children. Our trade is basket weaving and playing music for religious and marriage ceremonies. We play the drums for Mahlia Budha, and that's how I learnt music. In my young days I was a good singer. I had a harmonium and went to other villages to sing devotional and folk songs.

'My parents didn't send me to *chatashali*. Nobody from our settlement was studying. When I was eight years old I worked for my landlord. I kept his cattle and brought grass for them from the fields. When I got married I went to Calcutta because there was no work in the village. I worked for an English sahib as a gardener. He was a nice man. He lived in a bungalow with his wife and children. Sometimes his wife invited me to the house and gave me tea and biscuits. One of the other gardeners had a son who used to visit us. He played with the sahib's son.

'The sahibs didn't believe in the caste system. While I could go into the sahib's house, here in the village I was not allowed to enter the house of my landlord. The sahib was a nice man. He has given me a lot of certificates. He left when India became independent. The employees stood in a line and he came and talked to us. He said, "We are leaving but the black sahibs who are coming in our place will make your life difficult." That's exactly what happened. The atmosphere changed when an Indian sahib took over the company.

He and his wife treated us like servants. She shouted at me every day. Nothing was to her liking. She would pull the plants out, and then grumble. I had to replant them. I knew it would be difficult for me to stay there.

'My wife fell ill and I had to come to the village to see her. She persuaded me not to go back to Calcutta: "Why not stay here and do some farming?" My landlord asked me to cultivate his land and with the money I had saved in Calcutta, I bought a pair of bullocks and started to farm. It was hard work but I had strength in my body then, although God was always against me. The crops were ruined either by floods or drought. Now the prices of commodities are going up and I find it difficult to manage.

'I have three sons and two daughters. My daughters are married. I didn't send them to school because I couldn't afford it. I educated my eldest son, thinking that he would get a job and look after me and my wife but he couldn't pass his matriculation. He failed twice. He got a job for six months in a town and came back here: he said he didn't like it. He is married and has two sons but is now unemployed. The second son was not interested in studies. He wandered around doing nothing. I got him a job in the Karan settlement keeping cattle. But now he is helping me with farming. Some days, he works as a labourer and gets about ten rupees a day.

'My heart is always bleeding for my youngest son. He is mentally disturbed and cannot speak, but I think he can understand. I'm worried about what will happen to him when we are dead. His brothers have their problems and can't look after him. He is now twenty-two and eats a lot. He is always hungry. He eats twice the amount of food me and my wife eat. Sometimes he gets angry and starts beating his mother. I think he is frustrated because he can't speak. We love him. Although he is disabled, he is our son. He is part of our body. I took him to the hospital at Cuttack. A kind villager helped me. But his condition did not improve. I saw the local politicians but nobody would help me. Then people said, "Rajiv Gandhi is a good man. If you write to him he will help you.'' At election time Congress politicians came and told us to vote for Rajiv Gandhi. They said he was not like other politicians and we believed them and voted for him.

'One day, I asked a villager to write a letter for me to Rajiv Gandhi. He wrote it in English and I put my thumbprint on it. I got a reply saying my letter had been forwarded to the District Collector. I don't know who the Collector is and where he lives but I can't afford to leave the house because I have to work. When I don't work my family doesn't eat.

'My wife and I have grown old. I am seventy-five and she's seventy. Even at her age she has to go to the fields to work. When we're ill we go hungry and we often go without food. I have been suffering from a cough for the last month and I have a pain in my chest. I went to the health centre, wasted half a day to see the doctor but he gave me only a piece of paper. I have no money to buy medicines.

'There are seven families in my settlement and they are all suffering. We are always in want. We live from hand to mouth. Yesterday I went to the shop and could only afford to buy one biscuit for my grandson. But some villagers in other settlements have prospered. They've got electricity, television and motor-cycles. We have nothing. We have always worked hard but we will always remain poor.

'The caste system is slowly breaking down. In my childhood we had to avoid a Brahmin while walking in the village. Now we sit together, smoke and drink tea together, so it is getting better.

'I liked Calcutta because there were no caste restrictions there. Mahatma Gandhi called us Harijan, which was a good thing, but in the village I still feel I'm an Untouchable. But I like my village. My family is here and I know everybody. This is where I was born, so how can I speak against my friends in the village? If I am an Untouchable now, I must have done something wrong in my previous life. I am trying to be good in this life so that my next life will be better.'

Ravi is Sidhia's eldest son. He is twenty-six, married, with two sons and two daughters. He is well-built with a head of glossy black hair. Sidhia sacrificed a lot to educate him, but he failed his matriculation exams several times and had to give up. Once, I arranged a job for him at an officers' club at Rourkela. But because part of his work involved serving tea he refused. He said that his father hadn't educated him to become a servant.

'I got married when I was fifteen and studying for matriculation. I didn't want to marry but my father forced me into it. He needed someone to help my mother. My wife was only twelve then. After one year of our marriage we had our first child, a son. I got a dowry – a bicycle, a wrist-watch and a radio. I hadn't seen my wife before. My mother selected her.

'My wife cannot read or write because her parents didn't send her to school. But I'm trying to educate my children. I have no land and I realize that only through education can they prosper in life. My eldest son is studying in Class III and the youngest is in Class I. I regret not having taken my own studies seriously. There was nobody in our settlement who was studying, so there was nobody to guide me. My father had no money to support me and I could not complete my studies.

'We are three brothers and we live together in the same house. The youngest brother was born with brain damage and cannot speak or understand. But he's always hungry. He gets violent if he doesn't get any food and starts beating people. He was born like that. It is all God's will, what can we do? My parents are always worrying about him. They have taken him to hospital in Cuttack several times and even written a letter to Rajiv Gandhi for help, but no help has come from anybody.

'I used to work in the Land Settlement but now I'm redundant. I've been searching for a regular job for the last eight years, but in vain. I worked in a factory for a few months. I was operating a grinding machine. It was very hot and dusty inside and one day I started bleeding through my nose and fell unconscious. I was seen by the doctor who told me to go to the main hospital in Cuttack. I went there as an in-patient for ten days and I got better. But my parents and wife were worried and did not want me to do the same kind of job. When I asked the company to give me a different job they said there was nothing available. I was getting about five hundred and fifty rupees a month and was able to send two hundred rupees to my parents. I paid fifty rupees to share a room with a boy from another village.

'Since leaving that job I have been sitting at home. There is no work in the village and I cannot get any in the town either. I tried to do some tenant farming but the crops were destroyed by drought. My two-year-old daughter has had a fever for the last five days but I have no money to take her to the doctor.

'My other brother works as a labourer. He is not educated. He is married, with two children.

'I don't know who the government is and what it means. I saw the MLA for our constituency several times, but he took no notice of me. He simply pretended to listen. While I was telling him about my problems he was talking to somebody else. He said I should come back after a few days. But when I did he was not at home. I waited for twelve hours and as there was still no sign of him, I left. People say we are independent, but we are not free from hunger and poverty. Freedom has no meaning for Harijans, we are only free to suffer.

'My father used to work for a sahib in Calcutta. At least he was able to get a job, not like me. He worked as a gardener and sent money home regularly. Now the country is independent and I have no job. The government is not giving any help to the poor. If I could get a permanent government job then my problems would be over but I don't think I'll ever be able to get one. We Harijans have always been poor and we shall remain poor.

'I've never been to Calcutta, I have nobody there. Neither have I been to Delhi. Only once in my life was I able to hold one thousand rupees in my hand. My brother-in-law had given me the money to keep for him. After a week he took it away. I did not cheat him. I have a good record at the police station.

'The strictness of the caste system has gone by about 75 per cent but there are still differences between Harijans. The sweepers belong to the lowest caste; the fishermen are lower than us, but the washermen are higher. I was very young when my father told me that according to *Ramayana* the Brahmin caste was the best. We still believe it because Brahmins attend to the gods, but we also worship God ourselves.

'I have been to Puri and seen Jagannath. He is unfinished and his hands and legs are incomplete. I haven't been inside the temple in the village. One day when I was a child I tried to join my friends as they were going inside the temple but the priest wouldn't allow me. I came home crying and told my mother. She explained it had been like that for many years. "It's all right if they don't allow you. We can have a temple in our house." The next day she brought two brass images of Radha and Krishna and gave them to me to worship. They are still there in the house and my mother won't eat anything before she has worshipped them.

'I've seen television. We cannot afford to have electricity so the question of buying a television set doesn't arise. But on Sunday mornings we see television in your settlement, sitting on a villager's verandah. We watch *Ramayana*. I don't watch any other programmes. When the *Ramayana* is over the man takes the television set inside his house.

'I've also seen cinema. I took my wife and children to see a film about Krishna once. They liked it because it was in Oriya.

'My father worked hard to educate me. Now he is old and I wish I could provide him with some comfort in his old age.'

Kailash Jena is my childhood friend. We went to school together.

'The dreams of my childhood have vanished. I haven't been able to achieve anything in life; my hopes have faded and my dreams have been swept away in the flood water.

'My parents brought me up with love and care. They sent me to school but, I don't know why, I was not a good student. I didn't do well in mathematics and the teacher punished me. I couldn't pass my exams, I don't know why. If I had passed my matriculation I could have got a job. In those days it was possible. But I was not able to achieve even that much. Now I repent about it. I'm not lucky, so what can I do? My mother said it was my fate and I believed her.

'My father and his brother worked in Calcutta and sent money. We lived well. I had my grandparents. My grandmother looked after us and my grandfather worked in the fields. We had cows and bullocks. We had some farming land which my father had bought and a garden with mango and banana trees. There was a beautiful plum tree full of delicious fruit; it was my favourite.

'Then one day a storm came and destroyed it all. That day all my dreams were destroyed. Shortly afterwards, my uncle returned from Calcutta. He was ill and there was nobody to look after him there. He was spitting blood. We brought many healers to cure him but he died after a month. His wife left us and went to live with her parents. A year later my father died also. I was only fifteen. As I was the eldest the responsibility of looking after the family fell on my shoulders. I looked after the family land but I was not able to farm myself. My younger brother got a job with the government and that helped. He sends money home regularly and we manage, somehow. My youngest brother was married and worked for the electricity department. One day he was electrocuted while mending electric poles.

'The village has changed a lot during the last fifteen years. In the old days, everybody in my settlement was illiterate. They used to go to their high-caste neighbours to get their letters written by them. Now, with the help of the government, some children are going to school and can write letters for their parents. They are getting scholarships and financial help and some boys and girls have even studied up to matriculation. Slowly they are improving, but it's very slow.

'We can't see God, all we can do is believe in Him. You pray and if He listens, then you know there is God. At times of sorrow if I worship God I get peace. When I'm happy I also pray to God and that gives me contentment.

'Harijans are now going into the temple of Jagannath. There are no difficulties. There is a saying that your God is as big as your mind. God belongs to everybody, He doesn't say "No," to anyone. Whoever has fear in his mind will not go to the temple but if his mind is clean and pure he can enter the temple and find God. It is written in our holy texts that the world is in the mind.

'I have three sons and two daughters. I have tried to educate all of them. My eldest daughter is married but my eldest son is unemployed. He studied up to Intermediate in Commerce but could not pass his B.Com. and has been unemployed for the last two years. He has applied for many jobs and been to a number of interviews, with no result. The government says it is giving help and preferential treatment to Harijans but we haven't received any. My other children are going to school but only God knows what their future will be. I'm trying to do my duty.

'When I was a child I knew that we were Untouchables. I used to play with other children in the school but when we came back to the village I was not allowed to touch them or go into their houses. I couldn't understand why it should be like that. When I asked my mother about it she said, "It has been like that for generations. It doesn't matter if they don't allow you into their homes. If you study well you will do well in your life."

'But home was not a good place for study. The Harijan children don't do well because they don't get any support from their family.

'I've told my children that human beings are all equal, that blood is the same whether one is a Hindu, a Muslim or a Christian. Our blood and skin are all similar. We are Hindus and our caste is *pana*. We are basket weavers. The Brahmins do religious work according to their caste. But now they're not doing religious work any more. They're in business or administration. How can they still call themselves Brahmins? We *panas* will study, get professions and do the jobs which the Brahmins are doing. So why should we be Untouchable? I went to the blood bank to donate some blood. I didn't say it was a Harijan's blood. Do you think my blood will only be given to a Harijan and not to other people? But it was a mistake for Gandhi to name us *Harijan*. The caste system is slowly going and Untouchability is also going, but the label of *Harijan* will remain with us for ever. I don't like it.'

Kishore is small, thin and looks about four years younger than his age of fourteen, the result of chronic malnutrition. But his weak body contains an intelligent, questioning mind, deeply concerned about the welfare of his community. I have often tried to place myself in the Harijan's position, but listening to his description was a revelation.

'My name is Kishore Jena. I'm fourteen, the son of a poor Harijan family. The name of my father is Kartik Jena and my mother is Hiramani Jena. We have no land. My father works as a labourer, and he is sending me to school. When I was five years old he took me to the primary school. There I was enrolled in Class I. After Class III I walked to the upper primary school at Kusupur where I completed my middle English education. Now I am studying in Class IX at the same high school.

'There are ten members in my family and it is difficult for us to manage on my father's income. He gets about ten to fifteen rupees a day when work is available. If we eat one day, the next day we go without. My father cannot buy me books and papers. If I want to study at home in the evening and want to light the lamp there is no kerosene in the bottle. I get disheartened. Sometimes I wonder how I am going to complete my studies. The teachers in the school say I should get help by extra coaching, but when I ask my father he says, "Where is the money to pay the teacher?" He has five more children to educate and he hasn't got the money. Somehow I must remove the terrible word "poverty" from my family. I am the eldest son and my father, mother and grandmother love me. Sometimes I think that if I pass my matriculation, my young brothers and sisters will follow me. My mother used to say, "Wherever the first plough goes the next plough follows."

'I feel we are getting poorer every day and I have to face the poverty of my family and of the friends in my settlement. The government says through the newpapers and radio that it is helping the Harijans to get education and jobs. To some extent it's true, but it's like inviting a guest and serving him with the cheapest food. My father believed that through education he could get a job and prosper in life. He studied up to matriculation, but could not get a job. So when I think of my future I feel depressed. I have no backing and my father hasn't got the money to pay bribes for me to get a job. It's only propaganda that the government is giving priority to Harijans.'

There are many Harijan women like Guni in villages all over India, who can neither read nor write and are trapped in the prisons of poverty and suffering from which they cannot escape.

Guni was born into a fisherman's family and married a young man from the next village. When her brothers died she came back to Nanpur to look after her old parents. Now she is about sixty, but looks older.

'I was born in Nanpur. I'm the daughter of Suduria. There is something wrong with my head, it aches and I tremble. I can't go anywhere in the sun and find the heat too much for me. I have a son but he cannot work. His body is swollen and he sleeps all the time. He is married with four children.

'My parents were fishermen, now they are dead. I had three brothers and three sisters. Two brothers died of cholera in childhood. My other brother was quite healthy until he got mumps. He was twenty and married. One day he went to bathe in the river and when he came home his body went cold. He died the same evening and his wife left. Her father and brother took her away to live with them. She was a child. Her father got her married to another man. She reached puberty only eight days before her marriage. She had a son and then suddenly her husband died of a snake bite. Her son came to visit us several times during festivals, but the neighbours objected. "Don't allow him to come to your house, he belongs to a different family." Now he's married and has children. He's a good boy. He works hard as a labourer and looks after his family.

'Out of my sisters, two are dead. The eldest died this year. She had an abscess in her throat which went septic. I was not able to visit her but my son went to see her. I could only send her ten rupees. I am the next daughter. I married when I was fifteen and had reached puberty. My father arranged my marriage with the brother-in-law of a relative. In those days the girls didn't say anything. They married whoever their fathers chose for them. They accepted whether the boy was lame or disabled.

'My sisters told me that they couldn't look after my parents and that as I was living near by, I should look after them. I didn't like my husband's village. There the families went out to the jungle to cut firewood and sell it. That's how they earned their living. I couldn't adjust to their way of life. I never did hard work in my childhood. So myself and my husband came back here and stayed with my parents. They didn't have any land, neither did we. They used to fish but it was not enough to maintain the family. My father did some tenant farming and my husband helped him. Now my husband is old and cannot farm on his own.

'Once, my mother went to Kusupur to do some shopping. The midday sun was burning. It was the month of Baishakh. She collapsed in the heat and the people from the Karan settlement gave her water. She revived. They sent a message to me. I went there and took her home. But she didn't recover. She couldn't get up any more and died. Four years later my father also died.

'We used to live where the bridge is, but it was very congested, with about ten families living there too. The plots used to belong to a landlord who harassed us but fortunately when the road was built, the government gave us some land on the other side of the river and some money towards the thatch. Now we are independent.

'I have one son and seven daughters. First I had two daughters, then a son, and then five daughters. There was no birth control then. I wouldn't have had all these children if there had been. Now women are getting operated on after giving birth to two or three children.

'All my daughters are married; three are now widows. Their husbands died suddenly, accidentally. Two died of snake bite, the other was electrocuted. He was cutting bamboo with some of his friends and by mistake they cut an electric line. One daughter went mad. She has several children and is having a difficult time.

'The government gives us loans to buy goats. Some get the money but use it for food. But I'm frightened of getting money from the government. My father once did and the officers came and harassed him. They humiliated him in front of other people. I think it is better to die of starvation than receive humiliation from those strangers.

'Everybody in our settlement is suffering. We go without food for several days. Although we catch fish we cannot afford to eat it. We sell everything, including the spinach from our garden. But the families with more working men to help them are somehow managing.

'My son is married. My daughter-in-law is a good woman, she looks after me. She doesn't allow me to do anything in the house. They have three children – one son and two daughters, ten, nine and seven. They are not going to school. You need money for that. What can they do in their lives? They can only work as labourers. I never went to school. I didn't want to either. I was not interested. What was the point?

'My husband and I drink tea in the morning. We can't afford to buy any sugar or milk. We have it with salt. My daughter sent two kilos of wheat which I fried and made into flour. I kept it in a tin and used to add some of it to my tea. It's finished this morning. I have come here without eating anything today. I've got about five rupees after selling this fish. I'll buy rice from Kusupur and take it home. I'll make puffed rice for my husband, he likes it in his tea.

'I have been ill four or five times. Three times I thought I was going to die, but God kept me alive. I don't know why. It would have been better if He had taken me to His country. I don't know why He has kept me in this world. I don't know who God is and what He looks like. Once I went to Puri with my son-in-law. I walked all round the temple and saw Jagannath. We arrived at night and left at night, so I don't remember much about the other gods. I've never gone inside the temple in the village. God has created the poor and the rich. Everybody says there is God, so I say there is God and God has made everything. My husband is like God to me. He's a good husband. I have to look after him.

'I get worried when he falls ill and my children suffer. We have no farming land and there is nobody to support us. My son is an invalid. If we had some extra male relatives to help us our life could be better. But I am poor, my daughters are poor and their husbands are poor.'

Sashi is a fisherman, thirty-six, and lives with his wife and five children in a mud house built by himself. In his small garden he grows aubergines, spinach and bananas.

'Some people pray for children but to tell you the truth I never prayed. God created them. I did not know there would be a famine when I got married.

'I married in 1970. My friends were getting married and my mother wanted someone to help in the house. I have three sons and two daughters. The eldest daughter is fifteen

and now married. The son is twelve and studying in Class VI. I want to educate my sons so that they can live in comfort and get jobs. My two sons and one daughter are going to school. My father did not send me to school. Nobody from my settlement was studying and when I was a child I didn't know there were such things as schools. I used to go with other children to catch fish. But when I was ten and working as a servant for a landowner I saw his seven-year-old son going to school. Sometimes I had to take him there. But when I asked my mother if I could go to school she replied, "What good will you do by reading and writing? Our fore-fathers were fishermen and it was not necessary for them to read and write." Then I thought that if I had children I would educate them.

'My first child was a girl and I was disappointed. I wanted a son so that I could educate him like the son of the landowner. My second child was born after two years and I was happy that it was a boy. Then I had a girl and two sons. These days I'm finding it difficult to manage my household: I have no land and all I know is fishing. The ponds are dry and it is bad for us. We don't get much fish. Today my share of the catch is only half a pound. I work as a labourer sometimes but it is not regular. So we have to go hungry most days.

'We are seven in our family – myself, my wife, our four children and my old mother. We used to live with my elder brother and his family but now we are separate. My brother has six children. For seven of us we need three kilos of rice a day. I earn about ten rupees and a kilo of rice costs three rupees and fifty paisa: very little is left for me to buy cooking oil and kerosene for the lamp. Yesterday the oven remained unlit and we had no food until the evening when my wife got some wheat from a neighbour and made some porridge.

'I don't get any help from the government to educate my children. This year I could not afford to buy half the books for them and I borrowed some clothes from a landowner, so that they could go to school.

'I'm now almost forty and all my strength is gone. You see my skin? It is withered by the water. I spent four hours this morning catching fish in mud and dirty water. I have worked very hard but remain poor. I don't know what will happen to my sons. It's all in their fate.'

Anjali is the younger sister of Kishore Jena. Like her brother, she also suffers from malnutrition but poverty has not yet weakened her mind. Although she looks sad and resigned she is full of hope for the future.

'My name is Anjali Jena and my father's name is Kartik Jena. I'm twelve. I passed my upper primary exams from the village school and won a scholarship. The headmistress helped me a lot. Because I was a good student she coached me during her spare time and she also gave me books and paper. Thanks to her help I was able to do well in my exams. I want to study but my father is poor. Ours is a large family. I have my parents, old grandmother and four brothers and sisters. My elder brother is studying in the high school at Kusupur where I have joined him this year. We go together in the morning. We walk two miles.

'My father works as a labourer. He works very hard but gets only about ten rupees a day. Some days he gets five rupees and it is difficult to manage the household on that. We have no family land and no rich relatives. Some days we go without food. If we eat for four days we go without food for three. This morning I haven't eaten anything, only drunk some rice water.

'Some villagers eat well and dress well but my mother doesn't have a proper sari to wear. My father bought me a frock. He had to spend three days' wages on that. Several children from our settlement are not going to school because they have no proper clothes to wear. You can come to school with an empty stomach but you cannot leave the house naked. You feel ashamed. Everybody in my settlement is poor, they don't have enough to eat. The old people are always suffering from coughs, colds, fevers. When there is no money to buy food the question of medicines doesn't arise.

'People say we're Harijans. I don't know what it means. Do you think my blood is different from yours? My science teacher says that all human bodies are equal. So how can I be different from you? My grandmother says it has always been like that, but in her day there was no road and now we have a road. Things are changing. I want to become a minister like Indira Gandhi, then I could help the poor. But I will do a job first to get some money. I want to see that my parents live comfortably. My headmistress has given me a lot of support. She's from the village. She passed her M A, became a teacher and is now helping her family and others. She says that if I study well I will be able to earn a living.'

Naranama is the village washerwoman. She is dark, thin and has a sad and contemplative little face; she is totally immersed in her own thoughts. Her wrinkled face looks very old, and is marked with many lines, the experience of many generations.

She has come to my house to collect clothes for washing and sits silently on the verandah. There are six families of washermen in the village who perform this valuable service. They live next to the Brahmin settlement. While the Brahmins have prospered, the washermen have remained poor and mostly illiterate. Ironically they are considered Untouchable although clothes have to be washed by them to be ritually pure.

'You brought sweets for the children, what have you brought for me?' she asks.

I give her some biscuits and fruit which she eats with pleasure. When I ask her what she has eaten that day, she says, 'Nothing, only a cup of raw tea with salt.' It is already three in the afternoon.

The previous day, on a visit to the temples in Bhubaneswar, I had seen a group of cows eating straw and paper. A heifer was lying on the road, lifeless. A little way away a man was selling cucumbers. I bought a few from him, and held one near the mouth of the heifer. At once the cucumber disappeared. I gave her a few more, which she munched and then she struggled to get up from the ground. She pushed her head against me, asking for more. I bought some more cucumbers and she ate them all. Then she started to move slowly and walk across the road to join the others. It was like a miracle.

The food I give Naranama has the same effect. Her voice strengthens and she starts to tell me about herself.

'As I don't have a *jatak* I cannot say how old I am but people tell me that last year I was three times twenty and twelve. I was fifteen when I got married. In my day boys and girls did not see each other before marriage. Now it is different. They not only see each other but sometimes sleep together without marrying.

'My husband went to Calcutta to work and died there. I don't know what he looked like, I never saw him. I had to wear a veil down to my knees. He went out to work during the day and I was busy looking after the house and my in-laws. We only met at night in the dark. I cannot remember ever seeing him.

'It is not necessary to see your husband's face to have children. I couldn't see his face in the night. I used to get up before dawn when it was still dark and he went out to work. I cannot count how many children I have given birth to. I was pregnant every year. My eldest son died when he was twenty-two. He had gone to work in Calcutta. One day, he returned home complaining about pain in his body. He took my hand and pressed it against his chest. He had pneumonia. He arrived in the morning and died in the evening. I could not do anything to save him. It was all God's will. I don't know why I'm still alive and why the God of Death is not taking me away.

'Out of all my children only one is alive. He's now married with two sons. They are going to school but my son cannot afford to buy clothes and reading material for them. Their mind is not in their studies either, they are only interested

in play. The other day the teacher came and said he would
coach them. But he wants money. Where can my son get so
much money from? He goes out to work as a labourer and
earns a few rupees but it is not regular. My daughter-in-law
washes the clothes of the villagers and she works hard. I help
her by collecting the clothes from the houses in the village.
How can she manage unless I help her?'

7

EDUCATION AND AID

THERE are so many matriculates in the village that it would be impossible to count them. They are mostly unemployed and their prospects of finding jobs are remote. Even candidates with Master's degrees are applying for posts of office messengers. But there is always hope for the educated to find employment. Although the glamour of education is going, the respect remains. Parents are eager to educate their children.

There are three primary schools in the village, all built by the villagers themselves with their own money and labour. The primary school in my settlement started in 1967. It was built on land donated by the village and for several years the teachers were paid by the parents. The school building has been destroyed several times by floods and cyclones and rebuilt. There are three rooms, seven classes and two hundred students. Children bring their mats with them to sit on. Primary education is free but not compulsory. Books, paper and writing materials have to be bought by the parents and are expensive. As a result many parents cannot afford to send their children to school.

The school has been upgraded. English is taught from Class VI and the medium of instruction is Oriya. The children join the school at the age of five when they enrol in Class I. Their little brothers and sisters sometimes come to school with them and sit quietly while the lessons are being taught.

Chatashalis are only held in the morning but the school

starts at ten and continues until four, with a midday break. There are very few *chatashalis* these days in the villages because teachers cannot earn their living by running them. The government has not established any nursery schools in rural areas. Children from the higher castes are encouraged to study by their parents and families and usually do well. But the children from the lower castes, especially the Harijans, suffer.

'This is my village so I am very happy to be teaching here. I have been interested in education from my childhood. My father was a teacher and the idea of teaching came from him. I have a Master's degree in Oriya literature and a Master's degree in education. After my degree in Oriya I trained as a teacher at Cuttack and got my B Ed. Then I applied for a post as a primary school teacher. I was interviewed by the Inspector and offered a job in a rural area ten miles from here.

'I was already married and my mother-in-law came to stay with me. We rented a room in that village and stayed there. The school had been built by the villagers and the government paid the teachers' salaries. My father had arranged my marriage and my husband worked as a journalist, as sub-editor of a newspaper in Cuttack. Now he works as a field officer for Care organization. He and his parents have encouraged me to study and work.

'I came to this school in 1983. The previous year, the school was badly damaged in the floods and all three rooms were destroyed. Part of the land was under water. Now we are trying to rebuild the school but it's difficult: there's no money. We have no proper desks or reading and writing materials for the children. Officially there are about two hundred and fifty children but a number of younger children are attending who haven't enrolled. They are too young – three to four years old – and they come to school with their brothers and sisters. They are very eager to come and sit quietly next to them. Their mothers also like to send them to school to get them out of the house and make them interested in studies. It's a village school and we can't refuse them, we can only prosper with the involvement of the villagers. On Saturdays we have lessons in singing and dancing and the children enjoy it. There are also poetry readings and story telling, which are very popular. One of the teachers is a good story teller and the children listen to him attentively. He was telling stories from *Ramayana* and *Mahabharata* long before the T V serials started.

'There are seven classes but we are only five teachers. I need two more teachers. The school also needs a Hindi teacher. Apart from me there's another lady teacher. She lives in a village four miles from here. She can't ride a bike and walks here every day. It's good exercise for her, she says. I get about 1500 rupees a month. The other teachers get less, their scale of pay is 400 to 900 rupees a month. But we haven't received our salaries for the last three months and it's difficult to manage. None of the schoolteachers in Orissa have been paid so they went to Bhubaneswar and started an agitation. Still, nothing has happened and we have to borrow money and get groceries on credit.

'We cannot provide food for the children but we try to look after their health. We have a first-aid box containing Dettol, tincture, aspirin, cotton wool and other things. If a child is not well we usually send him home. A year ago there was a child coming from the other side of the expressway who met with an accident. He was almost run over by a truck. He was in a terrible state of shock. He fell from the embankment and injured his knees. Luckily one of our teachers was coming from that side and took the boy to the health centre. After a few days he got better. We have told the children to be careful while crossing the road.

'A health inspector has come only once to examine the children. He took their weight and height. Sometimes injections are given to poor and physically weak children but children are innoculated regularly against cholera.

'It's a happy school. There's no caste feeling among the

children. They dance and sing together. I have taught them to sing, "We're the brothers and sisters of the whole world. We must forget our differences." They know about the world and how many continents there are. The Harijan children get help from the government up to Class VI. They get money to buy books and writing materials. There are no feeding arrangements in the school and no clothes are given. There are lots of boys and girls who only have a pair of pants and a shirt or just a frock. Some days if their clothes have been washed and are not dry they cannot attend.

'Many children come to school without eating anything. During the break they tell us there was no food in the house and that they haven't eaten. Although they are hungry they are eager to study. We know from their appearance when children are hungry. They look weak and cannot concentrate on their studies. How can they sit quietly in the class when their stomachs are empty? They do not work well and at midday they say, "We want to go home, mother must have cooked something. We want to eat." We can't ask them to stay when they are hungry. They usually go home, eat, and come back to study.

'They tell us about their families, what their parents do, and how they are in want. The children are always telling us, "We haven't eaten anything today." Instead of getting three meals a day they only get one if they are lucky. When we see them looking weak we know the reason. They are mostly Harijan children. We feel sad, but what can we do? We're also poor and cannot help them. But we tell them to come to school.

'There are more girls than boys among the Harijan children. The boys usually help their parents in their work. During the harvest season they go and help cut the paddy, or the lentils, and some even do other manual labour. The girls study well. For the scholarship exams we sent four girls and one boy, but only one got a scholarship in Class III. There are only six scholarships for the whole of this area, two for girls and four for boys. Harijan children get preferential treatment. A Harijan girl is doing well in Class VII at the moment and I hope she'll get a scholarship. She's a gifted child and a good student.

'The children from the educated families usually do better. They get encouragement at home from their parents, while the Harijan children don't get the right kind of support.

'In October 1987 the Director of Public Instruction made a surprise visit to our school. He asked the children many questions. The Deputy Inspector has visited us once and the school has been audited twice. They have all made their reports.

'We have written to the authorities about the problems at our school. We need more teachers, more classrooms, and clerical help. The villagers help to maintain the building. We cannot ask them for money but they give us bamboo and timber and we collect one rupee a month from each child towards development charges. We need one more room urgently and are trying to build it. We have got the doors and windows and the estimated cost is about eight hundred rupees. We have arranged to receive four hundred rupees from the Red Cross, two hundred rupees from the development fund and two hundred rupees from the contingency fund. Somehow we must build this extra room.'

INSPECTORS' REPORTS

(Unless indicated, written in Oriya)

10 March '77 at 11.30 a.m.

Inspection was carried out this morning. Assistant teacher was on leave with pay. It was noticed that the other two teachers were present and were engaged in teaching.

Students present:

Class V	5	out of	20
Class IV	8	out of	23
Class III	5	out of	18
Class II	11	out of	27
Class I	10	out of	28
Total	39	out of	116

The low attendances are because Holi is still being celebrated in this area.

The classes were examined. The first year students were asked to spell certain words like *ascharjya, danta, shanti*. The students were able to spell the words correctly but clear pronunciation is essential. It was noticed that up to Class V children were not able to spell and pronounce correctly. It will be good if the teachers help the children practise faultless pronunciation and spelling. Three copies of this report should be sent to my office.

11 August '77 at 3 p.m.

I paid a surprise visit. The school was about to close and the children were preparing to leave. I was pleased to see the teachers and students working in a disciplined way. The students were studying with great interest. Some students stayed inside the classroom and were examined through games. Class V students were able to answer and read beautifully. Class IV students were unable to pronounce combined words. It is necessary to practise dictation. Class III students should practise arithmetic. Class II students should practise reading and writing. Class I students should be taught to recite poetry and tell stories.

Today's attendance:

Class V	23	out of	30
Class IV	18	out of	29
Class III	18	out of	26
Class II	28	out of	33
Class I	11	out of	11
Total	98	out of	129

27 January '86.

Today on 27.1.86 inspected West Nanpur middle English school. The headmaster along with the assistant teachers were present and were busy with imparting lessons to the students present. School building is not sufficient to accommodate the growing number of students. So appeal all the members of the administrative committee to appraise this crying need of the school. Block Development Officers to sanction funds for extension of school building. Maps of India and Asia and Europe have been engraved on the wall, which is highly praised.

Went through different records and found them properly maintained. I was highly pleased to find team spirit and co-operation of the teachers. The headmaster has published a magazine, *Pravati*, in manuscript form. This will create a new atmosphere for creativeness of the students. I was very glad to go through the articles of the magazine written by the students of different classes.

There is a very small but beautiful garden inside the school. Students work there during gardening period and take proper care of the plants they grow.

The school compound was kept neat and clean.

The school has been undergoing a great change after joining of the present headmaster who is very interested in the field of education. [Written in English]

28 October '87 – 11 a.m.

Paid a surprise visit to Nanpur middle English school today at 11 a.m. Found that all the 5 staff members were present.

The compound rooms and the office room were all neat and clean. The quotations and mottos written on the walls and hanging in the office room and the photos were all attractive and impressive.

The total strength of the school is 231 out of which 158 students are present today.

Checked up on the written work books of the pupils and found that they are properly maintained. But the correction work in some cases is not thorough.

Lesson Diary to be maintained by the teachers. The headmaster maintains an Inspection Book – which is quite commended.

The school has seven classes from I to VII. Results at the M.S.C.

examination 1987 are quite satisfactory as to the percentage of pass. But the quality must improve.

Admission Register may please be made up-to-date. From the Log Book I found that it contains some of the credits of achievements of pupils and records of Annual Sports prize-giving ceremony etc.

The pupils of this school have got scholarships at the L.P. and U.P. stage. One pupil has also appeared at the M.S.C. scholarship exam this year – the result of which has not yet been announced.

I along with the headmaster went round the classes and observed the teaching standard of the teachers and also tested the pupils which were found quite satisfactory and well.

Space for accommodation of the students is found inadequate. So concerned authorities are requested to give suitable grants and assistance for the completion of the building under construction and repair at the thatched shed.

The discipline and tone of the school is quite intact under the able supervision of the present headmaster.

Students be prepared and produced to be good citizens of National Spirit and serviceable mentality.

Scheme of lessons to be taught and the progress made are maintained in a record.

Gardening and drawing and decoration work by the students be encouraged.

A handwritten magazine is also published from the school.

The headmaster will please guide the students and the teachers in the line of education and building up of the future nation and their participation in the national pattern of education. Headmaster and staff members are requested to keep up their interest and sincerity intact as before.

Shortage of staff members breaks the discipline of the school at times – which may please be looked at immediately by the D.I. of schools concerned.

This school and area is of importance and under improvement so every help should be extended to this school and its well-wishers for the upkeep of its name and fame. [Written in English]

After primary school the children go to the high school at Kusupur, two miles away. It was built by the local villagers

and the children took part in the construction of the building. I was one of the first boys to enrol. There were two teachers who devoted themselves to the building of the school. The land was donated by some villagers, and money was collected from the local people who wanted to educate their children. It was soon after Independence and there was great respect for education. The teachers planted fruit trees and flowering plants and the garden looked beautiful with bougainvillaea and marigolds. The children and the villagers felt that the school belonged to them.

Now the government has taken over the management of the school. Teachers come from outside to teach for a few years and then get transferred. They do not feel that they belong to the village and for them teaching is merely a job. They are poorly paid and badly treated by the government, which does not pay their salaries regularly. They complain they have to live in holy poverty. The gardens are neglected and there are frequent quarrels between the teachers and the students as to who should enjoy the fruit from the trees.

The school looks like a prison with tall boundary walls around the grounds and an iron gate with a padlock to stop outsiders from entering. It used to be an integral part of the village but now the villagers feel it no longer belongs to them. A division existed before – the teachers were educated whereas the majority of the villagers could not read or write. But for parents the school represented a centre for learning and hope. They often came to discuss the future of their children with the teachers. Now there is such a high level of unemployment among the young educated that some parents have lost confidence in education.

Most children go to high school when they are twelve and stay until they are seventeen but there is no age restriction. When I was a student several of my classmates were married with children but this is not so common these days. Some of the students stay on until they have passed their exams, which is their only purpose in coming to school. The tuition is not free and the medium of instruction is Oriya.

The children are taught languages – English, Oriya, Hindi, Sanskrit – mathematics, science, history and geography. Before Cuttack was the centre for the final exam. Now the school itself has become an examination centre but local students cannot use it. They have to go to another centre fifteen miles away to avoid allegations of favouritism.

Most bright students want to become engineers or doctors and to go to Cuttack to study science at Ravenshaw College, built during the British Raj after the terrible famine of 1866. There is great competition to get admission to this college and it is expensive to maintain students in towns. Very few villagers can afford it. So a new college has opened at Balichandrapur, which has been of great help to local boys and girls. They can stay at home, eat rice and dal, walk to the college and get their qualifications. Afterwards the lucky ones get jobs, either in government departments or private organizations. The pressure of getting a job is immense. Some students go on applying for years and for them the hope of getting a job becomes a permanent mirage.

A few years ago a magazine in London asked me to write an

article on British government aid to India. When I met officials at the British High Commission in Delhi, I was given a long list of schemes which covered a wide range from public health to technical training. It was carefully pointed out to me that they were all Government of India projects that existed throughout the country. To investigate them all would have been far too gigantic a task so I tried to find out if any British aid had reached my own village.

When I asked Biswanath Jena, a village elder, if he knew of any aid to Nanpur from the British government he replied, 'We didn't know that Britain gave any help to India.' But he told me that the Save the Children Fund had been helping several children in Nanpur.

In October 1971 there was a terrible cyclone in Orissa and Nanpur was badly affected. Trees were uprooted, crops flattened and many houses destroyed. I had gone to the village to help and Biswanath Jena took me to see Shantilata Goswami, whose house had been completely destroyed. She was living with her two young sons in a little hut made of a few pieces of bamboo and some straw. Her youngest son was suffering from diarrhoea and dehydration and looked like a skeleton. Shantilata had fever and her children were hungry. I arranged for her and her sons to have food and medical treatment and after a while she got better and was able to look after the children. But she had no money and her future was dark.

Back in England I was describing my experience to some friends. Among them was a girl who worked for the Save the Children Fund and she said that her organization could help the family. I gave her Shantilata's address and she passed on the details to the person concerned in her organization. A sponsorship from the Save the Children Fund was arranged. That money was of immense help to Shantilata as she was able to buy food for her sons and pay for their education. She also worked in villagers' houses in order to earn some extra money. In time she saved enough to buy a cow; she needed milk for her children and she was able to sell some of it too. Shantilata was enterprising. She started a tea stall outside the primary school and sold homemade sweets to the schoolchildren. The eldest son continued his studies up to BA level and the youngest has enrolled at the local college at Balichandrapur.

Two orphan girls are also being sponsored by the Save the Children Fund. Their old grandmother is bringing them up and sending them to school. They are so poor that without this help the children would not have survived. When I first knew them they looked sad and suffered from malnutrition. Now they are full of confidence and have bright shining eyes.

The Save the Children Fund provides help until the children reach eighteen and leave high school but no assistance is given for higher education.

Kanak died leaving three children behind, all daughters; one ten, the other eight and the youngest seven. Her husband deserted her and disappeared, nobody knew where, and she had come to Nanpur to live with her old mother, a widow, who now has the responsibility of looking after the children. When the representative of the Save the Children Fund came to visit the village, Biswanath Jena told her about the helpless children. She arranged for two of the girls to enrol at the village school and got two sponsors for them. With regular financial help both the girls are now studying. Juni, the middle one, is fourteen and studying in Class VIII; the youngest, Kuni, is thirteen and in Class VI. Kuni has mischievous eyes which are dancing all the time.

'Do you like school?'

'Yes, but I got a Grade C in my exams.'

'Which subject do you like best?'

'Oriya literature. I'm also learning to read and write in English now.'

'What would you like to do?'

'I want to be a teacher.'

'I want to be a doctor,' Juni said.

Their grandmother is about sixty-five and anxious to get

the eldest girl married. The latter is now sixteen and cannot read or write. She stays at home to look after her two young sisters.

'We have been getting help for the last eight years. Otherwise we would have all died. I know the villagers help but they have their own difficulties. I'm so weak now, my head reels and I cannot see properly. Recently I fell down and became unconscious. My granddaughters brought a rickshaw and took me to the health centre. The eldest girl fell on the feet of the doctor and said, "Take whatever money you want." She had taken some money in her bag and put it before him and said, "We are poor people and we don't have enough to eat. Our mother is dead. We have nobody in this world, only our grandmother. Please make her better."

'The doctor examined me and prescribed medicines. He gave me injections in both my arms and they became swollen. He said I was ill because I had not enough to eat. I feel dizzy when I get up. The doctor didn't say what illness I had. He only wrote something on a piece of paper. You know we are all blind. We cannot read, so how do we know what is written on that piece of paper. But I took it to the medicine store and got the medicines. They cost a lot of money.

'When something happens inside my head I lie down, then I feel better. I was on my way to the God of Death, but he sent me back. Still, it's better to die than to live like this without enough to eat and proper clothes to wear. I have only one sari which is torn and when I have a bath I dry part of it while wearing the other half.

'I'm only living for these children. If I die who will look after them? I have to get the eldest married soon. I've found a boy who is a farmer and has some land, but his parents are demanding a lot of dowry. He wants a cycle, a wrist-watch, a radio and a gold ring and I don't know what to do. When we don't get enough food to eat where can we get money to pay for the dowry?

'I like tea in the morning. I used to get it for twenty paisa a cup at the tea stall, but now it's fifty paisa. In the winter it is so cold at night that I put rags over me to keep warm. I wait for the night to end so I can sit in the sun and keep myself warm.'

Naba Kishore Goswami is Shantilata's youngest son. When I first saw him I was shocked by his physical condition and wondered if he would survive but now he is a young man, full of energy and hope.

'Two years after I was born my father left home and disappeared. The villagers looked for him but he could not be traced. I cannot imagine how he could have left me. My mother looked after me and my elder brother. Our situation was precarious. We had no land and my mother worked as a servant in villagers' houses to keep us alive.

'I ate whatever food she was given by other villagers. We could not choose, it was like being in a state of famine. When I was four years old I ate something which poisoned my system and after a while I became a skeleton.

'Whenever the villagers see a sad situation they always help. There was a terrible cyclone and our thatched cottage was destroyed. At that time a villager working in London had come to help the village. During his stay some villagers told him about me and he came to visit. I was bedridden and he sat beside me in silence. He gave some money to my mother and asked her to take me to a doctor. My mother accepted those words as if they were orders from the guru. She walked four miles to the health centre every day carrying me on her shoulders. She didn't have the money to take me to Cuttack. With the treatment at the health centre I got better. On one side there was my fate and on the other there was my mother's strong sense of duty.

'Before returning to London the villager came to see us again. He gave me some money and promised to help. My mother got me admitted to the primary school and enrolled me in Class I. At that time I was five years two months and twenty-eight days old. I went to school regularly, carrying a slate and a piece of chalk in a canvas bag. When the school closed I always went straight home. After a year my mother received some money from the Save the Children Fund. She was so happy. It was as if she had found a boat while being swept away by a strong current. The dark clouds over the horizon disappeared and I was encouraged to continue with my studies. I shall never forget that villager who helped me. He's like my father and mother. I have accepted his advice and I shall always follow him.

'After completing my primary education from the village school I enrolled at Kusupur in the high school. The headmaster did not charge any tuition fee and the condition was that I should study well. I passed matriculation in 1985. I wanted to continue my studies but I didn't know how I would get the money to do so because my grant ended when I left high school. Some well-wishers advised me to join the college at Balichandrapur. I couldn't afford to buy proper clothes to go to the college. Other students were wearing good clothes and I wanted to be like them, but it was not possible. I could not buy books and had to borrow them from friends. Some days I went to the college without food. I did not have anybody to whom I could express my feelings and who could help me. My mother was worried all the time and I didn't want to trouble her further. However, I worked hard and passed my Intermediate in Arts in 1988.

'I want to continue with my higher education but poverty is against me. There is a saying that when a man wants to reach a goal he faces lots of difficulties on the way. I know if I face the problems with courage I shall reach my goal. I explained my situation to the Principal of the college and he allowed me to attend the classes without paying the enrolment fee. Then I wrote a letter to the villager in London who had helped me. He sent me some money and gave me moral support, which encouraged me. With that money I have now enrolled, bought some books and a shirt.

'I have done well in my I A exams and now I am studying for a BA. I have always lived in difficulties, always in want and I've never known what comfort is. But I am not unhappy. I realize that I was not born to die young. Although I was born into a poor and downtrodden family I have a lot of work to do for mankind. I like working. I have no sorrow or shame, and I will do any work to earn a few rupees. Now I am coaching some children in the village and I get some money from that. I don't like being idle and I don't like those who sit at home doing nothing. I understand the value of time. I can never remain unemployed because I want to do something.

'It is not because I want a job that I am going to the college. For me there's no connection between education and earning a living, the aim of education is enlightenment, to bring light to the darkness of ignorance. Education is for gaining wisdom. An educated man is like the sun: with his light he can enlighten other people. The world is lit by the rays of the sun and education helps to build a man's charac- ter. The blind man walks with the help of a stick and reaches his destination and in the same way, society and the country can progress through education. Through education he can learn about himself, his society, his country and foreign lands. An educated man can show the way to the people who have gone astray.

'I want to become a writer. Through writing I can express myself. I'm writing poems and short stories based on social events.

'My mother is only living for us and we are a source of inspiration to her. I have taken a vow to fulfil her ambition and to see that the rest of her life is peaceful and comfortable. My life has grown out of charity from other people and institutions and I want to devote my time to the service of mankind. I want to keep the name of my mother, my village, and India, and I want to be a good man.'

Raghu is twenty-one and an only son. His mother worshipped many gods and goddesses before she could have him. He passed his matriculation from the village school but his father was working as a postman in Bhubaneswar and took him and his mother there. It was difficult for him to manage two homes on his small salary.

After retirement Raghu's father stayed in Bhubaneswar with the family but continued to keep their family home in the village. It is now rented out to a man working for the bank and Raghu comes to the village once a month to collect the rent. Several families in the village have also rented their homes to outsiders, but these are mainly from the higher castes.

Raghu has a degree in political science from Utkal University. As he could only get a second-class degree he was unable to obtain admission for his Master's degree either at Bhubaneswar or Cuttack. He went to a college in another district for his MA but the local students would not allow him to enrol. About ten boys from other districts had also gone there to enrol but were surrounded by the local boys who did not want outsiders and detained them until the enrolment time for admission had passed. Raghu tried to enrol twice but each time was prevented from doing so.

'I don't know what to do, there's nobody to guide me. I want a job so that I can help my parents. My father has worked very hard to educate me. I have applied for several jobs. For each application I have to send a fee for tests and interviews. During the last six months I must have paid over two thousand rupees to government departments. It's a lot of money. I earned part of it by giving private tuition to two students for which I got one hundred and fifty rupees a month. My father borrowed the rest from a relative. I am also trying to sit for competitive exams and study in the evenings. Next year I'll sit for the Orissa Administrative Service exams.

'If I don't get a job I'll open a grocery shop on the outskirts of Bhubaneswar, not in the centre where the rents are high. But I need capital to start. The government has a scheme to lend a small amount of money to the young educated unemployed who want to start their own businesses. I have to prepare a plan and run after the government officers.

About 25 per cent of the loan goes towards bribes, it is asked for openly. If I pay I will get my loan. There are so many applications for loans that a lot of influence is necessary to get one.

'I desperately need a job, I'm prepared to go anywhere in India to work – Bombay, Delhi, Calcutta. I want to stand on my own feet, not depend on my father. He's retired and his pension is very small. I know shorthand and typing and I am practising a lot.

'My maternal uncle is a big government engineer. If he really tried I could get a job tomorrow, but he doesn't do anything for me. I hope a miracle will happen and I'll get a job. I can only keep on trying. But my future depends on my fate and on God.'

Although in the past there were Buddhist universities near Nanpur there was not a single college in the vicinity until 1973.

Sachi Jena, a local freedom fighter who took part in the movement to free India from British rule, tried to revive rural universities so that children could stay at home and continue with their studies. To start a college it was necessary to deposit 100,000 rupees with Utkal University which would affiliate the college and conduct the exams and he got support from the local villagers and businessmen. Politicians helped too because they wanted a platform to promote their interests, and a prominent one even donated 50,000 rupees. Sachi Jena also got 10,000 rupees from the Chief Minister. The rest of the money came from public donations.

During the construction of the expressway some buildings had been erected for storage and office space. They were then left vacant until the college management committee decided to use them for their purpose. Had they remained empty, they would have deteriorated but the college has transformed them. There are now gardens and fruit trees and the buildings are being used as a centre of learning.

Among the subjects taught are history, political science,

economics, education, sociology, English, Oriya, steno-
graphy, secretarial practice and tailoring. The college got its
finance from different sources including the cattle market at
Nanpur, the market at Balichandrapur and the contractors
from the nearby stone quarries. Now that the Nanpur cattle
market has been taken over by the government, its grant
has stopped. Each student pays a tuition fee of fourteen
rupees a month and a donation of one hundred rupees a year
at the time of registration. According to the Principal, the
aim of the college is to revive the ancient art and culture
of the locality, encouraging particularly contemporary art,
although there is also a great need for science, commerce and
technology. Local people sit on the management committee
but so far no women have been included. The lecturers are
now being paid by the government and the future of the
college is secure. Previously they were paid meagre salaries
by the management committee as the college did not have
enough money. Until recently the college remained a tool in
the hands of the politicians and it closed down completely
during the Emergency.

Most of the students who come to the college expect to
spend their time leisurely, hoping to get a degree at the
end, respect in society and maybe a job. Their value in the
marriage market goes up and a degree confirms that they are
educated. Although the rate of unemployment is high, a boy
with a degree stands a better chance of getting a job.

The college is an examination centre for Intermediate
and BA levels and is recognized by Utkal University. Both
regular and private students take their exams there. They
are checked at the gate and no outsiders are allowed in the
examination hall. Teachers work as invigilators.

Once a student was caught copying while his brother supplied him answers through the window. The invigilator went
out and caught hold of him but the student came out to help
his brother and together the boys tried to strangle him.
Alerted by the invigilator's cries, another teacher from the
next room went to the rescue. The brother stopped attacking

the first teacher and confronted the second and those who had also come to supply copies to their friends started throwing stones. There was nobody at the police station so the teachers could not do anything except expel the student from the exam. The order of expulsion was posted on the gate.

The student's guardian went to the governors of the college and together they came to see the Principal for a compromise. The boy came with them. The guardian said that when he was a young man he had fought with the British administrator, so this incident was nothing in comparison. 'He's your student and you are his teacher. If he has insulted you or beaten you he will ask for forgiveness.'

The boy was asked to apologize, but he just stood there playing with his moustache. All the teachers wrote to the Principal saying that if the boy was allowed to take the exams they would not work as invigilators. When this was reported to their secretary, the governors and some important local people tried to persuade the teachers to change their minds, but they were adamant. The students and their supporters threatened to place a bomb in the college and destroy it. The teachers were frightened to go out and stayed in their rooms. The incident was reported in the local newspaper and the next day, during the examination, a supervisor from the university arrived unexpectedly and saw books being used openly by some of the students.

The Principal explained the difficulties to him: how the students wanted to copy and how the local people were supporting them. The governing body was annoyed with the teachers and asked them, 'If a boy doesn't copy and pass his exams, can you guarantee him a job? If the answer is "No," why don't you allow him to copy and get a degree at least?' The teachers were worried that they had become unpopular. But if they allowed the students to copy, they knew that the university would take action and not permit the college to be used as an examination centre. That would prevent new students from enrolling. They stuck to their decision: the student was suspended and the examination continued.

Higher education has taken people away from their roots and made them totally unfit for Indian village life. Once a boy passes his matriculation he thinks it is beneath his dignity to do manual work. He discards the family trade and dreams of jobs in towns and cities. Some who leave the village and go to the towns to study, stay on there: working in the cities has glamour and prestige for the villagers. Those with higher education do not want to teach and be branded as schoolmasters, a label which an educated boy finds degrading. In spite of the low salary, becoming a lecturer in a private college seems preferable, as it at least confers a certain amount of status.

Kashi is twenty-four and the eldest son of a farmer. He received his Master's degree in political science at Allahabad University, but with high unemployment among the educated he hasn't been able to get a suitable job.

I suggested to him that he should do a teachers' training course because I knew he had all the qualities of a good teacher, but he vehemently opposed the idea. Although there was a job vacant at the nearby high school, he accepted a temporary lectureship at Balichandrapur instead. There he met young people of his age with whom he could communicate. He has a high regard for his parents, who are uneducated, but he feels he cannot talk to them about his life.

'If I get a job it will be a miracle. I have tried everywhere, in Cuttack, in Bhubaneswar, in Calcutta, and filled in hundreds of forms, but have only been called to a few interviews. They were only a formality, they had already made their minds up. They had chosen the candidates of politicians, ministers, or administrative officers. Once I was asked by a clerk to pay ten thousand rupees, but where could I get so much money? When my friends at the university talked about giving bribes to politicians for jobs, I didn't believe them, but now I realize from my own experience that without a bribe or influence you can't succeed in life. My father is a farmer and he hasn't got influence or money. All my dreams and ambitions in life have disappeared.

'When my father was a young man, people with English education got jobs quite easily and anybody with a good job commanded respect and authority in society. My grandfather was not educated so he didn't educate my father and in those days there were no schools in the village. His friends used to walk eight miles to attend a school on the other side of the river. My father was interested that I should be educated so that he could command respect in society. But just getting an education is not enough, I have to get a good job. The designation is important. What you do is more important than what you are. A district collector and a police officer command more respect than a teacher.'

While talking to Kashi I remembered a visit to a government minister in Bhubaneswar. His private assistant had asked me to fill in a form. For designation I put 'artist and writer'. He looked puzzled and asked, 'What is your designation?' 'I am an artist and writer,' I repeated. 'I know you paint and write,' he said, 'but what is your job?' It seemed that a man without a job had no identity. The job brings power and money. The more powerful the job the more respected is the person.

The young people who leave their villages and go to towns do so because they want a good job and a good life. The villagers think, 'Those working in the towns must be earning a lot of money, otherwise why should they leave the village?' People in my village think I can solve all their problems instantly. As soon as I arrive in the village, people come to me for all kinds of help. I find myself in the role of a social worker. It is difficult to refuse because I know their problems are real and much greater than mine: somebody is ill and should be taken to hospital, a family has no food or children need writing materials for school.

'There are no jobs here. I am working as a lecturer in Balichandrapur, but there is no money and very little respect in my job. You know the saying, "The local bride is not beautiful." The management committee wants money to appoint us, ten thousand rupees for a post. Instead of paying the lecturers they want to take money from us.

'My education alienates me from the village. I can't adjust to the present set-up of the village which is farming, the occupation of the villagers. The situation in the village is depressing. There are about twenty-five unemployed people like me with degrees. Sometimes we meet and discuss our plans, but the future seems uncertain.

'I'm the first boy from my settlement to have got a Master's degree. My relatives were expecting a lot from me but I haven't been able to fulfil their hopes. My father had invested a lot in me but I have become a failure. I am a burden to my family, I'm a dead investment.'

Saroj is twenty-four, wearing a clean pair of white trousers and a short-sleeved shirt. When he came to see me he was holding a video cassette of a Hindi film in his hand.

'I'm twenty-four. I have passed my Intermediate in Commerce and now I'm studying privately for my BA.

'I was a good student, got a first-class in my school-leaving exams. But my family had many financial problems and couldn't send me to a good college. I studied commerce but didn't do well. Unless I free myself from poverty we can't manage.

'My father is a farmer, but he can't farm now, he suffers from asthma. He can't work and I can't work either. I haven't done any physical labour since my childhood, my physique is weak. So we get our land farmed by tenant farmers and accept whatever they give us.

'I have been unemployed for the last six years. I need a job. I'm prepared to go anywhere to earn money. I was studying to become a magician but a lot of finance is required to become a performer.

'I've no money to buy cigarettes, my friends give them to me. I'm not working, so where can I get the money? This video tape belongs to a friend. He's the son of a trader in

Balichandrapur and they have a video. Sometimes I go and watch films, I can't stay at home, my parents are always grumbling at me. "You are wasting your time, mixing with bad boys," they go on and on.'

'How do you spend your time?'

Silence. He thinks. 'Just sitting, doing nothing. I'm not doing anything useful. I don't like it, I want to do a job and study in my spare time, and I want to help my father and mother but I don't know who will give me a job.'

'What kind of job?'

'I want to be a cashier in a bank.'

Biman is twenty-three and the son of a farmer. The villagers think he is established in life with a secure job in a bank in Cuttack. They do not understand his inner tension and longing for job satisfaction.

'I've been in Cuttack for two years. I work as a clerk in a bank there. I passed my matriculation from the village school and got a scholarship to study in Cuttack. As I am the eldest of five brothers I had to take up a job. My father is a small farmer and cannot manage on his income. At home I have my three brothers who are going to school. My other brother is studying in a college.

'I like Cuttack. There is electric light, a water tap, roads. I don't like the village in the monsoon. The paths get muddy and I can't go anywhere in the rain, I can only stay at home. When the river gets flooded it's difficult to go anywhere. I know it looks beautiful, the trees, the paddy fields, the hills, but is it possible to appreciate natural beauty every day? I only like to see it once in a while. I don't get the clean air of the village in Cuttack, there are mosquitoes, open drains, but at least there are roads.

'I live in a rented room and eat in restaurants. The food is not good, I miss my mother's cooking. I feel alone and nervous. I think I'm going to die and get frightened. Whatever I eat I cannot digest. Once when I was studying in the school, I went to the bank of the river with some friends. A breeze was blowing from the south. I felt light, as if I was going to float. I thought I was going to die. I had palpitations. Since that day fear has entered my mind and if I wake up during the night, I think my heart is going to fail. I do not know why I am so afraid of death.

'I went to the doctor and talked to him about my problems. He examined me thoroughly and said there was nothing wrong with me, prescribed some vitamins and said I should get married. But I don't want to marry now.

'I have my brothers to look after and I don't like my job with the bank. I work in the cash department, counting other people's money day after day. I want to change to a more satisfying job. I'd like to complete my MA and become a lecturer. That is my dream.'

Raj Kishore Goswami, the eldest son of Shantilata, is full of despair. He cannot get a job and feels unable to fulfil his duty of looking after his mother and brother.

'When I was five years old my father left us and disappeared. My mother did not know what to do. As the eldest son I have been looking after the family since I was a boy. It is my duty.

'As Vaishnavas we believe that man should not cheat, steal or kill to solve his own problems. It is better to beg than do harm to others. So my mother decided to send me out to beg and I accepted begging as a better way than stealing. I went to villagers' houses and asked for rice, money and vegetables. Everybody gave something but some children used to harass me by snatching my bag away. I always returned home in time to go to school. This became my daily routine for several years.

'While I was studying at school my mother cooked the food I had brought and looked forward to my coming home during the midday break. When I arrived she was very happy to see me. She fed me and sent me back to school. Only after feeding her children did she eat.

'My mother's only support was from God. But in spite of

all our difficulties I continued with my studies. She tried to educate me with the guidance of a neighbour and the headmaster of the school. They helped and encouraged me. I never wore new clothes, I always wore the discarded clothes of other children which were given to my mother by some better-off villagers.

'A villager helped us to get some money from the Save the Children Fund which gave us courage and hope. I continued to study and face life. Life is a battlefield. There is no point in just living like animals, eating and drinking. You must have an aim in life which will make you happy and give you joy. My aim was to study well, stand on my own feet, look after my mother and help the village.

'When I was studying in Class VII I started a pan shop selling pan and cigarettes on market days, that is Wednesdays and Sundays. I started with a capital of one hundred rupees which was lent to me by a villager. This meant that on Wednesdays I was not able to go to school.

'I passed my matriculation in 1980 in the second class. My mother was delighted. I wanted to study further but we did not have the money. The college was near by and I was interested in higher studies. I also realized it would be impossible for me to get a job as a matriculate, so with help from friends and donations from local charities I enrolled in the college. I did tuition in the evenings to earn some money to help my mother. I passed my Intermediate in Arts in 1982 and then I enrolled for a BA. I worked hard but unfortunately failed my exams. While studying I was also looking for a job, which distracted me. Due to financial difficulties I haven't been able to re-sit my exams since.

'I regularly read the newspapers and magazines for job vacancies and apply, giving all my biographical details. I get called for interviews and go to them hoping for a change in my fate. I thought it was a fair game in which many competitors took part, and that those who qualified were given certificates and called to join the service. But in Orissa the rules are different: interviews are only a farce. There are

three qualities a candidate must have: first, he must be very talented with political backing; second, he should have the money to buy the job in an auction; third, he should be a close relative of the head of the department advertising the vacancy. If you have one of these three qualities, then you can definitely get a job but because I do not possess any of them it is not possible for me to get employment. Apart from these, caste also plays a part. Brahmins will only support a Brahmin candidate.

'The other alternative is to start a business. But I am so poor, where can I get the capital? There is a government loan scheme from which you can borrow twenty-five thousand rupees, but I've applied three times and failed to be accepted. Here too, there's a lot of corruption. I have already written for help to the Prime Minister of India, the Chief Minister of Orissa, the State Industry Minister, the local MLA, the Collector, Cuttack; the Director of Industries, Cuttack; the General Manager of Industrial Corporation, Cuttack; and the Chief Secretary to the Government of Orissa, Bhubaneswar. I have written to them several times in the last three years but without any result. It is clear from my experience that in a democratic country like India a poor citizen has no right to live. You don't get justice or respect in return for your talent. I feel sad I haven't been able to fulfil the hopes of my mother. Her dreams just remain dreams, because fate is against us.

'While I was studying for my BA a villager working in Bhubaneswar said that if I went with him he would arrange a job for me. I went there and was employed as a temporary typist but the villager really wanted me to work as a servant in his house. I did not like it and left. So I could neither get a job nor complete my studies properly. Now I'm nowhere.

'Everybody has dreams of a better future. I used to have such dreams and so did several poor boys like me. I don't know what happened to them, but my dreams have vanished the way a lump of dust mingles in the river. They have disappeared in the river of life and the future for me is like a glow worm in a dark room. Hopeless darkness attacks my life like cancer. Yet I want to live. When I read the biographies of great men I find courage. I know I should remain strong and not break down. But I always ask myself, what can I do? And my future remains like a question mark.

'Once a teacher asked us in school, "What will you do when you grow up?" Like me, some said they wanted to be doctors, engineers, lecturers and administrative officers. They were dreams. But there was a boy from the last row who stood up and said, "I come from a family where both my parents are poor. My mother is ill, and although my father is old and weak he has to work as a labourer to send me to school. There's so much uncertainty about their lives that I have no confidence to say that I want to be this or that."

'From dawn till sunset our only worry is food and how to get it.'

8

FARMING

A COLLEGE in the United States used some chapters from my earlier book *My Village, My Life* for a course on culture. I was offered a fee but asked the college to send it to the headmistress of my village school. The cheque was sent and the headmistress deposited it at the State Bank of India, Balichandrapur. At first, the bank accepted it, but after a few days returned the cheque saying the date had expired. The headmistress wrote to me in London and I advised her to send it back to America for re-issue. This was done. When the new cheque was presented the manager of the bank still refused to accept it, saying that the name of the school had been written incorrectly. He wanted the headmistress to send the cheque back to America.

When I arrived in the village, the headmistress told me about her difficulties in encashing the cheque. She felt very embarrassed and did not feel she could send the cheque back again to the college in America. So I volunteered to take the cheque to the manager and talk to him. An assistant teacher came with me. It was around midday and the bank was being audited. The auditor had come from the head office in Calcutta and the manager was busy looking after him. It was lunchtime and the auditor was personally being served with mutton curry and sweets while the bank clerks watched him eat. The manager was polite and offered me a seat. I introduced myself. When I told him about the cheque he said there was another school in Nanpur and they may say the money is meant for them. 'But there's only one middle English school,' I said. I explained that I had made a mistake by asking the college to send the money direct. 'Since you have come personally, I'll get the cheque cleared,' he said. We left, but it took another month for the school to receive the money.

I asked the manager to give me an interview about the function of the bank which I could include in my book. He said he would have to get the permission of his head office in Calcutta. He made several dates and many excuses and I knew he was trying to avoid me. Then, in a friend's house I met a field officer who worked for the bank, negotiating loans for the villagers and businessmen. He was from a nearby village and was keen to talk to me.

Over fifty lakhs of rupees are lent to farmers every year. A villager with a family income of three thousand rupees a year can get a loan for agricultural purposes – two thousand to five thousand rupees, at a fixed interest rate of 12.5 per cent. This loan is only given for six months but can be extended for three years if there is a failure of crops. If the first crop fails finance is given to raise the second crop. If that fails further finance is given to raise a third crop. If that fails the loan has to be repaid by any means. The failure of crops depends on the monsoon over which the farmer has no control.

'The minimum age for applying for a loan is twenty-one and the maximum age is sixty. Finance is given to buy seeds, fertilizers, pesticides, and some cash for labour. It is also given to buy cattle. The buyer selects the animal and the veterinary officer makes a recommendation to the field officer from the bank. Money is then paid to the owner of the animal. Cows cost between five hundred and five thousand rupees. No security is required but legal documents are drawn up. The term for the loan is three and a half years and the animals are insured for a small fee. If they die the veterinary doctor has to issue a certificate on the strength of which the purchaser can get finance for another cow. If the borrower cannot pay the loan then he is taken to court. This is a rare thing as the bank doesn't want to frighten the farmers into not taking loans.'

But the villagers complain that they have to pay a fee even to see the bank official and that the banks are the major source of corruption in the country. In the old days when people wanted money for anything – from buying a cow to getting their daughter married – they either mortgaged their land or pawned their gold jewellery to the moneylender. The rate of interest was extremely high and very often the borrower was unable to pay back the loan. In that case the land was auctioned and the jewellery was forfeited. There is now a greater demand for money in the village to get daughters married.

When Shyam wanted to get his sister married he needed five thousand rupees. He came to me and asked if I could talk to the bank manager about a loan. He was going to say that he wanted to buy a cow but he was really going to spend it on the wedding of his sister. When I didn't agree he told me that many people in the village were doing what he wanted to do and getting money on false premises.

Rama Jena is a farmer and my childhood friend. He was named Rama by his grandmother so that by calling him she would utter the sacred name of God every day.

We went to school together but he left his studies when his elder brother died of cholera. He was only ten but his father needed him to help with the farming. Sometimes he would come to our house in the evenings to borrow books from me. 'I want to study, but my father says it's a waste of money: you don't need to read and write to be a good farmer. Our forefathers were not educated, but they were excellent farmers.'

Rama lives in a house made of mud walls and a thatched roof. He is married with four children, two sons and two daughters. His father died five years ago and his seventy-five-year-old mother lives with him. The house revolves around his mother who, since her husband's death, has become very religious. She spends most of her time performing rituals and keeping the house clean and tidy. The walls are meticulously plastered with cow dung and decorated with rice paste.

Rama is about fifty but looks older. I remember he had a beautiful complexion. But now his skin is dark and withered, the result of working in the sun and the rain.

'Rice farming is hard. To work with soil you have to become soil.'

Rama learned to farm by watching his father. He is considered a good farmer and some villagers ask him to cultivate their land. People from the higher castes like Brahmins and Karans are not allowed to do manual work. Now, the educated feel that working in the fields is not only degrading but lowers their image in society. So their land is cultivated by tenant farmers who get 50 per cent of the produce.

Rama has one acre of his own land, though his plots are scattered. Some are two miles away from the village. But his work as a tenant farmer for several other families gives him about seven acres altogether to farm.

'That's all I can manage on my own. Unlike my father, I am sending my children to school. There's nobody else to help me except my wife, but she can't work in the fields.'

The government has a plan for land consolidation and distribution to help the farmers to get all their land in one area. The Settlement Officer has been working in the village, registering land. The task is difficult because not all the land is irrigated. The plots near the canal are more valuable than the plots liable to flood.

Rama starts ploughing his fields from the middle of April, which is the beginning of summer and the new year. The date and time are fixed by Dharani Naik, the astrologer. The ploughing is done by bullocks using a wooden plough made by the local carpenter and blacksmith. There are no tractors and even if they were available, it would be difficult to use them as the plots are small. 'For rice farming wooden ploughs are the best,' Rama says.

Ploughing is an art which his father taught him. Not all farmers are good at it. A lot of skill is required to manoeuvre the plough while controlling the pair of bullocks. The farmer has to be in charge otherwise the animals will carry him away.

A regular supply of water is essential for rice farming but too much rain can damage the crop. In the summer it gets so hot that the fields dry up and crack, making ploughing difficult. Some showers are then needed to dampen the soil.

Nanpur is in the coastal belt with a network of rivers, all flowing into the Bay of Bengal. During the monsoon, which starts in June and continues until October, the rivers overflow, often causing severe floods. If the flood water stays for about a week and it rains while the water subsides, then it is good for the paddy. The leaves are washed and a fertile silt is left which kills weeds and stimulates growth. But if the flood water stays longer the rice plants are completely destroyed.

'My mother is constantly praying for the right amount of rain to fall at the right time.'

It is a wonderful sight to see the farmers going to the fields. The bullocks are decorated with sandalwood paste and garlands of flowers. A ceremony is performed to greet Mother Earth by lighting an oil lamp and breaking a coconut to invoke good luck. There is a feeling that new life is beginning.

By the middle of June the fields are prepared. The farmers sow the seeds and pray for the rain to fall. Then the whole village rests for three days when no work is done. It is the popular festival of Raja, when the villagers only eat and play.

Raja was originally a peasant festival to celebrate the wetting of Mother Earth by the first raindrops. It symbolizes fertility and menstruation. Raja is an enjoyable time for the unmarried girls. For three days they live together in one room, playing on swings and singing folk songs. They wear

new saris, decorate their faces with sandalwood paste and adorn their carefully prepared hair with sweet-scented jasmine flowers.

Every day Rama gets up before dawn, washes his face and feeds the cattle with chopped husks and rice water, which his wife stores regularly in a large earthen pot. She sweeps the courtyard and prepares breakfast for him and the children. Rama's breakfast consists of *pakhal bhata*, a bowl of water rice with chutneys and raw onions. He has a small garden at the back of his house where he grows spinach, aubergines and green chillies. Some days his mother makes rice cakes for the whole family.

After breakfast Rama goes to his fields. Chinta the Harijan helps him. Chinta has no land of his own and does tenant farming. He worked hard and saved some money to buy two bullocks. Last year one died suddenly. He has not been able to buy another bullock and borrows Rama's animals to plough his fields.

Rama stops work at noon and returns home after taking a bath in the river. He washes the animals and gossips with his friends. He says his prayers before eating his meal, and then he rests until the sun loses its strength, at about three in the afternoon. He returns to the fields and works until sunset, around six in the evening, when his wife lights the oil lamp to welcome the night.

He has not got electricity: he is frightened of it. 'It is not suitable for my modest thatched house. My children have been persuading me, but when I saw a young man electrocuted in the other settlement I decided against it.'

He fetches water from the well, feeds the cattle and tethers them in their shed. While drinking a glass of tea with roasted rice sprinkled on it he tells his mother about the day's work, listening to film music on the radio. Some evenings his friends join him and he discusses the wedding of his eldest daughter, who is sixteen and has just left school.

'It is not good to keep a mature young girl unmarried in the house,' his mother constantly grumbles. But Rama has already bought the dowry, including a television set.

Rama goes to bed at ten and that is the only time he gets to talk to his wife. They have no need to talk to each other during the day. She does her work inside the house and he goes out to the fields. It was an arranged marriage and I remember going to see her after the wedding. She was brought before me by Rama's mother, who lifted the veil to show me the bride's face. Her eyes were closed. According to the custom newly married women do not look straight at the guests. Passing by Rama's house, whenever I stopped to enquire about the family she always hid behind the door and replied in a soft voice.

If the rain does not fall at the right time to germinate the paddy the farmers become desperate. They have to buy more seeds, which is expensive. After harvest a certain amount of paddy is kept aside to be used for seeds, but often most of it is either eaten by rats and insects or cooked for food. Although there is electricity in the area, there is no provision for cold storage.

Rice seedlings are cultivated specially for transplantation and the process needs a lot of care. First, the seeds are sprayed with insecticide and dried in the sun. Then they are soaked in water for twenty-four hours, taken out and kept in bamboo baskets covered with straw and sprinkled with lukewarm water. Gunny bags are spread over them and after three or four days the seeds begin to sprout. By then the farmers have prepared special plots of land with manure and the seeds are sown. The seedlings take three weeks to grow to a height of one foot and they are ready to be transplanted. The fields are levelled and the soil must be like mud. The seedlings are planted in rows, eighteen inches apart. The rice plants need a constant supply of water. Two weeks before harvest the fields are drained dry.

'It takes four months from the day I plant the seeds until the day of the harvest. There are lots of problems. If the wind blows strongly at the time of flowering, the rice is damaged. Insects eat the plants and I have to spray them with insecticides, which are expensive. But we don't use them after the paddy has come up.'

The intense green fields ripple in the breeze like green waves. Gradually the colour changes to deep green and then to golden yellow. If it is a good crop the plants bend down under their own weight. A successful crop brings happiness to the village.

'It gives me a lot of pleasure to see the fields full of crops. I'm glad that I'm a farmer so that my family can eat pure food grown by me. The foodstuff we buy in the market is adulterated. In the winter months I grow lentils, potatoes and vegetables and sell some of them in the market. I like market days, when I meet my relatives and friends from the other villages. I also grow a second crop of rice during the summer.'

Rama does not know what the Green Revolution is. The farmers are encouraged by the government to use high-yield rice, fertilizers and pesticides to produce a second crop. But it can only be achieved from November until May. A few acres of irrigated land are cultivated, the rest remains barren. Previously cow dung was the only form of manure, but the village women burnt most of it as fuel. Now, fertilizers and pesticides are sold in the market place without any restriction. Most farmers are not aware of the harmful effects the pesticides can have on crops and health. They are so poisonous that they have killed off much wildlife. The jackals have disappeared, the frogs who used to fill the night air with their croaking have gone. Several young people have committed suicide by taking pesticides.

'I spray pesticides while covering my face with a cloth. I hire a pump from the government. It would be easier if I could have my own pump, but it costs a lot of money. The government has introduced new seeds producing more per acre than the local seeds. The rice is white and cooks well, but there is no taste in it. I grow different kinds of rice, some with long grains, some with short, and all with different flavours and typical to our area. My mother insists on growing them. Otherwise we will lose them in a few years, she says. I harvest the rice in November. I cut the paddy and leave it in the fields for a few days to dry. I then tie it into bunches and carry home the bundles on my head. I feel a wonderful sense of achievement and very proud.

'On Thursdays during the harvest season the village women clean their houses, give the floors and walls a coat of mud plaster and decorate them with rice paste to welcome Laxmi. They prepare an image of the goddess by putting a bowl of rice in the middle of a room and decorating it with coins and flowers. The first rice from the field is offered to Laxmi and only shared among the family members.

'That night I can sleep well, but my problems are not over. Whatever I get from the land is just enough to maintain my family. With seven people to look after I have to buy clothes, medicines, and pay for the education of my children. I can't afford to buy a new shirt for myself. I haven't the time to go to the cinema or see television. The only time I saw a film was when the cinema opened with a religious film in Oriya, depicting the life of Krishna. I have seen television in Hindi, but I could not understand it.

'I have only been to Cuttack once and to Puri twice. But my mother has gone to see Lord Jagannath several times. I am religious but I haven't got the time to practise religion. God will listen to me wherever I am. It is the sincerity that counts.

'If only my eldest son could get a job, my problems would be over. He has completed his studies from the local college but so far hasn't found a job. He is applying and running to the towns. I spent money on his education and now I am spending money for him to find a job. I understand you have to give a bribe, but where can I get so much money? It is difficult for me to get ready cash. We eat whatever we grow and very little is left over to sell.

'I educated my son because I thought he would get a job and send me some money. Moreover, there is a respect for education. People respect you because you are educated. Do you think they respect me because I'm a good farmer? No. When I went to see the bank manager to get a loan he did not even ask me to sit down. I had to stand two feet away from him. But when our friend Raja – do you remember the boy who was two years junior to us at school? He is now a big government officer – came to the bank while I was there, the manager offered him a chair and they spoke to each other in English, ignoring me. Raja pretended not to recognize me. I felt very small. If I had been educated and had a good job I am sure the bank manager would have treated me with respect.'

'All my crops were destroyed by drought. Last year it didn't rain at all. Most of my plots are on high ground and it was not possible for me to lift water from the river. The paddy had a very stunted growth. Instead of growing to a height of four to five feet it only grew to two feet. If it had rained I could have produced a lot of rice.

'I have no electricity in my house, but I do 420 and get the power. My neighbours do the same. We give something to the line man, who closes his eyes while passing by our house, but it has got no value. I can't say openly that I have electricity. I give him five rupees a month and sometimes a glass of milk. But he's very clever. Before I can offer him either a cup of tea or a glass of milk he will say, "I have just had a cup of tea and I'm not hungry, so I won't eat anything." He's an actor. If he sees you he will say, "Sir, when did you come? I haven't seen you for so long. Have you brought any nice things?" To get electricity I have to deposit three hundred rupees and get my house wired. But if I had that money to spare I would rather spend it on my farm.

'I have no TV. But others have got it. They are not going to their neighbours' houses any more, so the friendliness which was in the village before has now gone. They are mostly staying at home and watching television. A trader is getting married next month. He'll get a colour TV as dowry.

'I don't go to the cinema. You can only go to a cinema hall if your mind is happy. But I'm always worried about where to get money to manage my family. My health also suffers because of my worries. I'm constantly worried. Two of my cows suddenly died.

'My son is studying for his BA at Balichandrapur. He's really the son of my younger brother, but we live together, so he's my son. I've got no sons of my own, I only have daughters. My daughter Jilli is a good student and very keen on her studies. I want to educate her. She also sings very well. The headmistress is very happy with her and gives her extra coaching in the evening.

'I have got my two other daughters married. There was no problem in getting bridegrooms because they were good-looking. For my eldest daughter's wedding I spent fifteen thousand rupees. I gave a wrist-watch, a radio and a gold chain for the bridegroom. They came and selected her. I was not keen to get her married because she was studying for her matriculation exam. But when I went and saw the boy's house and the farm they have, I agreed. From the back of the house you can see their paddy fields and their land is irrigated and produces a lot. His mother works as a social worker, so my daughter is living in comfort.

'I left school before I could complete my primary education. My eldest brother died of typhoid and my father needed my help. I was a good student. If I had continued I could have become a government official. But it didn't happen. Some of my friends went to work in Calcutta. They worked for Dunlop, got ready cash and educated their children.

'I wanted to go to Calcutta but my father said, "No." There was tension between Hindus and Muslims then, so I couldn't go. One of my contemporaries, whose father was selling coconuts in the village, went to Calcutta. He was not a better student than myself but he got a job there and has built a concrete house in the village. He has educated his

three sons. But my problem is to get ready cash. I cannot
manage my household. Altogether we are eight, my two
brothers and our families. I have to take all the decisions in
the house. My younger brother does nothing. He says, "If
the sons are not doing well in their studies, let them do some
kind of business." But I say, let them complete their studies
first and then whatever is written in their fate will happen.
I remain half-educated and I don't want that to happen to
my children. I want my daughter to study. I want her to do
M A. Now she can pass her B A because the college is near
by.

'Before Independence it was a dark age. People were not
so clever. Now you get a vehicle as soon as you step out of
the house. Then, people used to walk everywhere. You could
get fifteen *gaunis* of rice for a rupee in those days. Now you
have to pay fifteen rupees for one *gauni*. It was impossible
to get one rupee; now some people have got thousands of
rupees. We didn't have a single concrete building here, but
now there are several houses made of sand and cement. Most
people are getting their verandahs cemented.

'But farmers haven't prospered, it's only people with jobs
and big businesses who are doing well. The contractors building roads and the dealers who sell controlled sugar, rice and
flour are doing well. They are putting money in their pockets.
There is also a lot of corruption. There's no government now.
Everybody takes the law into his own hands. You can kill a
man, give a bribe and walk free. During the British days
there was a respect for authority. The Untouchables didn't
come near us. Now they want to put a hand on our shoulders.
There's no caste now. The Untouchables are called Harijans
and they say, "Your blood is like our blood and work is
related to caste." So why are there so many sub-castes and
divisions among the Harijans? They won't mix with each
other but they want to mix with the Karans, the Khandayats
and the Brahmins. Why? Why do they want to mix with us?
Now they come and sit beside us. The other day I was
drinking a cup of tea at the tea stall. A Harijan came and

sat next to me and he started talking to me as if he was my friend. I got up and left. If he sits beside me, why should he think he's my friend?

'Now the government says it has done so much – roads, electricity, hospitals, television, radio. But you don't get electricity free, we have to pay for it. Epidemics are under control, but not because of the government. It's because the scientists invented cures. There are still villages where people are suffering from cholera and typhoid.

'Now we are not cultivating jute, so the land around the village is clean. As a result we have less pollution. It is not the government who has done that, it is the people themselves.

'I don't like the Congress government. They only help their own people, the people who support them. They run the country according to their whim, as if it was their father's property. Since 1977 I've only voted for Janata, I've never changed. But all the M L As are the same. They'll come to the village before the election and then they're rarely seen afterwards. They're only concerned with their self-interest. Let the country go to hell. They're interested in getting houses, cars, silk saris for their wives. One of the M L As was starving, he didn't have any food in his house. The villagers gave him food and votes. He was elected but didn't do anything for the villagers. Now he has a concrete building, several trucks and a car. Where did he get all this money from?

'I've seen Rajiv Gandhi on television. There's no gain in seeing him and no harm in not seeing him. Indira Gandhi ruled for some years. Congress ruled, then Janata ruled. You can't blame the government because people arc corrupt. Corrupt people can only have corrupt government. If a man has a one-storey concrete house he wants to make it two-storey. But nobody cares for the man who is living in a mud hut.

'The expressway was built by the leader of the Janata party when he was in power. People say he's also corrupt but at least he did something for the province. Because of the road people have benefited. From that main road we can have branch roads reaching out to interior villages. I helped to construct the road. There were no mechanical rollers to level the soil and they were pulled by bullocks and buffaloes. The engineer asked several farmers to do the job for him. They brought their bullocks but could not pull the roller. The engineer came to my house and said, "People say you are a good farmer, would you help me?" I took my bullock and like magic the roller moved. I said, "I can't work for ten rupees a day." He said, "Work, and I'll see." I worked for a month and he gave me a cheque for two thousand rupees. I went to Cuttack and got it cashed in a bank. There was no bank in the village then. Now there is a bank, I've got no money to put in it.

'You have to give a bribe at every step these days. A farmer can get a three thousand rupee loan from the bank at a low interest, but out of that he will have to pay four to five hundred rupees as a bribe and that, too, beforehand. Otherwise they'll keep you waiting. If you buy a bullock with government money and it dies before you have repaid the loan, you can get extra money to buy another. But the veterinary doctor has to give a certificate saying the animal did not die of neglect or old age. You give money to the veterinary doctor to get the certificate. Even then you have to run after him. For everything you have to give money.'

Gauduni Mausi, the milkmaid aunt, died ten years ago at the age of eighty. I asked her when writing *My Village, My Life* how old she was. She said she did not know because she did not have a *jatak*. She could not remember how many children she had given birth to but the memory of her eldest son dying of cholera was still painful. Although she could not read or write she was expert in milk products, like making curd, cheese and ghi. As a boy I went to her house to collect milk and she would give me some butter to eat. Her husband, a tall, well-built man, looked after the cattle and did tenant farming. He died, leaving her a widow, but her authority in the house did not diminish. She got her two surviving sons married. They were my childhood friends. Their joint family house stands at the entrance to our settlement.

Kundera, the eldest son, went to school with me for a few years but then stopped after the death of his brother. Now that he is the eldest, the responsibility of managing the household is upon him. He does the farming and Hadia, his younger brother, looks after the cattle. Hadia studied a little but discontinued. He knows everything about looking after the cattle and the villagers consult him. He is always eager to help. They live together in a house of mud walls and a thatched roof.

Kundera has only daughters, while Hadia has sons. The children are treated equally by both the brothers. They have educated the eldest son, who is now attending the college at Balichandrapur. Then he will look for a job. Kundera once told me he wished he had a brother who could go out to work in a town and send him ready cash. It seems his wishes will be fulfilled through his brother's son.

'Is there any difficulty in living in a joint family?'

'No,' Kundera replied, 'why should there be? My brother looks after the cattle and I do the farming.'

'Do you ever quarrel?'

'Why should we quarrel? We live together, helping each other.'

Hadia said, 'We are educating my sons so that they can prosper in their lives. There is prestige in education. I could not continue with my studies whereas you went to school and college. People respect you, but they say I'm a milkman.'

'Why didn't you study?'

'My eldest brother died and my father was an old man, unable to work. There were so many cows to look after and if I had continued with school, how could we have managed? My mother said, "What is the point of studying, our business is milk." But I am determined to get my sons educated. I want them to be respected and not remain inferior milkmen.'

Kundera added, 'Farming is difficult, we either have floods or drought. At the time of an election the government says, "We will do this and that for you," but when we need help they do nothing. The water pump arrives after the rice plants are dead. We could produce a lot if we could get help at the time of need. Farming is my life. I only know that, I can't do anything else. Because I haven't got money I depend on government help. Last year we got seeds from the government. The rice plants grew healthily but they died before ripening. Thousands of farmers were affected. Later on we found out that the Chief Minister had taken money from a dealer and given him the contract to supply seeds. They were not proper seeds. Instead of supplying seeds he supplied eating rice, which is cheaper than seeds. We worked hard and got nothing, no compensation either from the government. We suffered for two years because I had invested all my money in buying the seeds.'

9

FOOD, DRUGS AND MEDICINE

FOOD means rice to the villagers. The poor eat it with spinach and the better-off with dal, vegetables and fish. Goat meat is popular but expensive, and very few can afford it. Eating beef is unthinkable as the cow is sacred. Without processed and packaged food only freshly cooked food is eaten. In my childhood wheat flour was used only for festive and special occasions. When a villager ate chapatis or puris he said, 'I have eaten only snacks, not a proper meal.' Now nearly everybody in the village eats chapatis for the evening meal because flour is cheaper than rice.

Food is cooked mainly by the women and the kitchen is under the strict control of the housewife. It is the most important room in the house and kept scrupulously clean. No animals are allowed inside and women should have a bath and change into fresh clothes before entering. The ancestors live there, kept in the shape of small mounds of earth in one corner of the room. They are worshipped every day and offered food. At death anniversaries an elaborate ritual is performed when all the ancestors are remembered.

Rice is cooked in earthen pots. The ovens are made of clay and wood is used as fuel. Now a few villagers are using electric stoves and gas cookers. The gas comes in cylinders but as they are supplied only to town dwellers, only those villagers with relatives and friends working in Cuttack can get them. In my childhood metal pots were not used for cooking as it

was believed they caused stomach illnesses. Now this
restraint has gone.

No food is eaten in the morning before cleaning the teeth
and washing the face. Women do not eat anything before
having a bath and attending to their religious rituals. The
first face seen by the villagers dictates the events of that day.
It is believed that if you see the faces of certain persons in
the morning you won't get anything to eat that day and
everything will go wrong.

The morning meal consists of rice pancakes with sugar, or
water rice with onions and chutneys. The housewives feed
their children first and send them to school. Tea drinking has
become popular and it is now common to offer it to guests.
The majority cannot afford milk and sugar so they drink it
with salt. Only a few years ago my old relations would gather
around me in the morning to drink cups of tea and gossip.
Now there are tea stalls where the villagers can buy a cup of
tea for fifty paisa and have a chance to gossip with their
friends.

At midday boiled rice is eaten with curried vegetables. The
left-over rice is soaked in water and eaten as *pakhal bhat*. If
kept for a day, it ferments and induces sleep. It is refreshing
in the summer, eaten with yoghurt, lemon juice and fried

vegetables. Roasted and puffed rice is popular as an after-noon snack. It is delicious when mixed with peanuts and slices of coconut. Potatoes, aubergines, plantains and pump-kins are the main vegetables. Cauliflowers, cabbages and tomatoes are grown in abundance in the winter months but during the dry season it is difficult to get any vegetables except potatoes.

Tomatoes came to the village when I was a child. I remem-ber when a friend of mine came to me with a large red tomato and told me it was full of blood. His mother gave him glasses of tomato juice every day in the belief that the blood in his body would increase. Another friend, who was thin and anaemic, was given tomato juice by his grandmother to improve his health. I was very thin and my friends persuaded me to drink tomato juice too. I tried some but did not like the taste, it did not seem like blood to me. Blood represents life and strength to the villagers, but after drinking glasses of tomato juice we still remained thin and weak.

Oriya cooking is simple, mainly steamed and boiled, using delicate spices in small quantities. Onions, mustard seeds, garlic, root ginger, coriander, cumin and turmeric are the main spices. These are locally grown. The food offered to Lord Jagannath is considered the best. Gods are vegetarian and steamed food cooked in clay pots is offered to them. Onions and garlic are forbidden. Only vegetables indigenous to Orissa are allowed, so potatoes, cauliflowers, tomatoes and cabbages are not offered. In the old days *dali bhat* was always served at wedding receptions with rice pudding and tra-ditional cakes. Now the food has become more sophisticated and fish and meat are included.

In my childhood I ate hand-pounded brown rice, bean sprouts, yoghurt and molasses. Everything was grown without using chemical manures and pesticides. The oils were pressed locally, there was no adulteration.

When I went outside the village I found that educated people ate white rice, white flour and white sugar. Everything was refined and village food was considered inferior. When I came to England and saw health food shops and restaurants, it confirmed my belief that the village food of my childhood was better. Unfortunately there is no teaching about nutrition and the old practices are disappearing in the name of modernism. It is now impossible to get hand-pounded rice and freshly pressed oils.

Adulteration is widespread and the government has not been able to control it. Sand is mixed with sugar, sawdust with flour, petroleum products with cooking oil, small stones with rice to make it weigh more. Traders go to great lengths to adulterate food. A few years ago a group of salesmen arrived in the village selling ghi. They were from outside Orissa and had come to the market place at Balichandrapur. They had cans of ghi which smelled and looked like pure ghi and were inexpensive. My father was persuaded to buy a kilo and the family consumed some of it. But after a week my mother complained that the ghi had no smell. My father thought she had lost her sense of smell but when the other members of the family tasted it, they found my mother was right. But when my nephew went to the market place to look for the salesmen they had gone, after cheating many other villagers.

Since the road was built vegetables and fish are sent to Cuttack and other centres. The traders buy them direct from the farmers. Therefore the demand for food has increased, very few villagers want to remain farmers. As a result the food production is not sufficient. This creates an increase in prices, which are often higher than in the towns.

There are strict rules about eating Milk should not be taken with meat or fish. On certain days, such as Thursdays and other auspicious days, only vegetarian food is eaten. Until recently eggs and chicken were not allowed into the house and women from the higher castes never ate them. They were considered dirty and associated with the eating habits of the lower castes. But it was a common belief among men that eggs gave strength and vitality. So some villagers drank egg yolks with milk and sugar. When I was a student I was told that the proteins from vegetables and fish were inferior to the proteins from meat. That was why Westerners were stronger than Indians. Now even the Brahmins have started to eat chicken curry and eggs.

Those who have the money can afford to eat well. In India eating well means eating rich food – oily, spicy, sweet, fried and full of ghi and butter. This has created certain health problems associated with cardio-vascular diseases.

I do not know of any scientific study of the food habits of an Indian village, but it always amazes me how the poor can keep alive and mentally active on so little food. Many live to a great age. I am sure this is because they are mainly vegetarian, do not eat fatty food and take plenty of exercise as part of their work. They live in close relationship with nature, with a strong sense of belonging to a community.

Lord Shiva, the God of Creation and Destruction, was the first hippy. He left home and spent his nights in the cremation ground, smoking hash and dancing in ecstasy. If it was all right for Shiva to smoke hash, it is considered good for his devotees. They have been smoking hash, singing and dancing for centuries. It is a religious ritual, and in the village a *puja* is often performed, dedicated to Shiva or Trinath. The shopkeepers on the bridge have erected a shrine for Trinath and in the evenings villagers gather there to listen to a story:

Once upon a time, there was a Brahmin called Madhusudan. He was married with a baby son but his wife did not have any milk of her own. She was worried. 'How is my son going to live?' she asked her husband. 'Please go and buy a cow so that I can feed my baby with her milk.'

The husband replied, 'I'm a poor Brahmin, where can I get a cow? Nobody cares for the poor Brahmins any more.'

The wife started to cry, 'O God, why did you give a son to poor Brahmins? If I can't feed my child and it dies, I'll be committing murder, a great sin.'

The son cried out for milk and the Brahmin became anxious. He sold all his possessions in the market place in order to buy a cow but could only raise five rupees. With that money the Brahmin went from village to village in search of a suitable animal. Eventually he reached the village of a wealthy merchant who had a herd of beautiful cows. Among them was an unruly cow called Baula, who ate vegetables from the neighbour's garden. He was so angry that he shouted, 'If I could find somebody who would pay me five rupees I'd sell you to him.'

The Brahmin was resting on a neighbour's verandah and overheard. 'I'll pay you five rupees,' he said.

The businessman replied, 'Are you mad? The price of my cow is fifty rupees, how can I give it to you for five?'

The Brahmin said solemnly, 'You are a great merchant and you trade in the name of truth, so you must keep your word.'

The merchant thought to himself, 'What a coincidence the Brahmin should be there to hear me. If I don't keep my word then I'll commit a sin.' So he took the five rupees from the Brahmin and gave him the cow and her calf.

When the Brahmin's wife saw the cow she was so delighted that her face beamed with joy like a full moon. She looked after the cow and was able to feed her son. Unfortunately, a few days later the cow went to the grazing ground and did not return. The Brahmin looked everywhere but could not find her. He and his wife were so unhappy that they could not eat or sleep. In the morning the Brahmin took a stick from the house and went out in search of the cow. He had only gone a little way when he came across a banyan tree in which lived Trinath – Brahma, Vishnu, Maheswar. When Trinath saw the Brahmin they asked him, 'Why are you so sad? Tell us where you are going.'

The Brahmin said he was going to the market place to find out if anybody was trying to sell his cow. So Trinath asked the Brahmin to do some shopping for them – hash, pan, betel nuts and oil, for one paisa each. The Brahmin said, 'I live by begging, where can I get the money to buy your shopping?'

'The money is under the bush,' Trinath replied.

The Brahmin pulled the bushes and found three copper coins. He went on digging, hoping for more money. Trinath laughed and said, 'Don't be greedy. You have got whatever was there.'

The Brahmin walked a few yards and then stopped to think. He returned to the tree and asked Trinath, 'How am I going to bring the oil, I haven't got a container?'

Trinath said, 'In your towel.'

'How can I carry oil in a towel?' the Brahmin replied.

Trinath said, 'Just utter our name.'

After reaching the market the Brahmin looked for his cow but could not find her anywhere. He bought betel nuts and hashish and then went to the oil men and asked for oil. The oil men refused when they saw the towel. At last an old oil man thought, 'This is a mad Brahmin, I'm going to cheat him. I'll take his money and not give him any oil.' He poured the Brahmin a little oil from the pot using the wrong measure and the Brahmin collected it in his towel. When the Brahmin left the oil man discovered that his full pot was empty. He started to cry and people gathered around him. He said a Brahmin had bought a little oil from him and as soon as he had left the pot became empty. Other traders said he had also come to them for oil but they had refused to serve him. Soon a group of men went running to the Brahmin and told him what had happened. He came back and returned the oil to the oil man. Immediately the pot was full and he was happy. This time the oil man gave him the right measure.

When the Brahmin reached the banyan tree, Trinath asked him to perform the *puja*. He said, 'If you and your friends do it, all

your sins will go.' Trinath explained to him the procedure for the
puja – three pipes for the hash, three lamps and the three betel
leaves with nuts. 'In the evenings, invite your neighbours and
worship Trinath.' The Brahmin wanted to perform the *puja* there,
under the banyan tree. He made pipes with leaves but did not
know how to prepare the lamps. 'What shall I do for making
wicks?' he asked Trinath.

'Use your towel.'

'I'm a poor Brahmin. I earn my living by begging. My cow is
stolen, my wife must be waiting for me. How can I tear my towel
to make a wick for the lamp? What am I going to do?'

Trinath said, 'Don't worry. You'll find your cow and your family
will live in comfort.'

'If this is going to happen, I promise to perform the *puja*,' the
Brahmin said. After preparing the lamps he asked Trinath, 'How
do I light them? I have no fire.' Trinath replied, 'Close your eyes
and the lamps will light.'

He performed the *puja*, paid his respects to Trinath and left. On
his way home he found his cow and when he arrived in the house
it was full of wealth. The neighbours were amazed. The Brahmin
explained to them what to do. Everybody in that area worshipped
Trinath and all the poor became wealthy. They were so rich that
they had no need to borrow. The merchants were worried and went
to see the king. They complained that the Brahmin had started
this *puja* and everyone had become so wealthy that they had no
need to come to them.

The king announced to his subjects that whoever worshipped
Trinath would pay a heavy fine, go to jail, or have his head chopped
off. That night, unexpectedly, the eldest son of the king died. The
whole country was in mourning. The boy's corpse was taken to the
bank of the river for cremation. Trinath thought that if he could
bring the boy back to life then people would have faith in him. So
disguised as an old Brahmin, he came to the bank of the river and
asked the attendants what had happened. After listening to their
stories he said, 'If you think of Trinath the boy will live.' The old
Brahmin whispered 'Trinath' seven times into the boy's ear and
the prince came back to life.

The king was delighted and worshipped Trinath regularly.
People from all over his kingdom came to watch the ceremony.

A blind man wanted to attend. He told his friends, 'I can't see

Trinath, but you can. Come back and tell me all about it.'

'If you pray to Trinath you'll get your eyesight back,' they replied.

The blind man started to walk slowly. On the way he met a lame man who also wanted to see Trinath. He said to the blind man, 'I can see and you can walk. Let me sit on your back and guide you. Together we can reach Trinath.'

The lame man sat on the blind man's shoulders. They both prayed to Trinath. As they moved along the blind man said he could see and the lame man said there was new life in his limbs.

The villagers believe that by worshipping Trinath miracles can also happen to them.

Hash can be bought openly from a government-licensed shop, as well as *bhang* and opium. Opium and hash are more expensive than *bhang*. My grandmother used to take opium and sometimes it was given to pets to make them docile. *Bhang* is drunk in the summer, mixed with sugar and fruit juice. Nearly everyone in the village has tasted it. When drunk in small quantities the experience is uplifting. But there are unpleasant experiences if too much is taken.

Hash, or ganja, is smoked and is considered stronger than *bhang*. Those who smoke hash regularly are described as *ganjod*, a derogatory expression. But I only know of one addict in the village. His father used to smoke and he smoked with him. After his father's death the problem of looking after the family was too much for him and he took to hash as a means of escape.

The villagers are not worried when their children take *bhang* but they get upset if they find out they are drinking alcohol. Toddy, or palm wine, is drunk by the Harijans and, if not fermented, is good for health. Whisky, brandy, rum and beer, called 'foreign liquor', are now manufactured all over India. They are a source of income for the government through the excise duties. Vast sums of money are invested in the manufacturing process and the industry is expanding. Everywhere you can find shops licensed to sell foreign liquor.

Although there is a government health warning on the bottles, it is considered fashionable to drink alcohol. Most Indians I know drink to get drunk, not for enjoyment. There is no licensed shop in the village but alcohol can be bought illegally in the market place at Balichandrapur. This has become a cause of crime. People steal money to buy alcohol and under its influence lose their self-control.

In the village theatre, drunkards were introduced as figures of fun, waving bottles of red water, singing and speaking incoherently. Now these characters are more serious and portrayed as criminals, even rapists and murderers.

'I'm sixty-eight. I retired from my job when I was fifty-eight. I used to get forty-five rupees a month as pension but now it has gone up to one hundred and sixty-six rupees. But I have to go to Cuttack to collect the money. It's not enough to manage on. I have to look after my wife. She is ill all the time; she suffers from rheumatism and is almost bedridden. We have no children, so there's nobody to look after us.

'I enjoy smoking hash and drinking *bhang*. I got the habit while working in the town as a *havildar*. In the evening the others smoked and I smoked with them. Now I cannot do without it. But hash and *bhang* have no strength these days. The other day while buying some hash, I asked the shop-keeper, "I'm spending twenty-five to fifty paisa every day but I don't get intoxicated. What's the matter?" He said, "Why are you smoking every day?" I think the supplier extracts all the power from it. It's adulterated, so what can the shopkeeper do?

'I've never liked opium because it gives me tummy-ache. I only like *bhang*. I mix it with milk, sugar and tea and drink it in the evening. I also add some spices to it. It increases the intoxication if you add spices. I have taken foreign liquor – whisky and brandy. In the army there were some British officers and I used to play hockey with them. They liked to enjoy life and after the game they drank rum and brandy – very good quality – and used to offer me some.

Now you can get it in the market place, but manufactured in India. A little bottle costs twenty-five rupees.

'I have no money to spare so I can't buy any. But I take *Ayurvedic modak*, like a small *ladu*. One *modak* costs seventy-five paisa. If you take one at night you have a good sleep. One makes you feel merry, but after two you become silent. I take about one and a half. Our gods smoked and Shiva was very fond of ganja, so I don't see any harm in taking it. At the end of the day I need something to relax my mind. But I don't get enough money to buy foreign liquor.

'When I was working in the army, the police had gone to arrest a holy man. We took our rifles in case there was any trouble. But the holy man did such magic that the Collector couldn't give any order for his arrest. We stayed there for ten days and nothing happened. One of the disciples told me, "You have come here, you shouldn't go back empty-handed. Take the name of God from the holy man." He arranged for the holy man to whisper a mantra in my ear. He said, "Whenever you get up in the morning say 'Narayan', before eating say 'Narayan', before sleeping 'Narayan', so Narayan will be always with you, giving you joy and peace." So I take my *bhang* and say "Narayan", and the world is beautiful.'

In 1973 I was in the village. One evening, I had severe pains in my chest. My brother-in-law, who works as a doctor in Manchester, was also visiting Orissa and had come to see my parents. He wanted to examine me but unfortunately, he did not have the necessary instruments. A relative went to the health centre but it was locked and the doctor had gone on leave. At Balichandrapur he found a pharmacist who came with an old faulty stethoscope. My brother-in-law did not want to take any risk and decided to take me to the hospital at Cuttack. There was no ambulance or vehicle to take me there, so we fetched a taxi from Chandikhol.

The countryside was dark and the old taxi shook and rattled as we drove the thirty miles to the hospital. We got there after midnight and the duty doctor was in bed. He was woken up, and after examining me he admitted me to a medical ward. The specialist was not available until the next morning. I was given a pain-killing injection but it had no effect. Medicines supplied to hospitals are often adulterated, my relative said.

The ward was crowded and patients were sleeping on the floor. As there was no adequate nursing service, patients were required to have their own private attendants who slept beside them. There were no mosquito nets or proper bedding and I felt I had come to a living hell.

In the morning my brother-in-law came to see me with a doctor friend. They took my E C G, but the machine was old and as the voltage fluctuated the reading showed there was something wrong with my heart. I was immediately given treatment for a heart attack.

As soon as the doctors left, I heard an attendant say to another patient, pointing at me, 'People get admitted to this bed complaining of chest pain during the night and in the morning they're gone.'

When the doctor came to see me in the afternoon, I requested him to shift me to another bed. Soon everybody in the hospital knew I lived in England and went out of their way to give me special treatment.

All the tests were carried out and I was referred to the cardiologist. I was taken on a stretcher to his department and put on the floor to wait. As soon as he saw me he exclaimed, 'Prafulla, what are you doing here?' We had studied science together at Cuttack and were meeting after many years. He examined me thoroughly and said that my chest pain was connected with my stomach and not my heart.

Last year a fifty-year-old engineer, married with six children and working in Bhubaneswar, was visiting his family home in Nanpur. In the middle of the night he had a heart attack and died without any medical help.

There is no ambulance service and patients have to be carried to the hospital or the health centre in whatever condition. Consultation is free but patients have to buy medicines, which are very expensive. Usually doctors demand money before seeing the patients.

I was staying with friends in Cuttack when a group of people arrived from my village, looking worried. They had brought a young man to the hospital who was the victim of a road accident. They had already paid money to the surgeon who had examined the patient, but he was demanding more money to admit him to a bed. The superintendent of the hospital was a friend of mine and I sent him a note before going to see the patient. When I went to the hospital the young man was lying on the floor, and there were many like him. The superintendent, who had been trained in England, was embarrassed that the surgeon had taken money from a patient. He told me there were several similar allegations made against the surgeon but he was helpless as he had the backing of an important government minister. The surgeon had already paid the politician a large amount of money to be posted there and he was recovering it, I was told.

In my childhood we did not know that there were places called hospitals. People suffered silently and used local remedies including herbs, strict diet, massage and spiritual healing. When my old relatives in the village had aches and pains, I used to massage them. Nursing was the only means of relieving suffering. A *baidya* from a distant village came to treat us. When my sister was recovering from typhoid he prepared a tonic for her which had a miraculous effect. Now the villagers are not using herbal and local remedies. They want to take a modern pill and get an instant cure. The doctors maintain that herbal remedies cannot be scientifically proved. So much money is being spent for the research of modern drugs, yet the government of India is only paying lip service to the ancient traditions of herbal treatment and healing.

Anybody with a little knowledge of medicine can practise as a doctor. There are several stores in Balichandrapur where medicines can be bought without prescription. When I am in the village, people come to see me for all kinds of problems –

headaches, stomach pains, colds, fevers. I always have a stock of medicines with me – paracetamol, cough syrup, antacids and digestives. In emergency cases I take them to the hospital. As they are not used to taking lots of medicines, antibiotics work like magic. With inoculations and vaccinations, epidemics and infant mortality are under control. People are living longer.

Young doctors are reluctant to work in the villages because there is no money. Basant Jena is an exception. He wants to devote his career to Nanpur, where he was born and brought up. His grandfather was a farmer, but his father worked as a factory worker in Calcutta and was able to educate Basant to become a doctor.

'I decided to become a doctor when I was young, studying for matriculation. I wanted to help the sick. After studying science for two years at Cuttack, I enrolled in the medical college. For my father there were only two respectable professions – medicine and engineering. He knew about lawyers, but they had a bad image. They extracted money from the villagers and promoted litigation. Young boys then wanted to become doctors or engineers. So my father was happy with my choice.

'After qualifying as a doctor, I came to live in the village and started my practice. I was the only doctor and people came to me in the middle of the night for help. I would be asleep but I had to go and see the patient. I was never offered money. They thought that because I was a village boy it was my duty to help them. If they had called a doctor from the town or another village he would have demanded money. I felt too embarrassed to ask them. I knew they didn't have money, so how could they pay me? I used to give the patients free medicines from the samples I received from the pharmaceutical companies. What could I do? I can't see other people suffer. My father said, "How are you going to manage? One day you'll get married and have a family. You cannot become a charitable institution."

'I rented a room at Balichandrapur and started my clinic. I named it "Kalpataru", after my grandfather. It was a room with a verandah but no washing facilities. It was located centrally near the canal. The businessman who let me the room had his own personal interest, he thought he would get a family doctor free. He told his friends about me and my practice started well. About one hundred patients came to see me every day. I also went to patients' homes to visit them. I had all kinds of patients – young, old, men, women and children. I didn't ask for any fee and accepted whatever people gave me. Somehow, they knew that if they came to see a doctor they would have to pay. The poor would come, put the money on the table first and beg me to see the patient. I knew they were poor and had sold whatever they had – jewellery or utensils – to get the money for the treatment. Often, I didn't accept.

'I was only able to carry out a few basic investigations. With my microscope I examined blood, urine and stools. But if a patient had an accident and had broken a leg, it was not possible for me to get it X-rayed. The nearest X-ray machine was in Cuttack. I found that many had worm infections – hookworm, roundworm – caused by bad drinking water and bad sanitation. Their illnesses were also caused by poverty and malnutrition. These were problems I could not solve with medicines. I wanted to help them but didn't know how to. If the government could provide clean drinking water and proper sanitation, at least 75 per cent of our diseases would go. Whatever people eat is sucked away by worms and infections, so the body doesn't get the nourishment and becomes anaemic. Most of the villagers suffer from this condition.

'I also carried out simple operations like hernia and abscess. When major operations were required I sent the patients to Cuttack. Often I went with them to make arrangements for admission to the hospital. Going to hospital is expensive. You have to pay the doctor or the surgeon, otherwise they won't see the patients. Although it's a government hospital, the doctors demand money. It's a business for them.

There are agents who work for these doctors. They wait at the railway and bus stations and as soon as the villagers arrive they approach them and take them to the hospital. The villagers feel totally lost in the town and the agents extract money from them.

'The children suffer from gastro-enteritis and rheumatic fever, which can affect the heart. There's also a lot of leprosy in our villages, but it's curable. Usually people hide the disease, as it is considered a stigma. There is some TB, but not much. The most common illnesses are dysentery, diarrhoea and typhoid, all caused by bad sanitation and infected water or food. But many people suffer from malaria and filaria, which causes swollen glands.

'I have treated several cases of VD. It's a new disease in our village now, all due to prostitution. There are some very sad cases. A young woman with several children became a widow. She was poor and had to look after her children. The only way she could do it was by selling her womanhood. Men and young boys visited her out of curiosity and for pleasure. Then she became pregnant. An abortion was performed on her by a local quack, but she got tetanus. Nobody had told me about it, and I was only called to see her when she was in a state of collapse. I arranged for her to go to hospital but she died. Now there are several other women doing prostitution. They all live near the bridge, which is a meeting place for the local men with all the tea stalls. After attending prayer meetings, some men will go to the prostitutes before returning home.

'A young woman was staying in Balichandrapur. She was a refugee from Bangladesh. She had come there as a little girl and was adopted by a businessman who gave her a job to work in his sweetmeat stall. As soon as she was grown-up, he raped her. When she started meeting other men he threw her out. She rented a room and started selling tea. But she was actually selling VD. Young boys, married men and even some local important politicians came to me for treatment after visiting her. They confessed, "We have difficulty in

urinating, pus is coming out." The older men knew of the
danger but the young boys didn't. None of them used con-
traceptives. They feel embarrassed to ask the chemist and
anyway they don't plan the encounter with the prostitutes
in advance. They would be passing by, meet the woman; she
would agree and it takes place in a minute. Where is the time
to get the contraceptive? I have also treated a number of
lorry drivers. They are from other areas. Prostitutes usually
charge five to ten rupees, but they give a concession to regular
customers.

'When I saw young boys suffering from VD I became
worried. I brought it to the notice of their parents and talked
to some of my friends. Together we employed guards near
the prostitutes' homes to stop young boys entering. Once
they caught a father and his son. But some boys supported
the prostitutes and fought with the guards. One came to my
clinic and scolded me. I said, "Don't come to me if you get
VD." But six weeks later the same boy came to me and said,
"Please help me. I have difficulty in urinating." As a doctor
I had to treat him although he had insulted me and I was
angry with him. Now he has become one of the guards. I
cannot blame the prostitutes, they are doing it for money. I
cannot blame the young people, they are curious about sex.
But the children should learn about their bodies and the
dangers of promiscuity.

'There's also incest in the village. Due to overcrowding,
children sleep together. As they grow older they become
curious about the changes that take place in their bodies and
want to explore. There's no sex education at school and
nobody tells the children how their bodies function. Parents
know only how to scold and not to guide. Children learn from
their friends and if the friends are misguided, they are also
misguided. Until my second year at medical college, I did
not know how men and women had sexual intercourse and a
child was conceived. When I asked the tutor how a child
came out of the mother, everybody in the class laughed. I
felt embarrassed.

'Sex education should be introduced in our schools, particularly about pregnancy, and how it occurs. Many girls are made pregnant by their teachers. It's a social problem but nobody thinks or talks about it. Parents are worried that if others knew their daughters were pregnant, it would be difficult for them to find a husband for them. Once, while I was a student at medical college, a friend brought a girl from his village, accompanied by her parents, to be examined by our tutor. She was twelve and her stomach was swollen. Her parents complained that she had a disease. When our tutor examined the girl he found that she was pregnant. My friend told the girl's parents what was wrong, but they refused to accept his opinion and went back. My friend returned from his village after spending the weekend there, looking very upset. When he arrived in the village he saw the dead body of the girl being taken to the cremation ground. Her parents had carried out an abortion on her secretly, but it went wrong.

'In the high school, there was some homosexuality. Handsome boys were always the victims. Even the teachers were after them. In some cases there were romantic attachments and boys would go together to the river-bank in the evenings. But I did not know there were lesbians until I went to medical college. There were two girl students who stayed together, did their shopping together and never mixed with boys. The boys used to call them "les".

'Many boys and girls in the medical college chose each other and got married. Somehow they found partners from the same caste. I had a girl-friend whom I liked very much. She also liked me and we wanted to get married. She was from Maharashtra. When my class teacher saw that I was attached to her he said, "Keep the relationship, but don't go any further than that." After I qualified, I asked her to wait because my parents were anxious to get my sister married first. But she went to Bombay and got married there. Her husband was chosen by her parents. I did not feel heart-broken. There have been no more affairs since then. I'll marry whoever my parents choose. I cannot marry this year because I am preparing for my MD.

'My cousin Kanu, who is two years older than me, got married recently. He used to tell me, "Don't talk to girls, they are bad." He never talked to a girl and I was surprised when some of the villagers said he was going to marry a girl from Assam. "He has fallen in love with her." His parents are very strict and usually keep to the moral order of the village. As Kanu is the only son, his father agreed to the marriage. The villagers say she belongs to a lower caste, but they accepted her. But the neighbours from my settlement said, "Give us two feasts – one for getting married and the other for marrying into a lower caste." Kanu got annoyed. But I told my cousin, "If you come to the village you will have to face the problems. If you stay in the village don't complain, accept the caste feeling. Try to change it through your example."

'When I was a student, my Communist friends used to mix with Harijans and eat with them. I thought it was wrong. The villagers used to sneer, "That boy is eating with Harijans." Now it doesn't seem wrong. First you sit with them, then eat together, have friendship, love and marriage. Kanu's wife is very beautiful and attractive. She charmed the whole settlement. She had already enchanted Kanu. There is a belief that women from Assam turn men into goats during the day and enjoy them as men at night. Kanu certainly takes a lot of interest in her. She cannot speak Oriya and doesn't like Oriya food, even our delicious rice pancakes. Kanu has to go to the market place to buy eggs, bread and biscuits for her breakfast.

'After working for eighteen months in the village, I decided I should have some experience in other places. I worked in a dispensary belonging to a factory at Dhanmandal, ten miles from the village. I needed the money to get my sister married and to educate my two young brothers. There I spent most of my time writing medical certificates. The factory workers, instead of going to work, would go home to their villages and say they were ill. They would come to me and demand certificates. Sometimes I was offered money. If I didn't give certificates they'd get angry and threaten to beat me up. I gave them certificates but never accepted any money.

'Once I was having tea at a roadside café when a newspaper reporter approached me and said, "I understand you are taking money from the factory workers, so why don't you give a donation to our newspaper, we are celebrating the birthday of our editor." I refused. He threatened to publish a story against me. I said, "Go ahead, do it." Then he started quarrelling with me. There were other people watching us. When I said that journalists were using their power to get money from people he got upset and lodged a complaint against me at the police station. He said I had assaulted him. I talked to the police officer in charge, who sympathized with me because the journalist had often taken money from him.

'The reporter went to his editor to publish his story against me. My friends told me to try and see the editor of the newspaper, but when I went to his office he wouldn't see me. A false report was published in the newspaper, saying that I had assaulted the journalist. Those people who read it said I had done the right thing by assaulting him because he harassed people and extracted money from them. He would often go to government officers and ask for a donation. He would say, "People are complaining you are taking bribes, but I don't take it seriously. I know you are an honest man. I can never write against you." So the officers have to give him money, otherwise if stories appear in the newspaper, their superior officers would have to take action. The atmosphere is so dishonest that people won't believe you even if you shout in the middle of the street that you are honest.

'I didn't like working in the dispensary and wanted to do my post-graduation. I enrolled for gynaecology and I'll complete this year. I want to start a nursing home in the village with X-ray and other facilities for investigation. But there's nobody to help me. In the village it's difficult to get good friends and companions. The educated people go to the towns to work. Only the illiterate and half-educated stay in the villages.

'This is now changing because those who went to work in towns thirty years ago have retired and are returning to live in their village. They don't want to stay in the town because it is expensive, but they don't like the village because the facilities of the town, such as water supply, are not there. Also they don't like the atmosphere in the village, which has been polluted by the uneducated politicians. Some of these retired people used to remain aloof, but now they are taking an interest in village affairs, like my own father. He worked in Calcutta for thirty-five years and finds that the loving atmosphere of the village of his childhood has gone. So he and his friends are trying to bring about some changes through a village development committee.'

Pitamber is a *baidya*. His forefathers have always dealt with herbs which they sold at Balichandrapur on market days. But Pitamber has taken it up as a profession and combines *Ayurveda* with homeopathy and modern medicines.

'I knew about herbs from my childhood, while helping my father prepare medicines. But now I face competition from quacks and modern doctors. People want to take a pill and get cured instantly. With herbal treatment certain illnesses can be cured quickly, but chronic illnesses take time. People don't live in the right way and don't eat the right food, so they get all kinds of diseases. There's a saying that right diet is equivalent to ten *baidyas*.

'I understand all the herbs which grow in our village and the surrounding fields. Now because modern drugs have come, the younger generation has almost forgotten them. Yet our civilization is based on eating fruit and vegetables grown in the forest. The animals and birds live happily in the forest by eating those fruit and vegetables, but we human beings suffer because we have lost the understanding of them. There are herbs and leaves which can cure us. A number of people have the knowledge but they do not give their secrets away. As a result the knowledge is dying out. The government has not carried out the necessary research to give people confidence in the traditional methods. Everything is scientific in *Ayurveda*, based on experience. The Chinese have developed their own remedies, such as acupuncture, which is accepted as treatment for curing all over the world. But the knowledge of *Ayurveda* is diminishing.

'Everybody should be educated on how to produce healthy children. In ancient times people had sexual intercourse in order to have children but now they are doing it for pleasure and not observing the correct rules. A woman is fertile for sixteen days after menstruation. Parents wanting healthy children should avoid intercourse for four days after, and on the eleventh and the thirteenth day. The other ten days are suitable but the later days are better for producing strong, healthy and intelligent children with long lives. Apart from those ten days, no sexual intercourse should take place on Sundays, no-moon days, full moon days and on the first, eighth and fourteenth day of the month, because on those days the seeds of men and women are not pure.

'If a child is conceived during the early part of the night it cannot live long. The middle parts are not very good, but the later parts are better. If couples have intercourse on the sixth, eighth, tenth and twelfth nights after menstruation they can have sons. Children conceived on the later dates are better, and when couples have intercourse on the fifth, seventh, ninth and eleventh days, then they have daughters. On the even nights the male seeds are more in number than the female seeds, and on the odd nights the female seeds are more than the male ones. Thirteenth, fourteenth and fifteenth nights are not good at all and should be avoided. Only Mondays, Thursdays and Fridays are good for intercourse. Dawn, dusk and afternoon are harmful.

'Sexual intercourse should only take place when the

couples are fit and well and free from negative emotions such
as sadness, anger, jealousy and any kind of worry. Sexual
intercourse should be avoided when the stomach is full or
empty and the partners are hungry and thirsty.

'The life of a pregnant mother is important. If she has
religious thoughts, then the child becomes religious and
healthy. It acquires the qualities experienced by the mother.
During pregnancy mothers should not fast, grieve, stay
awake at night, sleep during the day or have any sexual
intercourse. The women should be encouraged to work and
not sit idle. Those who work and do physical labour do not
have difficulty in giving birth. The mother's wishes should
be fulfilled, like visiting places or eating a particular type
of food. If all these rules are observed, then healthy and
intelligent children will be born, who will grow up to
be healthy human beings. If you start from that point and
then live correctly, eating the right kind of foods, then
you will have a healthy life and not need expensive treat-
ments.

'The most valuable herb we have got in our garden is
tulashi. It can cure cold, cough, fever and tonsilitis. *Tulashi*
leaves can be drunk as tea, with lemon as a digestive. When
swallowed with water it can cure tonsillitis. The spices which
we take in our food are all good for us. Turmeric is a dis-
infectant, coriander helps in digestion and chronic gastritis,
cumin seeds are digestive and roasted cumin seeds with honey
can check diarrhoea.

'Garlic cures inflammation of the nerves and lowers the
blood fat. Four cloves of garlic should be taken in the morning
and four cloves in the evening, but not on an empty stomach.
Onions have the same properties as garlic, but raw onions
help with heat stroke. *Amala* has vitamin C and is also
digestive, it improves vision and immunity. It has the power
of rejuvenation and it relieves duodenal ulcers – one tea-
spoonful twice daily in warm water. *Harida* is a laxative and
also a digestive – two spoonfuls thrice daily with warm water
gives relief in piles. *Amala* powder with sultanas and sugar

made into pills and sucked cures vomiting, particularly
during pregnancy.

'Tamarind juice with sea salt for children – one teaspoon
thrice a day and for babies ten drops – is good for cold;
also *tulashi* with honey. Mustard oil massaged on the face,
forehead, chest and feet, relieves cold, cough and body-ache.
For indigestion, small pieces of ginger should be taken with
sea salt one hour before eating food; also three to five whole
black peppercorns chewed and drunk with a glass of warm
water fifteen minutes after food. For cholera and dyspepsia,
one leaf of *amarpoi*, plus twenty-five black peppercorns made
into a paste and drunk four times a day. Cholera patients
will definitely be cured. For a blister in the mouth, apply
lamb's milk.

'For cuts, wash the wound with the juice of marigold
leaves, apply crushed marigold leaves and bandage it with a
clean cloth. Any kind of cut or sprain will be cured. For
burns, make a paste of potatoes and apply it on the area –
no blister will come out. Also apply running cold water,
coconut or sesame oil. For stomach problems, *bael* powder
should be mixed with water, and taken twice daily; also
isabgol mixed with water. For back-aches, take laxatives like
harida powder, massage with castor oil, foment and swim in
the river. For lumbago, stand three feet away facing a wall,
bring the feet together so that the toes and the heels touch
one another; rest on the wall, touching with one finger and
then stand on the toes, lifting the heels and count to one
hundred and eight. Then stand on the heels and count to one
hundred and eight – twice in the morning and twice in the
evening for three months.

'A good aphrodisiac is *urid dal* made into powder, fried in
ghi and taken with honey for six months. This will increase
sexual potency and strength; taken regularly it cures impo-
tence. There are other herbal preparations which can give
sexual strength.

'So you see, all these cures are within our reach. The
remedies don't cost much and can all be found near the

sult the Kumuda market almost closed down and
ittee took out a High Court injunction to stop
ur cattle market from operating on Sundays and
ys. The *panchayat* committee contested the case
urt found in favour of Kumuda. The committee
nge the Nanpur dates to Mondays and Thursdays.
da committee then plotted with two other villages
cattle market at Kusupur. The importance of
a business centre was decreasing, so some of its
re eager to start a cattle market there and decided
ays and Sundays. The management committee
 gnored the High Court order and changed its
Wednesdays and Sundays.
rs preferred Nanpur as it was the most con-
nd situated on the bank of a river where they
er for their cattle. The Kumuda and Kusupur
te together to the police complaining that
lisobeyed the order of the High Court. There
nquiry and the sub-divisional officer said that
arket could not be held on those days. But the
obey the order and hundreds of them came
tle. It was impossible for the police to stop

ommittee applied for a daily market but the
sed permission. This ruling was also ignored
arket and the cattle market continued. To
government took over the management of
t, to which the villagers were unable to
s difficult to employ honest people to collect
in India and there are frequent allegations
government agents. The newly formed
proved to the government officer respon-
ts used two receipt books, one for them-
r for the official record.
een taken against the agents it is believed
must be getting his cut from them. The
ollege at Balichandrapur was receiving

village. The only problem is to understand them and to have
faith in them. With faith we can heal people.'

When I asked my sister-in-law to boil some water for drinking, she said everybody in the family now drinks boiled
water, particularly the baby. My brother suffers from chronic
dysentery and has to be very careful. A large pot of water is
boiled daily, strained and stored in an earthen pot to keep it
cool. In my childhood boiled water was only given to patients
as part of their treatment, but the practice was never
extended to the whole family. Now several people who have
returned to the village after working in towns are drinking
boiled water. But it takes a lot of time and money, as fuel is
expensive. In a hot climate, the villagers drink large quantities of water.

When I am in Orissa I carry a flask of boiled water with
me wherever I go. A few years ago a politician friend who
had just been made a government minister invited me to
lunch in Bhubaneswar. Glasses of water were placed on the
table and when I was told the water was not boiled I took
my flask out and drank from it. My friend was sarcastic. 'He
has become a sahib by living in England and cannot adjust
to our system,' he said.

During my next visit I was again invited to have lunch
with him. When I took my flask of water out he said, 'We
only drink boiled water now.' I was surprised by this change.
He explained that when he went on long tours, he had to
drink water from different places. As a result he caught
dysentery and jaundice. Now he always carries boiled water
with him.

In an environment without proper sanitation, water con-
tamination is common. The majority do not have latrines
and the left hand is used for cleansing. There is a strict
division – the right hand does good works, the left dirty
works. Very few people use soap and disinfectants and the
right hand is easily contaminated by the left. Even the act

of worship, when the hands are joined together in prayer, can be a source of infection.

In my childhood there were no latrines, we went into the field. Women often went together, it was a social occasion for them and a chance to gossip. In the summer the fierce heat dried everything up quickly, but in the monsoon the water-soaked ground soon became contaminated. I had chronic dysentery, as did everybody in the village, and several of my cousins had worm infections. Nobody told me that these diseases were caused by infected water.

When my brother worked as a police officer, he was provided with government quarters with latrines. Visiting him gave me the opportunity to use them for the first time. While studying architecture in Bombay I was taught how to design and construct latrines. I suggested to my mother that we could have one in our house, but she said she liked the open air.

When an English friend visited the village in 1966, we decided to build a temporary latrine for him in the garden. I dug a large hole in the ground and put two planks across it for a foot rest. After each visit soil was poured down. My parents liked the idea and constructed a permanent latrine for the family. During my next visit I noticed that my cousins had latrines in their gardens. A latrine is expensive to build and not many villagers can afford it.

10

BUYING AN

IN 1972 a group of vill
tree for a spiritual
relationship of man wit
in flowers and trees. For
bhang and hash. They
they decided to hold it
could start a cattle m
from the traders. As th
it was ideal for a mar
the running of the m
for its management
comed the idea. Fc
site. They could b
Orissa along the
market twice a we
fee would be colle
mers went round
market.

But there wa
four miles up t
and Sundays.
the new mark
notice. In th
obtained a li
it was able
Balichandr
ties for the

As a r
its comm
the Nanp
Wednesda
but the c
had to cha
The Kumu
to start a
Kusupur a
villagers we
on Wednes
at Nanpur
days back to
The trade
venient site
could get wa
markets wro
Nanpur had
was a police e
the Nanpur m
traders did no
to sell their ca
them.
The Nanpur
government refu
and the daily m
take revenge the
the cattle mark
object. It is alwa
government taxe
of fraud against
village committee
sible that his age
selves and the oth
As no action has
the officer in charg
money which the

has now stopped. But the cattle market has helped some shopkeepers and tea sellers in Nanpur, including Padan.

Padan is the only dwarf in the village. He is liked by everybody because one of the incarnations of Vishnu was Baman the Dwarf. So some villagers affectionately call him 'Baman'. He is a Karan, thirty-three and married to a dwarf from another village. The villagers think it is God's plan. He created Padan, so He made a girl for him. Padan's first child died soon after birth. When his wife became pregnant again he took her to Cuttack to be examined by a gynaecologist. A girl was born, perfectly normal. It was felt to be a great achievement by Padan, who was worried that his children would be dwarfs like him.

Padan is a man of independent spirit. He does not want to consider himself disabled and started a tea stall under the bridge twelve years ago. When he was small his father was asked by the villagers to dedicate him to Lord Jagannath at Puri. Even some circus parties wanted him to join them. But his father said, 'No, my son will stay with us.'

'When I was five years old, I was studying in the primary school. All the children were tall and I could not understand why I was so small. I asked my mother and she said that God had created me like that. He Himself was once a dwarf like me. My grandmother was alive then, and she would decorate my face with sandalwood paste and put flowers on my pigtail. She said I looked like baby Krishna.

'Everybody loved me, my friends, my parents, the villagers. Whenever there was a feast I was invited first. Whenever there is a marriage or sacred ceremony now, they take me with them. The villagers believe that I bring good luck. Some call me "Bhagwan". There are seven stalls here and sometimes the stallholders ask me, "Bhagwan, will it rain today?" I smile at them and say, "Yes, it will rain." I just say that to make them happy. I know there are clouds and it will rain, so it rains. But people think I have the power to know the future. I'm not unhappy that I'm a Baman, I have accepted it. It is God's creation. I am free to move about, I can earn a few rupees and be independent.

'My father helped me to start the shop fifteen years ago, when he retired from his job. My elder brother had got married and moved away. My father asked me to stay at home and look after the family affairs. I had decided to leave my village after my parents' death, but when my sister got

married my father asked me to marry. He found a girl for
me, another dwarf. But I don't think of her as a dwarf, only
small. Her father was very poor and could not feed her
properly.

'I did not want to marry but my mother said, "Who's
going to look after you when we die?" So I reluctantly agreed.

'I like my wife. She not only looks after me, but looks after
the whole family – there are twelve of us. When she became
pregnant I was worried that the child would also be a dwarf.
Our first child was a boy but he died soon after coming to
this earth. When my wife became pregnant again I took her
to the hospital at Cuttack for a check-up. All the doctors are
interested in me and my wife. They could not believe that a
dwarf could have a child. My daughter was born on April
14th in the hospital – on New Year's Day according to our
calendar. The doctor said she was a normal and healthy
baby. I cannot believe I'm a father. At the name-giving
ceremony I distributed lots of sweets among my friends. My
mother has named her Laxmi because she will bring us
prosperity.

'The road has helped me. I've got this stall, selling tea,
sweets and snacks. There are six other stalls selling different
things. We help each other. If there was no road it would not
have been possible for me to live.

'I sell about fifty cups of tea a day. A special cup costs
fifty paisa. I buy milk, about six *seers*, at four rupees a *seer*.
So I spend twenty-four rupees on milk. Ordinary tea is forty
paisa a cup. I sell about two hundred cups of tea on market
days. I also sell snacks, sweets and biscuits. I had my tea
stall under the bridge and moved to this side of the road two
years ago. The land belongs to the government and they
have asked for an explanation. An officer came and took our
names, addresses and signatures. All the other stallholders
agreed to give the information so I agreed and put my
signature on the piece of paper.

'I start work at five in the morning and go on until eight
in the evening. On market days I stay longer. A young boy

called Suresh helps me. He is thirteen and the son of a weaver. He was naughty, stayed away from school, chewed pan and smoked *bidis* all day. He cannot read or write and has forgotten whatever he learnt.

'Although I can swim and ride a bicycle, I cannot walk long distances. I cannot walk like other people. I can only walk up to Balichandrapur. I don't want people to treat me in a special way, I want to be like everybody else. I'm always worrying about my wife and daughter, how I can earn some money and look after them properly. I need a regular job with a regular income. Before I was married, I thought of going to Puri after my parents' death, but now I cannot go anywhere.

'In the monsoon I cannot open my stall. My father is old and unable to help me. I wrote a letter to Rajiv Gandhi to give me a job. He wrote to the Chief Secretary to the Government of Orissa and I was called to see him at Bhubaneswar. When I went to his office his assistant told me it was not necessary for me to meet the Secretary. There was a post of Class-IV messenger in the Children's Hospital at Cuttack and he had forwarded my name to the appointing authority. I went for an interview. They didn't give me the job, they appointed a girl without an arm. It is my fate, I don't know when I'll get another interview. I'm waiting.

'I have tried hard to get a job and spent a lot of money. Each time I went to the town I spent fifty rupees and had to close my stall as well. I'm fed up with this government. They don't help people who really need it. They call you for an interview, give you hope and then turn you down. I don't want to do a job any more. Whatever is written in my fate will happen. I must have done something wrong in my previous life that I am born like this.

'All the time I think about my daughter. I don't know how I'll be able to educate her and get her married. I need a minimum of twenty thousand rupees for the dowry. Without it it will be impossible to get a good bridegroom. Sometimes I wish I was not married, but when I look at

the beautiful smile on my daughter's face I forget all my
worries.'

'Have you ever been to a town?' I ask a young boy of fifteen.
   'Yes.'
   'Which one?'
   I expect him to say 'Cuttack' but he says 'Balichandrapur'.
   Only a few years ago Balichandrapur was a weekly market
place held under a banyan tree. Farmers from the surrounding villages came to sell their produce, beautifully
packed in cane baskets. Only about a hundred people came.
Money was a rare commodity and the majority did not have
any. Farmers exchanged goods among themselves.
   A woman came to our house to sell puffed rice and my
mother bought two measures in exchange for a measure of
paddy. Most villagers grew vegetables in their gardens and
had no need to go to the market. Now, Balichandrapur has
a bank, a police station, a high school, a college, and a number
of government offices. The post office has been upgraded with
facilities for telephones and telegrams. It has a pin code –
754205   a system of numbering post offices in India. There
is a cinema, a video hall, shops selling luxury goods, two
photographic studios, several tea stalls and restaurants. The
market is held daily. Naturally, for the young boy Balichandrapur is like a town, yet it has no water supply, no
sanitation and the buildings have grown like mushrooms
without any plan or design.
   The first tea stall belonged to a sweetmeat seller nearly fifty
years ago. He catered for workers returning from Calcutta on
their way to villages near the coast. The tea stall has now
become a restaurant with several branches inside the market
place.
   Balichandrapur is the centre for several villages, with a
total population of around one hundred thousand. It is situated between the expressway and a canal and surrounded by
paddy fields liable to flooding during the monsoon. Brick
structures are being erected on raised platforms protecting

them from flood water. People are building indiscriminately on paddy fields and the demand for land is so great that prices are going up. Balichandrapur is growing rapidly and very soon will become a mini-Cuttack, with open drains, noise and pollution. But people do not seem concerned. They have no concept of an ideal town. Their knowledge is based on Cuttack and Calcutta.

Balapatra's stationery shop is the oldest shop in the town. Balapatra is ninety, bent down with old age. But he still manages the shop with the help of his grandson. He sleeps there and food is brought to him by his children. His mind is alert and he remembers everybody and everything. He doesn't use spectacles and his eyesight is clear. It was a moving experience for me when, during my last visit, I bent down to touch his feet. He stroked my head and said, 'God bless you, Sriman Prafulla.'

'The market place has now become a town, but I have no strength to go and look. I have no time. The site belongs to Lord Jagannath. The local landlords donated the land and the priests collect the tax from the stallholders. Now we pay tax on everything to the government. The sales tax officer comes regularly and makes our life difficult.

'The first shop started fifty years ago. That was the tea stall. Then I started my stationery shop. We had a cloth store before, our family business. We sold all kinds of mill-made cloth from Britain, very little handwoven. Pistol Marka dhotis and saris from England were very comfortable to wear and only cost twelve annas – seventy-five paisa. Labourers earned twenty-five paisa a day – that is, four annas. There were no pants or shirts. I have never worn any shirts or vests, only dhotis and chaddar. Some people had only a dhoti and a *gamcha*. Now dhoti and chaddar are out of fashion. People want to wear shirts and trousers and go everywhere wearing shoes, but in my shop nobody is allowed to come inside wearing shoes. This is Laxmi's place, it is her temple. There was no silk, nylon or *terrycot*. Now they're available but I don't wear them. But my grandson likes *terrycot* shirts and trousers and my son has to pay a lot for them.

'I sold cloth on market days and also went around the villages selling. I used to travel in a radius of ten miles. People paid in money. If I could sell ten to twenty rupees worth of goods a day that was a lot. Now people come to me to buy. My son goes to Calcutta to do the shopping so our prices are cheaper than Cuttack. We supply to traders and store everything for which there is a demand, from needles to electric fans.'

A Brahmin once sold books and paper to schoolchildren from his house. Now his son has opened a bookshop at Balichandrapur selling college books, notebooks, pens, pencils, English language magazines and newspapers published all over India.

The cinema hall was started in 1983 by a man who people

say has the support of local politicians. A licence is necessary and the District Collector at Cuttack is the issuing authority. Only those with political backing and financial influence can get licences. But the video hall was the brainchild of a young unemployed man with a little money to invest. He shows Hindi movies in a small thatched hall with electric fans. He is operating illegally, as the owner of the cinema has put pressure on the District Collector not to grant him a licence.

The cinema is situated by the side of the road connecting Nanpur with Balichandrapur. When the film shows start the road gets congested with rickshaws, cycles and pedestrians. Ticket prices are high – five rupees, equivalent to a labourer's wage for half a day. Oriya films are popular and run for several days. For the Hindi films, many Muslims come from nearby villages. In the afternoons, Muslim women in burkahs come with their children and male relatives to watch them. The films are in colour, full of song, dance and fantasy. The cinema hall is a modest structure with a thatched roof and has two hundred uncomfortable wooden seats, infested with bugs. Once I went there to see a mythological Oriya film depicting gods and goddesses. It was badly made and boring and I left after half an hour. But for the villagers it was an exciting experience.

11

CRIME

THE police station stands on the other side of the canal in Balichandrapur, away from the main centre of the market. It has become important and under the charge of an inspector because of the main road and the increase in crime. The road has brought crime to the local villages; the area was peaceful before. Dacoits come in vehicles from Calcutta and other places with bombs, go into the villages, terrorize people, rob and leave.

Before the police station started in Balichandrapur, no children or young people were ever handed over to the police. Stealing fruit and small items was considered a part of growing up. God Krishna used to steal butter and is affectionately called *makhan chor*. The children were controlled by relatives and it was considered damaging to the image of the village to hand them over to the police. Several of my childhood friends used to steal but they all grew up to be decent human beings. Village disputes were settled by wise men, the village elders. Now every little disagreement is reported to the police and people take pleasure in getting their enemies arrested. Political parties support these divisions, encouraging quarrels among villagers.

During my recent visit I went to enquire if I could buy some films for my camera. A young man running a photographic studio showed me some rolls of Japanese film. They had come through a man on a ship at Paradip and were much cheaper than the London price. I was with an English friend who was fascinated by the elaborate backdrops used for the studio portraits. I persuaded him to be photographed against a colourful lake in Kashmir with a starlit sky.

As the young man prepared the camera, there was a power failure. We waited in the darkness. Suddenly we heard shouting and the sound of people running. When the lights came on again, we were told that there had been a robbery. A trader had collected twenty thousand rupees which he put in a leather bag. He had been sitting in a teashop, drinking tea and talking to his friends. When the electricity went somebody snatched his bag and ran away, disappearing in the crowd. People ran after him but he could not be found. The police were informed, but they were helpless.

To steal in the market place was considered a sin because it belonged to the beloved god, Lord Jagannath. Everybody tried to be honest. Now dishonesty is the norm.

There was a sensation in the village when the police came and arrested Bhima Nayak, the rice trader. He was accused of murdering a businessman from another village, ten miles away.

His name was really Bhramarbar, but the villagers call him 'Bhima' because he looks like the character called Bhima the Wrestler, in the *Mahabharata* – short, fat, dark, with a round face. He used to collect rice from different places and store it in the market place at Balichandrapur. Then he negotiated with dealers and supplied them by truck, making a good living for himself. Some unemployed young men in the village helped him. He gave them money and entertained them in roadside eating places with mutton curry and whisky.

The businessman was supplying Bhima with rice on credit and the debt accumulated to twenty thousand rupees. He had come several times to collect the money but was always given false excuses. Bhima did not want to pay and thought that if he killed the businessman, he would be free from debt.

There was a young boy of twenty called Tutu. He was

unemployed and living with his parents in the village. He was quiet, well-behaved and looked so innocent that you would not think he could ever cause harm to anybody. Bhima invited him to an eating place one day and promised him five thousand rupees if he would kill the businessman. That was a lot of money for Tutu and he could not resist the temptation. Together they made a plan. Bhima would arrange to meet the businessman one evening at a place near Paradip, under the pretext of repaying some of the debt. There Tutu would be waiting with a chopping knife.

On the appointed day the businessman came to Nanpur on his motor bike. He and Bhima went to Balichandrapur where Bhima got a few hundred rupees from a trader and gave them to the businessman. He said he would collect the rest of the money from another trader near Paradip. They set off on the businessman's motor bike. On the way they met Tutu. He also got on the motor bike and they all went off together. It was around six in the evening, dark and drizzling. They stopped at a roadside restaurant, ate meat curry and drank a lot of whisky. Bhima paid and left Tutu and the businessman, saying he was going to collect the money from a trader. After half an hour he returned and said he could not find the man, so they decided to return to Nanpur. They had only gone a few miles when they came to a bridge over a wide river. Tutu complained he was feeling sick. The businessman stopped the motor bike to help Tutu, who suddenly pulled the chopping knife from a canvas bag and pushed it into the businessman's stomach. Bhima and Tutu together killed him and threw the dead body into the river. It was August and the river was flooded. On the way back they threw the motor bike into a canal but forgot to dispose of the chopping knife until they reached the village. This was around midnight. Tutu threw the knife into a pond at the back of the Harijan settlement and went home.

The corpse floated down the river and landed at the mango grove of a flooded village. When the villagers saw it they realized it was a case of murder. They did not want to inform the police as they were frightened of being accused of the crime. With a bamboo pole, they pushed the corpse away and it went on floating down the river to another village a few miles away.

A week had now passed and the corpse was badly decomposed. Some villagers found it and informed the police. A diary wrapped in a plastic bag was still intact and a watch was still on the wrist.

When the businessman did not return to his house his wife became worried. He had frequently spent a night away on business without telling his family, but never longer. As he had told his wife he was going to Nanpur to collect some money, they sent a man there. Bhima told him the businessman had come to see him but had no idea where he went afterwards. The traders of Balichandrapur had seen them together but did not want to get involved and kept quiet. Looking through the diary the police discovered the identity of the corpse. They also found the addresses of several people, including that of Bhima. They came to Nanpur and took him away for questioning.

He was kept in a police cell and interrogated but said nothing. After a couple of days he was still silent. One night, while a police constable was keeping watch, Bhima started talking in his sleep, 'Tutu, where have you put the knife?' The next morning the constable told the investigating officer what he had heard. The investigating officer immediately went to Nanpur and asked if there was anybody in the village called Tutu.

In the meantime, Tutu had been feeling nervous and agitated. He had asked his relatives if the police would arrest him because of his friendship with Bhima. As soon as the police came and started questioning him he immediately told them the entire story of the murder in the presence of some relatives. This was recorded on tape. When Bhima heard of Tutu's confession he also admitted the crime.

At the trial Bhima and Tutu pleaded not guilty. Surprisingly, the knife recovered from the pond and the bloodstained clothes found in the homes of the accused disappeared. The police recordings of the confessions were not properly authenticated and not accepted by the court as evidence. There were no eye-witnesses to the murder. Bhima and Tutu said they had confessed because the police had tortured them. They were acquitted.

The villagers were dismayed, because they felt justice was not done. Bhima's father-in-law was rich and must have bribed the police and the court, they believed.

There is now a saying in the village: 'Give a thousand, commit a murder and walk freely in the market place.'

12

DAILY LIFE IN THE VILLAGE

A L L the year round the sun rises around six in the morning and sets twelve hours later. There is a clear division between day and night, with brilliant sunrises and sunsets. In my childhood we woke up at dawn, when the cock crowed in the Harijan settlement and the crows started their loud chorus. But things have changed. In the mornings there is now the noise of television and film songs from radios in neighbours' houses.

I go to the river for my bath. Friends and children follow me, wanting to talk. I can no longer experience anything on my own. I have to share. If I want to be by myself the villagers think there is something wrong with me – I must be unhappy, worried, otherwise why should I want to be alone?

The river of my childhood has changed. The river-bed has silted up, small islands have developed and farmers have started growing vegetables on them. Very soon the river-bed will rise to the level of the bank. The road and the concrete bridge stand between me, the paddy fields and the distant range of hills. When I return home there is bread and eggs for my breakfast. I had asked for a traditional village breakfast of rice pancakes, but there's nobody to grind the rice and lentils.

The sun has moved up and it is bright and hot. Neatly dressed children go to school, holding books and papers in their arms. The school starts at ten and they have to keep

to time. Each period is marked by the ringing of a bell. The banks and the post office keep to the official times using clocks and watches, but many villagers do not have them. But if they want to catch the first bus to Cuttack they have to be at the bridge by seven in the morning.

Day and night are divided into four main periods – *Sakala*, sunrise until midday; *Dipahara*, midday to sunset; *Sanja*, sunset until about nine in the evening; and *Rati*, from nine till dawn. There are no strict divisions within these periods. When people say that we will meet in *Sakala*, they mean any time between eight and twelve in the morning. When an educated villager complained that a labourer did not come to his house at seven in the morning, I wondered how he could be blamed when he didn't have a clock. But more and more people are beginning to have clocks and watches, and these form an essential part of the dowry. For some it is a symbol of modernity as well as a means of decorating their wrists.

Around ten in the morning a singer with a melodious voice enters the village, followed by small children. He is the *jogi*, the traditional ballad singer. As he goes from house to house, people give him rice, money and vegetables. He is often provided with shelter for the night. He plays a one-stringed instrument which he has made himself and sings in Oriya:

> A cow goes to graze in the forest and meets a tiger.
> The tiger says, 'I want to eat you.'
> The cow says, 'I have a small child who is hungry. Let me feed her first, then you can eat me.'
> The tiger says, 'If I let you go, you won't return.'
> The cow says, 'It is the Age of Truth. I promise by saying three times that I will return.'
> The tiger agrees.
> The cow goes home, feeds the calf and tells it, 'I have promised to go to the tiger. He wants to eat me.'
> The calf says, 'If you leave me I won't have any food and will die. It is better the tiger eats me as well.'
> The cow and the calf go to the tiger and offer themselves to be eaten.
> The tiger thinks, 'If I eat the cow, the calf will die. If I eat the calf I will be killing a baby and be disgraced for ever.'
> The tiger decides not to eat them and lets them go free.

This song is a part of Oriya village culture and very popular because it describes the love between mother and child and the kindness of the good man.

The *jogi* is thirty, married with three children, and tells me about his problems. He comes from a village of *jogis* and leaves home for several days during the dry season. But he finds there is no respect for his singing any more. He is educating his sons to become clerks.

The postman comes at eleven with my mail. Among the letters there is one from a friend in England. The English envelope and stamps stand out from the other letters. I have known the postman for many years and he is a family friend.

After the midday meal, I go to the school. I have been invited to its annual sports day function. As I approach I hear loud Hindi film music coming from a loudspeaker. The school has no electricity but a temporary supply has been especially installed to give importance to the occasion. The noise is overwhelming and I ask the headmistress to stop it. The children present short sketches with words, songs, mime and movement, describing their difficulties in the school. They are aimed at the local politicians, who were invited but didn't turn up.

As I return home I stop to watch a group of villagers playing cards under the banyan tree. A few feet away a man is lying on the ground, sound asleep. The potter arrives. His thin dark body, balancing the load of pots on his head, looks like a piece of moving sculpture. He's our family potter and I have known him since my childhood. He talks to me about his problems: the villagers prefer plastic, aluminium and stainless steel. His handmade grey pots cannot compete with them. Some housewives use gas and electric cookers and find his pots unsuitable. To supplement his income he does tenant farming. He had no money to educate his son, who is helping him. He enjoys being a potter but receives no help or guidance from the government.

I walk to the market place at Balichandrapur to buy a sari for my niece. She is a student and must wear something new for the Saraswati *puja* celebrations. I carefully select a beautiful handwoven cotton sari and give it to her. To my amazement she throws it on the floor in anger, complaining that I have insulted her by buying a handwoven sari: all her friends are going to wear nylon saris and she says they will make fun of her when they see her wearing a cotton sari. 'Your uncle lives in London and can only give you a cotton sari.' I explain to her patiently why cotton is better than nylon and why we should support our own weavers. She bursts out crying, picks up the sari and leaves. She wears it for the *puja* celebrations but the next day I see her mother wearing it. The village weavers complain they cannot compete with synthetic and mill-made fabrics and are forced to weave only towels and fishing nets.

In the evening I go to the river-bank to watch the sunset, an experience I have always enjoyed. But large electric pylons and the noise from the road disturb my peace and sense of unity with Nature. The sun goes down, darkness spreads, cattle return from the grazing ground, a line of birds flies across the sky. There are no flickering oil lamps to welcome the evening, only the harsh electric lights.

I come home and try to write my book. Suddenly the dim electric bulb becomes bright and I watch it becoming brighter and brighter. Suddenly it explodes with a loud noise. All the houses become dark but there is a beautiful moon outside. I sit in the courtyard to write my book by moonlight.

One Sunday morning I went to the house of a neighbour who had a colour television set. On the verandah a crowd of about twenty people had gathered to watch *Ramayana*. The television set, decorated with garlands of flowers, was placed on a wooden table. An oil lamp was lit to welcome the programme and a plate of fruit offered, as a man blew a conch. There was a feeling of anti-climax when the television was switched on and there was no image on the screen. The owner went on adjusting the knobs but nothing happened. The crowd got impatient and cried out loudly, '*Sitaram ki jai*' – 'Long live Sitaram.' Immediately the programme appeared on the screen.

That morning millions of people throughout India saw the same programme in Hindi, depicting the story of Rama, Sita, Laxman, Ravana and Hanuman, produced by Doordarshan, the Indian television authority. This happened every Sunday morning during the serialization. Many stories appeared in the Indian press about the programme. The actors who played the roles of Rama and Sita were worshipped by the viewers. It was reported that in a village a group of monkeys used to come and watch the programme, silently watching Hanuman, the Monkey God, build the road to Sri Lanka with the help of other monkeys. Another story was that a bride was two hours late for her wedding because she and her mother had been watching *Ramayana*. The programme turned out to be the most popular of all programmes, and when it stopped there was a protest.

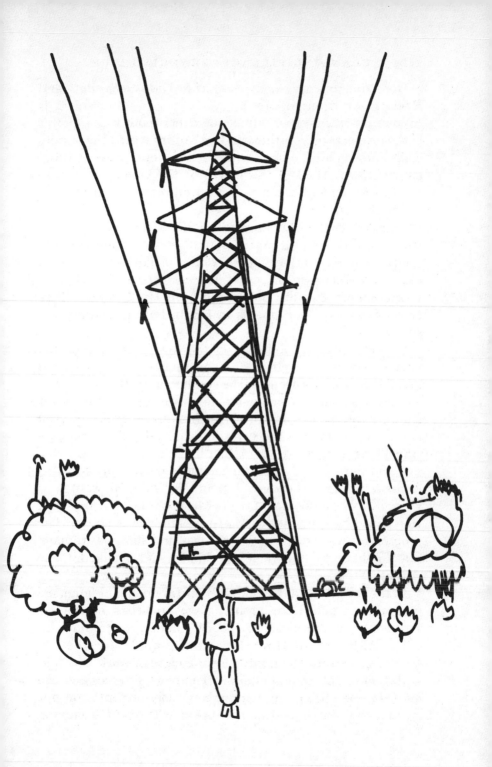

Doordarshan are now serializing *Mahabharata*, and *Ramayana* is being repeated.

Soon after the programme was over, there was a power cut. The electricity authority dare not interrupt the supply while these epics are being shown. In several parts of India crowds have attacked the offices of the government electricity department when power cuts prevented them from seeing the serial.

On Sundays there are always two films. One is in a regional language with English subtitles, but the more popular one is the Hindi movie in the evening. This is usually a well-known old film with lots of songs and dances. Once a week there is a programme showing pop songs from Hindi films. There are at least two soap operas in Hindi, imitating American sitcoms.

Cricket is eagerly followed in the towns and among the village children. Television coverage of international matches is widely watched. The stadium at Cuttack has been accepted as a suitable venue for one-day international cricket matches and the English and West Indian teams have played there. These matches are very popular and college students travel long distances to try to get in.

A journalist friend in the village asked me if I had seen *Yes, Minister*, which is shown on Indian television. He wanted to know if it was a documentary because it was so real to him. He seemed disappointed when I told him it was fiction. The programme was criticized when it was first shown as it made fun of politicians, but when Mrs Gandhi said she liked it, the criticism stopped.

In the early weekday evenings there are regional-language programmes and Doordarshan have opened a station at Cuttack which broadcasts poorly made programmes in Oriya. Although the Hindi programmes are better, they do not compare with the quality of the camera work and presentation of the Indian cinema. The news programmes are most disappointing, imitating the West in presentation but lacking co-ordination. Images appear with mouths moving but no sound, and pictures appear unrelated to the particular news-story. Undue coverage is given to the Prime Minister and government ministers. Watching television you would think that in India there is only one party with no opposition.

Programmes are interrupted by advertisements, usually of glamorous young men and women using cosmetics and wearing beautiful clothes and jewellery in luxurious dream-like settings. Most of the villagers do not understand them as they are in Hindi. They think that the advertisements, which are totally unrelated to their lives, are part of the programme. But they create expectations in the minds of the young and the unreal world of the Hindi film has come to the village home. I felt uncomfortable when I saw an advertisement for spices showing plates heaped with chicken curry and pilau, watched by silent villagers who did not have enough to eat.

Television can inform, entertain, educate and enlighten, but in India it has not yet found a purpose. At present, apart from encouraging consumerism, it is being used to promote the Hindi language and the government.

My fear is that, as in the West, the villagers will lose the ability to entertain themselves and depend on television to do it for them. It will also divide the community into separate families, each one centred around its own set and experiencing life and the world through it. That will be the end of Indian culture.

'I'm ninety. I'm ten years younger than your father. All my friends are dead. I'm the only one who is alive. I almost died in my youth, when I was only nineteen and had cholera. But Mahlia Budha saved me. The medium gave me sherbet and blessed me. That's how I lived. Then everybody respected the medium. But now that devotion has gone. People are not pure any more. They eat chicken and drink alcohol. They also smoke cigarettes and take drugs. I've never smoked in my life. My friends smoked and tried to persuade me but I didn't like the smell of tobacco. It made me feel sick.

'When I was twenty I went to Calcutta to work. There I helped to manage a hotel. I got married when I was twenty-one. My elder brother arranged it. I hadn't seen my wife. It was not like these days when boys and girls see each other before marriage. Then you could only see her after marriage. When you married, you married a bundle of cloth, because the girl came to the wedding platform all covered and you couldn't even see her feet. Whether there was a tiger or a bear inside the bundle, who knows? People accepted, they didn't ask any questions. But there was a great curiosity. What was there inside the bundle? I was happy with my wife. If I hadn't liked her, who else would I like? Whether she was blind or hunchback, I would have to accept her. Somebody has to marry her. Now men want to marry *apsaras*. They may be ugly to look at, but they want beautiful wives. But what will happen to girls who are not so beautiful? If the girls refuse to marry ugly boys, then what will happen?

'Now people are divorcing. A bride from this village left her husband a month after the marriage. She went and stayed with her parents. She's educated and works. In my day only people from the lower caste had divorces but now the educated people are doing it.

'I left Tata and went to Calcutta to work. I worked in the jute factory but my health was affected. My wife asked me to return to the village. I like the village, I didn't like the town. I didn't have a proper room. Here at least I can bathe in the river and go out in the open. There I felt suffocated.

'My family had a few acres of land and I farmed. Although people from my Karan caste don't do manual work I had no such inhibitions. I knew I had to work for myself so I bought a plough and two bullocks. I felt very happy when I brought the first crop of rice into the house. I enjoyed farming but we always have floods or drought. How can you farm if you have to depend on the weather? The government is not helping the farmers. Because there's no profit in farming, the farmers are educating their children to do jobs.

'It's difficult to get labourers, too. They charge a lot these days. The Harijans in our village used to provide some free labour because we had given them our land to build their houses on, but now they are demanding high wages. They are the new Brahmins of our society. You can't tell them anything.

'I had three children, a daughter and two sons. But my sons died in childhood. Only my daughter is alive. I've got her married and now her children are also married. So now I'm a great-grandfather. My wife died fifteen years ago and I live alone. I used to cook some days, but now a neighbour looks after me. My daughter says, "Why don't you come and stay with me? I'll look after you." How can I go and stay with my daughter in a different village? What would people say? This is the village where I was born, I'll stay here and die here.

'I sit here on the verandah and keep an eye on the children. I know who is going to the river, who is playing in the fields. I keep an eye on their activities. You see my *lathi*? They are frightened of it. Their mothers say, "*Oja*, we give you permission to control them. You are helping us a lot." But I can't control the older children. They have no respect for their parents any more.

'Every evening, I go to a tea stall near the bridge and sit there until nine. The stallholder gives me tea and snacks. Then I return home, sometimes alone, and go to bed.

'I believe in God but I don't do any religious rituals. I don't know how to do them. It's enough to have devotion in one's heart. It's not necessary to show it to the outsiders.

'This village has changed a lot, not for the better. Politics have ruined the peace of the village. Now there are three or four different parties and they are all fighting with each other. Before, people respected the old, but now politicians and bureaucrats are respected. The more corrupt you are, the more respected you are. I don't know what is going to happen to this country but I won't be alive to see it.'

13

OUTSIDERS

A RELATIVE took me to see Bimali, an old woman living under the bridge. She looked like a skeleton covered with a piece of torn cloth. I asked my relative how the villagers could have allowed her to starve. 'She would have died a long time ago if they hadn't helped her,' he replied. The villagers will not knowingly let people die for lack of food, but they have their own problems.

Bimali spoke in a very soft voice. 'Arrange food for me, otherwise I will die.'

She was born and brought up in a village in the hilly districts of Orissa. When her husband died she came to live with an older man in a village four miles from Nanpur. His wife had died and he needed a woman to look after him and his children. She lived with him happily for several years until one day he drove her out of the house. She doesn't know why. She had nowhere to go and walked to Nanpur. A tribal woman living under the bridge took pity on her and gave her food and shelter. The next day a villager asked her to work in his house. In the night she slept under the bridge and later, with the help of the tribal family, she made herself a room next to them. Gradually she grew older and weaker. When she fell ill and was unable to work, there was nobody to help her.

I arranged food for her but she said she had lost her appetite. The next day I sent her to the health centre. I wanted to find out if she had TB or some other disease. The doctor examined her and gave her a prescription for liver extract injections and vitamin B with iron. I thought he was callous. When a person hasn't got the money to buy food and is suffering from malnutrition, where would the money come from to buy vitamins?

I went to see the government officer in charge of looking after people in need to find out if he could help Bimali. Looking through his files he said, 'Her name is not on the voters' list, so she is not eligible for government help.'

In India, a person does not exist unless their name is on the voters' list. A vote gives the power to bargain. At election time the Janata party accuses the Congress party of buying votes – 'Take a note, give a vote.'

Bimali has never voted in her life, but would like to if it would help her, she said. She does not know there is such a post as the Prime Minister of India, let alone what his name is.

There are five families of *Adivasis* living under the bridge. I have seen families living under bridges in the cities, but this is a new phenomenon for Nanpur. They use the bridge as a roof and have enclosed the space with bamboo and mud walls. They came to work on the construction of the road in the sixties and stayed on. There is a demand for their services in the village. The men help with the farming and the women work in villagers' homes. They have no land of their own. The land under the bridge belongs to the government. The rooms are neat and clean and the families live together with their cows and goats.

Jadu Munda is forty-five, a tribal, and helps a farmer to plough his land. His physical features are negroid and different from the villagers'.

'Why did you come to Nanpur?'

'To look after my stomach. I do not have any land of my own in the forest. My father was farming for a landlord, but when he died the land was taken away. They said, "Your parents and grandparents were working for us but you are

not helping us in any way, so leave." I was married and had three children to look after. One of my friends was working on the road and told me about it, so I came here.

'My wife and I were childhood friends. We liked each other and got married. We danced to the drums and drank a lot of *handia*. When she was grown-up I asked her, "Will you marry me?" She said "Yes."

'Were there other girls in the village?'

'Yes.'

'Why did you like this particular girl?'

He laughs. 'Our minds became one.'

'Do you have a dowry system?'

'No, not like this village. We make rice wine and when it matures the drums are beaten and the marriage takes place. When men and women become adult they live in separate rooms and dance together in the evening.'

'What about here? Do you do that?'

'No, I have sent my daughter back to the forest, where she can meet one of our own people and marry him.'

'Do you observe your festivals here?'

'The villagers invite us to their festivals, but where is the money to celebrate ours?'

'Do you drink *handia*?'

'No.'

'Why not? You drank it in your village.'

'I don't have enough money to fill my stomach and look after my family, so how can I drink? I haven't been able to educate my children. This land is not mine and the government officers harass me. They demand money. I earn about ten rupees a day and the work is not regular. Where can I get the money to give bribes?

'But I like Nanpur and I have friends here. In the summer months I go back to the forest where I can be alone.'

The villager's attitude to outsiders has changed over the years.

The first foreigner to visit Nanpur was an Englishman,

during the British Raj. He was the sub-divisional officer from Jajpur who came riding on an elephant to settle a dispute. The villagers hid inside their houses.

The next Englishman to visit was Tom, my friend in Bombay. It was in 1959. There were no proper roads then and we came by cycle rickshaws from Cuttack, along the canal embankment. It was thirty miles and took us over five hours. We stayed with my parents for a week and wherever

Tom went, children followed him, observing his every movement. Although Muslims and Christians eat beef and the
villagers think of them as *mlechas*, Tom was greeted by my
parents and invited to enter the house. But while serving
food, my mother avoided touching Tom and dropped the
food on to his plate. He noticed it and I felt embarrassed.

When my mother visited Bombay, we were lent a flat by
a friend. The cook was called Lalu. He was a kind man and
looked after my mother. He took her around and showed
her Bombay. Although they couldn't speak each other's
language, they were able to communicate. During her stay I
took her to visit my friends, among them a Muslim family.
I did not tell my mother they were Muslims, but somehow
she realized who they were and refused to eat or drink in
their house. She might have guessed by not seeing Hindu
gods and goddesses in the house or the vermilion spot on the
women's foreheads. I explained my mother's behaviour to
my friends and they understood.

When my mother returned to the village she told my sister
how good Lalu was to her. My sister exclaimed jokingly,
'Lalu? He must be Lalu Mian, a Muslim. You ate food cooked
by a Muslim? You have lost your caste.'

'It doesn't matter whether he's a Muslim, he's my friend,'
my mother replied.

Over the years her attitude to my non-Hindu friends
changed. Gradually, she started inviting them inside the
house and it was a touching experience for me when she
caught hold of their hands and said, 'God bless you.'

In 1966 when I visited the village from London an art
dealer friend came with me. He wanted to experience Indian
village life. One morning we went to see Mahlia Budha and
he took photographs. The next day I saw Kanhai Barik, the
attendant to Mahlia Budha, talking seriously to my mother.
She looked very worried. I went up to them and asked what
the matter was. Kanhai said, 'Mahlia Budha came to me
during the night and said he was angry. I had taken a beef-
eating foreigner to see him without permission and he had

taken photographs. The whole area was polluted and should immediately be purified by burning ghi and performing a *puja*.'

I said, 'Mahlia Budha also came to me during the night. He said how pleased he was to see us.'

Kanhai looked puzzled and left.

That evening I had invited some friends to dinner to meet my English friend. It was a dark night and I was cooking lamb on the verandah, as no meat is allowed into the kitchen. Suddenly, I heard some women scream. My father, who had been recovering from a severe attack of pleurisy and was extremely weak, had gone outside to urinate without telling anybody. He had stumbled and fallen over. There was a deep cut on his forehead and blood was pouring out. I panicked.

A friend had a jeep and we took my father to the health centre four miles away. As we drove through the village and the countryside, I thought that because Mahlia Budha was angry the accident had happened. I prayed to him and offered a *puja*. When we got to the health centre the doctor had gone on holiday and the pharmacist was away in Cuttack. We took my father to another health centre, twelve miles away. Luckily, the doctor was there. He was asleep and we had to get him out of his bed. He attended to my father and stitched the wound. He also gave him an antibiotic injection. When we returned home it was past midnight. The lamb was cold. We ate a little and went to sleep.

When I woke up in the morning the sun was shining and my father was sitting up on his bed. He said he was feeling better, and I forgot all about giving a *puja* to Mahlia Budha.

In 1972 I was in the village with another English friend. He had constipation and consulted a homeopath who had recently come to practise there, after qualifying in Calcutta. It was his first opportunity to try his hand on an Englishman and he wanted to show, not only to himself but also to the village, how good he was. After consulting his books, he gave the best remedies he could think of, together with instructions. My friend returned to the house happy. But instead of following the instructions properly, he went on taking the little sugar balls as if he was eating sweets.

I had invited some villagers to meet my friend, but he had already started having diarrhoea and was in bed. When they saw him they remarked, 'Doesn't he look like a piece of white log?' In the middle of the night his condition deteriorated, with violent attacks of diarrhoea and vomiting. I gave him whatever medicines I had and prayed to Mahlia Budha. The village was dark and silent and there was nothing else I could do. In the morning his condition improved and he soon got better. Everywhere I heard villagers whisper that the poor sahib was ill. This time I remembered my promise and gave a special *puja* to Mahlia Budha. Kanhai Barik, who performed the *puja*, cut my friend's hair, attended to his feet and massaged him. He had never massaged a sahib before and wanted to show his strength. My friend cried out in pain. When I went to see what had happened, I saw red marks all over his body. They had become friends.

Since then, several foreign visitors have come to the village and have been accepted. They include Canadians, Australians, Japanese and Americans. Most of them come because they have read *My Village, My Life* and want to see the village and meet the people I have written about.

In 1983, just before my yearly visit to the village, I met Ben in a friend's house in London. He was nineteen and had just finished school. Before joining his university he wanted to go and work in India for a few months to experience life there. He said he wanted to come to my village and I gave him my address. I did not think he was serious, but a couple of weeks after I had reached the village, a telegram arrived from Bombay. It was from Ben and he was on his way to Nanpur. I met him at Cuttack and brought him to the village.

I realized that if I stayed there with him, I would stand between him and the villagers. So I made arrangements for his food, introduced him to a few boys of his age who could speak a little English and left the village. When I returned a couple of weeks later Ben had been accepted as a village

boy. He was loved by everybody and invited to villagers'
houses to eat with them. He also attended festivals and
wedding ceremonies and the villagers treated him like their
son. Ben now thinks of Nanpur as his village and has gone
back there several times. He says his stay in the village
changed his life. At university he met an Indian girl, fell in
love and married her.

14
ELECTIONS AND POLITICS

E LECTIONS are usually held in the dry season and particularly after a good harvest, when the villagers are
happy and content. An election brings excitement to the
village. The campaign is conducted like a carnival. People
dance, sing and distribute pamphlets. Politicians come and
make speeches. 'Vote for us. We will do everything for you –
build roads, dig wells, educate your children, give loans and
jobs. You will have a better life.'

Congress, Janata, Communist and various Independent
candidates, all come with loudspeakers. As the majority of
the villagers cannot read, recognizing the party symbols
on the ballot paper is important. At the 1977 election the
Congress symbol was the cow and calf, and the Janata symbol
was a farmer and a wheel. As Janata party workers explained
to the villagers how to mark the ballot paper, they said, 'If
you are a man, vote for a man; if you are a beast, vote for a
beast.' In 1979 the Congress (I) symbol became a hand. The
Janata party workers were sarcastic: 'The hand is not to
bless you, but to slap you.'

The campaign in the 1977 election was important when
the freedom of the individual became the major issue. The
villagers did not approve of Mrs Gandhi putting old politicians in prison simply because they objected to her policies.
So they voted against her. Just before the election the price
of mustard oil, the only oil then used by the villagers for
cooking doubled. The Janata workers took advantage of this

and told the villagers, 'You can only afford to use it as medicine.'

At the time of the election campaign in 1979 the price of kerosene went up and Congress (I) workers had their chance to exploit this. They also convinced the villagers that the Janata politicians were only interested in personal gain and were obstructing the country's development. They said Mrs Gandhi was right to put them in prison during the Emergency. The villagers voted for Congress (I) and Mrs Gandhi came back to power.

When she was assassinated in 1984 the villagers were shocked. The educated were afraid that India would be attacked by China and Pakistan and that the security of the country was at risk. When the election was called, the police and the bureaucrats wanted Rajiv Gandhi as Prime Minister to ensure internal stability and helped the Congress (I) campaign in Orissa. Just before her assassination, Mrs Gandhi had visited the state. A film of her visit to Orissa, made by the state government publicity department, was shown to the villagers during the campaign. It ended with the sound of bullet shots. The screen went blank and the voice of Mrs Gandhi was heard saying she was prepared to sacrifice every drop of her blood for India.

I was in the village at that time. A police inspector had come to supervise the polling booths. When a four-year-old boy sang, 'Rajiv Gandhi has no father, no mother, no brother, vote for him,' he brought out a packet of sweets and gave some to him. Mrs Gandhi's death filled the villagers' hearts with sympathy for Rajiv Gandhi, and Congress (I) came to power with a massive majority.

The villagers had included my name on the electoral register and for the first time I was able to vote in India, an experience I shall never forget. The primary school had been chosen as the polling station for Nanpur. It was a bright sunny day. A long queue gathered outside the tiny schoolroom, with only one door through which the voters entered and left. Ten people were let inside at a time, and women were given priority. The voters were required to sign or give their thumb prints against their names in the list before getting the ballot paper. Only 20 per cent of the villagers can read or write but some have learnt to sign their names. To show that they were educated they insisted on signing. This took two or three minutes for each person. As a result only ten voters were able to cast their votes in half an hour.

'Who have you voted for?' I asked a Harijan who was standing barefoot outside the polling booth. He was about forty-five, well-built and his body was weathered by sun and rain.

'Who the other villagers have voted for.'

'Who is he?'

'Biju Patnaik.'

'But he is not the candidate here.'

'He may not have stood, but his man is the candidate.'

'Why didn't you vote for Rajiv Gandhi?'

'I don't want to be castrated.'

'He doesn't want to castrate people.'

'His mother did, his brother did, and it's in the blood. What's the point of voting for him? As soon as he gets my vote he will sit on a cushion under an electric fan. Who is going to care for me? He will be in Delhi and I will be here. I've never seen Delhi, neither can I afford to go there. It is better for me to vote for you. Then I'll come to you with my problems and you will listen. Biju Patnaik is a local man. I can go and see him, talk to him. Whether he does anything is a different matter, but at least he's an Oriya from Orissa.

'My situation hasn't improved in the last thirty years and I don't expect any benefit from the government. I'm uneducated, illiterate. My father didn't know there was a place called school and he died of cholera when I was very young. I worked as a servant in your settlement. I carried the children on my shoulders and took the cattle to the grazing ground. That is how I could eat. My son is also doing the same thing. He was born after Independence, but I was not able to educate him. There is a school in the village now, but I didn't have the money to feed him, let alone buy clothes and writing materials. So you can understand how I have benefited from the government. All politicians are the same. Indira Gandhi was castrating people to reduce the population and these politicians are doing it by starvation.'

A Harijan boy was holding a rickshaw. He was about twenty-two but looked younger. Malnutrition had affected his growth. His father was a rickshaw-puller and he took over from him.

'Who will you vote for?'

'Whoever will control the price rise.'

'Who is that?'

'Rajiv Gandhi.'

'Who did you vote for last time?'

'I didn't. My parents did, they voted for Indira.'

As we were talking a well-dressed man got into the rickshaw and sat down. 'Don't you recognize me?' he said.

His face looked familiar and I pretended I remembered him. But when I said, 'Yes,' he asked me what his name was. I felt embarrassed and admitted I had forgotten it. As soon as he told me I remembered he was two years junior to me at school. He was a good poet and used to bring some of his poems to show me. I was meeting him after more than thirty years. In the meantime he had got a Master's degree in political science and was working as a professor in a nearby college. He was married and had several children. When I asked him if he had decided who he was going to vote for he said emphatically, 'I'm not going to vote.'

'Why not?'

'They are all thieves. You vote for one and after he is elected he changes his party and joins another. A lot of money changes hands. It makes a mockery of the voters. You can't trust anybody now, they are only interested in themselves.'

Before Independence there were no politicians in the village. I did not know what politics were or what a politician looked like. A man from Kusupur joined Mahatma Gandhi in the freedom struggle and had gone to jail several times, I was told. After Independence, he was garlanded and a procession led him through the village, chanting 'Long live India!' He belonged to the Congress party and had political ambitions but he was never selected as a candidate either for the legislative assembly or parliament. He wore a Gandhi cap and called himself a freedom fighter. He was interested in social work and was involved in building a college at Balichandrapur. Several of his friends had become ministers in the government and he was able to exercise his influence to get things done for some of the villagers.'

Now politics are discussed everywhere. Even little children talk about politics and take part in canvassing.

Sama is the son of a farmer and went to school with my nephew. He was an idealist and interested in social reforms. He rebelled against injustice and spent most of his time organizing student protests. During my annual visit Sama would come to our house and talk to me about socialism. I thought he had the makings of a political leader but he failed his exams several times and to support his family he had to go to Calcutta to work in a factory.

'I don't like Calcutta. It's crowded, noisy, and full of slums. I can't breathe there, I feel suffocated. I have no friends in Calcutta and my wife stays in the village, I can't afford to take her with me. What would she do there when I go to the factory, where I work like a machine? She stays here with my parents, brother and sister. In Nanpur there's clean air and a beautiful river. It's so different from Calcutta. I'd like to come back to the village and have a small farm, not to make money, but just to live. The countryside around Nanpur is peaceful. In Calcutta people are always in a hurry and they are so mercenary.

'I want to be free, but I never feel free there. They tell me I'm an Oriya, but I don't like geographical boundaries. We're all human beings. I don't believe in provincial, national or religious restrictions.

'People are mean. They only think about their personal gain. They say freedom is only in the mind, but you must understand what freedom is. It's not abstract, it's both physical and metaphysical, like love. Love is a feeling, it's abstract in form, you can't hold it or touch it, it has to be felt right inside yourself. But the demonstration of love is different. Some express it by kissing, but for me holding hands is enough. I have seen Western films. They give so much importance to demonstrating love that they've turned it into pornography. In Calcutta you can buy it for ten minutes for ten rupees. But the love between husband and wife and parents and children is divine. We should respect it because we happened out of love.'

'But we can happen out of a rape.'

'It's very rare.'

'Now we watch life on television. We can sit in front of the set and see the world. We don't have to go anywhere and we don't have to imagine anything. It's a television world: my sense of colour and form is controlled by what I've seen on the television screen. Through it, I can experience the sunset in Bombay and the blue sky over Greece. I don't have to watch the sunset by the river. But the colour isn't real. When I watch a real sunset I can feel that there is somebody behind it.

'I like my village but there's still a lot of poverty and suffering. Some people have done well and now have cars and television sets, while others don't get enough to eat. Marx said that everyone should have enough and equal opportunity. He did not say that you should kill your own brothers. Thousands of people were killed at the time of the Chinese Cultural Revolution. We need a revolution in this country, but we should have one without bloodshed.

'I think that there will be a revolution. People are not going to accept the present situation for much longer without food in their stomachs, or an umbrella over their heads to protect them from the sun. Stomach rumbling, and heads throbbing in the heat – these are the experiences which will force people to revolt. Those without anything will try to snatch from those who have something. There'll be fighting and a river of blood will flow. The other day I was in my manager's office. It was air-conditioned, although the factory itself is full of dust and heat. I wanted to scream to the manager, "You are selfish. You only think about yourself. What are you doing for the poor workers? Have you ever thought about them? Our country is only for the selected few. The majority don't get enough to eat yet you go around in cars. There are people lying on the pavement and you sit comfortably in an air-conditioned office. Is that good? If you don't change, we, the workers and the peasants, will make you change."

'But our people won't unite, they can't live or work together in peace. If they could work together they could build a new society. But they're always fighting; Punjabis with Sikhs, Hindus with Muslims; there's always envy. The moral strength of India has collapsed. There are no human beings here, they're pieces of stone.'

A group of unemployed young men sat on the bank of the river and talked about the village.

'There's no unity among us and no organization. We're all interested in our own self-development. The self-employment programmes of the government are not working. Some young people get the money and spend it in other ways. It's not easy to get money from the bank either. You have to prepare a project and give a bribe to the bank manager. Only then will you get the money. Some take money for projects which only exist on paper.

'The population of the village has increased. When I was studying in Class III, there were not so many children. Now the death rate has come down and people are looking after their health. But many are suffering from malnutrition, so they have stunted growth, and the majority are the living dead, without any hope. Those who have jobs prosper a little. But the small farmers, daily labourers and small traders have suffered. They haven't prospered during the last fifteen years because the land is not cultivated properly. People from the high castes, those who have jobs in the towns, and the educated are not working on the land. They get their land farmed by tenant farmers. But they don't benefit from farming because there is no water for irrigation. Now many people have stopped farming and a lot of land remains uncultivated.

'Previously a lot of people died in childhood, but those who survived were healthy and strong. Now lots of people are living because of modern medicine, but they are not growing. Each generation is becoming smaller in physique than before because people don't have enough to eat, and whatever they eat is adulterated.

'The price of everything has gone up. We think twice before buying fish or meat because we have no money, we're always in want.

'There are roads now, so communication is good. This is good for the people who have the physical strength to travel and work. For them the road is beneficial but not for everybody. Those who cannot work don't get any money. Money is not coming to everybody because they don't know what the opportunities are.

'Everybody has become commercially minded. They want money. If they have a litre of milk, they sell it. The farmer sells all his vegetables. Before, people consumed whatever they produced at home but now they're selling everything for money. They spend it on luxuries. The first thing they buy is a television. If you eat well, nobody is going to see, but if you ride a bike or a car, have a radio or a fancy wristwatch and go to cinema then you can show people you have money and are spending it.

'Now dowry has become a drug. Television, motor-cycle, scooter are included. Although the government has made it illegal, the bride's parents are planning how to give more and get more. When people saw on television a government minister's daughter getting married in luxury, what do you think they thought? If your leaders spend crores of rupees on their daughters' weddings and you show it on television, what will be the effect on ordinary people? What sort of examples are they to the public? Those who are supposed to enforce the law against dowry are helping them. The police, the administration, and the Prime Minister attended the wedding and the representatives of foreign countries came there. Also the press and the television. The road that was built for the wedding was paid for by the government. Yet the government says it has to be done, it was part of a development scheme. If it had to be done it could have been done five years later or five years earlier. Why to coincide with the wedding?

'Our leaders are only making speeches, not doing anything. The other day I was sitting at a tea stall at Balichandrapur. The local MP came. I said, "*Namaskar.*" He asked me the way to a certain village and I directed him. This is his constituency and the village is an important one, yet he didn't know how to get there.

'I worked for my MLA during the election campaign. I didn't ask him for any money and he didn't even thank me. I went to his house a couple of times. Although he was there he didn't have the time to see me.

'They don't want to do anything for the unemployed. The MLAs are only interested in their careers. They're busy making money for themselves, how to build houses and buy five cars in their five-year term. They are busy looking after the interests of their families. Where is the time to look after the welfare of the country?

'It applies to all the politicians. They speak with one voice. They teach people all the bad things.'

'Don't you ever want to revolt against the system?'

'We don't think there's anything to gain from revolution.'

A villager said, 'You have never revolted, how can you know whether it is good or bad?'

'One man cannot revolt against the system, we have to do it together.'

'Is there unity among you?'

'We have unity in the village, but there is no unity at the national level.'

'We can buy newspapers in Balichandrapur now. All the important English language newspapers published in India are available here. We also get the news from radio and television. It's a big jump in mass communications. If something happens outside India or inside India we hear about it immediately. TV is mainly in English or Hindi, but there are some programmes in regional languages. It is controlled by the government and they use it for propaganda. It is also being used for political purposes. What happened in Tamil Nadu at the time of Assembly when the politicians attacked each other? It was shown on television. Didn't it produce a bad effect on the public? The government decides what should be shown on television for its own benefit. Television and radio should not be controlled by the government.'

'What are the changes that have occurred in the village during the last fifteen years?'

'We have telephones, a bank at Kusupur and a bank at Balichandrapur. More and more people have electricity. We have cinema, television, video. The roads are better. We can go by bus to Calcutta.'

'The relationship between neighbours has got worse,' said a villager.

'It's not the fault of our government, it's the fault of our society.'

'We are not discussing our government, we are discussing our village.'

'But hasn't the government carried out all these development works?'

They would have happened anyway. Ministers are going on aeroplanes but we don't have the money for our bus fares. We don't have clean drinking water. Last year a girl died of

malnutrition. If the country has made progress, why should the girl die?'

'She died by eating adulterated food. She was small. If she had been a little older she wouldn't have died.'

'Parents can't afford to purchase cow's milk.'

'Why should a child die anyway? This question should be answered by the government.'

'We are told we are free and independent, but we are only free to suffer and die. If we had got Independence through fighting then we would have understood the meaning of independence. There is a difference between the freedom you get through pleading, and the freedom you get from demanding justice. They're not the same. The poor will go on praying to God and die but there won't be any changes in our society. We need a bloody revolution to bring about change. Either we kill or get killed. How long can we go on starving and praying to God? We can't go to the men with power and say, "Don't kill us, allow us to revolt."'

'We're all in one boat. We're all Indians. While one is dying of starvation, the other is prospering. While my neighbour is enjoying life and sleeping on a Dunlopillo mattress, I haven't got the money to send my son to school or buy sugar for my baby. If you're a government officer you'll get several kilos of sugar, because the trader depends on you for his licence. When I go to him, he says he has no sugar. My son dies without proper food. Is this happening in our country or not? Is it true or a lie? Before Independence three or four people in the village were wealthy and had enough to eat, now that has increased to ten, but that's all. The others go hungry.'

The villagers clapped.

'Why don't you express your views on a political platform?'

'I have no courage. You listen now, but you won't support me if I make such a speech in public. If I speak like this outside the village, someone will start a case against me. I don't want to die now, I want to live a little longer. This is all the fault of politics. The politicians who used to come here on foot, begging us to vote for them, have become M L As and go around in cars. We voted for them, we helped them to be where they are now, but we have remained as we were.'

'Politics has become a profession.'

'I'm saying the same thing, I'm not saying anything different.'

'The moral strength of our society is declining. In the past, politicians entered politics to develop the country, but now they cling on to power. They want people to depend on them, to run after them. Our people are like dogs, they run a little, bark a little, and when a little piece of meat is thrown at them, they fight among themselves. This is what has happened to our political system. There is no honesty, no integrity. All these killings that are going on all over India – all politicians are responsible for them.

'The election system has created these problems. Politicians are only interested in how to get elected. The politicians and the bureaucrats have ruined our country.'

Krushna is my childhood friend. He belongs to a business

family and the traders' caste. He is the youngest of three brothers and they are all interested in music and drama. At school his elder brother used to direct plays and compose music and songs. He was well-known in the area. The family had prospered through business and was well-to-do. But his two elder brothers wanted to give an educated image to the family. So while other children left school to help their parents in business, Krushna continued with his studies. He passed matriculation from the village school and then went to Cuttack where he did his Master's degree in arts and a degree in law. Acquiring the qualifications was enough for the family. They did not want Krushna to work as a clerk or an officer, which would mean carrying out the orders of politicians and other bureaucrats.

The eldest brother, who was a local politician, had political ambitions for Krushna. But Krushna was not interested in active politics. He wanted to do social work.

'I have been interested in music and acting since my childhood. My brothers had a clothing shop. They went to Calcutta, brought cloth and sold it in the village. My brothers worked hard. They went to different market places to sell cloth, but now they are both old and weak and not able to carry on. I have to help them, but my mind is not in business. My heart cries when I see poor people suffer and go hungry. I try to help them as much as I can.

'A few years ago, the houses in our settlement caught fire. Our house also got burnt down. We got a loan from the government and rebuilt ours and I also helped other villagers to get a government loan. Most of them could not read or write and did not understand the government machinery. Nobody from the government came to help them either. The other boys in the village were only interested in politics. The villagers were divided. Those who supported the ruling party got the loan; those who had not voted for the ruling party were discriminated against. I could not tolerate it. I went to the Member of the Legislative Assembly for my area. He was sarcastic. "Why don't you go to the politician you voted for?'' he said. But he arranged for everybody to get the loan anyway because he wanted their votes in the next election.

'Politics has corrupted village life. It happened in 1971. Young people came into politics without any inclination for social work. So quarrels and fighting entered the village and houses were divided. The wife supported Congress and the husband supported the opposition. People from different parties came and distributed money, persuading people to vote for their candidates. I was trying to establish a girls' high school. That became a cause of conflict and there was tension between the different castes. At the time of the election, young children went round canvassing; eight- to ten-year-old children were involved. They liked distributing pamphlets and speaking through the microphone and loud-speaker. When politicians came to give lectures, they usually spoke against the rival candidates. But in the end there was a feast and lots of sweets were distributed among the children.

'As the election day came nearer the atmosphere in the village became tense. People were afraid of leaving their homes and going out because as soon as they came out canvassers from the different parties approached them, putting pressure on them to vote for their candidates. The day of the election was like a fair. The parties had arranged cycles and rickshaws to bring the voters from their homes. On the way to the polling booth people from different parties would stand by the road, pulling the villagers' hands to persuade them to vote for their candidates. Sometimes they even threatened. They got so involved in winning elections they forgot there were poor people suffering. Winning the election was enough for the politicians as that gave them power. After the election they rarely came back to the village. When I went to see them in Bhubaneswar to ask them to inaugurate a function in the village, it was impossible to meet them. There were peons and clerks to guard them.

'Politics has entered the grass-roots. The village elects

the *grama panchayat*, which consists of ward members and a *sarpanch*. It is not supposed to be a political election but politicians want to have their base in the villages. So they put in their people to support them. There are three parties fighting against each other: Congress, Communist and Janata but educated people do not enter into this kind of politics. They stay away because of all the fighting that goes on. The *panchayat* election is supposed to be held every three years but recently it was suspended for five years as people were against the ruling party. When the government required public support the *panchayat* elections started again. They are not really interested in helping the village or the villagers, they are only interested in helping themselves.

'There was a politician who used to come here on a bike. I know him. He was not a good student but he was involved in college politics. He failed his exams several times but joined a political party. He stood for the election and was elected as a Member of the Legislative Assembly. Immediately, he went round in a chauffeur-driven car and in a few years I found that he had built a house in the village, one in Cuttack and another in Bhubaneswar. He had bought a bus for his relatives and given several people licences to start businesses. Politics is business here; because politicians know their political life is only for a limited period, they want to make the most of it.

'The road has brought prosperity to the area. It has made Balichandrapur into a commercial centre. Several people have started shops there, and along the main road they have a chance to earn their living. Earning my living is difficult because I don't have a regular job, but I'm religious and I pray to Jagannath and offer myself to him. I have written several poems dedicated to him. In one of them I said, "Lord Jagannath, you hear what I say, you give me what I want. I need nothing else. I speak because I have a need to speak and you hear because you want to hear. Otherwise you would say, 'Goodbye, see you again.' You give me everything I ask for." For instance, I say "O Prabhu, I need five hundred rupees." It comes, somehow. Or if I say I want to be the Prime Minister, I know it is impossible to be a Prime Minister in real life because I have to be elected as an M P first. But in the night I have a dream I become the Prime Minister for five minutes, that is enough for me.'

15

THE VILLAGE COMMITTEE

TIRED of being exploited by politicians and bureaucrats, in 1987, the villagers decided to form a welfare committee. They elected Fakir Charan Mohanty, a retired police inspector, as the president. The committee has been registered under the Societies Act of 1860.

'From 1941 to 1946 I served in World War II in the Royal Indian Air Force. I was released in 1946 and joined the Orissa State Police in the middle of 1947. I retired as an inspector of police in 1980. I was in charge of many important police stations, both in rural and urban areas, including some important cities. My life in the police was unpleasant, hazardous and unrewarding. I always raised my voice against injustice and would not obey any unlawful orders. As a result I did not get any favours from many of my superiors. Some of the superintendents of police, with their IPS badges, considered themselves to be sole monarchs of the forces they commanded, yet having little experience of the investigation of criminal cases. I had a particularly bad time with this type of officer. I lost promotion due to adverse comments in my confidential character reports. But I was widely respected by my colleagues as an efficient investigating officer.

'There was a wide gap between life in the Air Force and life in the police. I regretted having left my military service when I could have continued, had I exercised my option. My juniors rose to the ranks of Wing Commanders and some of them even became Group Captains.

'While in the police I had to work day and night under many hardships with scanty remuneration. Therefore police officers in the lower ranks had to extend their hands to others. Of course there were also corruption charges against some of the top-ranking officers, despite their adequate pay and privileges.

'I had little time to look after my family and my sons did not come up to my expectations. I used to return to my quarters very late at night, after midnight, when my children were asleep. The following morning, I went on duty at about seven. I had no time to take care of my children and look after their education. I had no social life and my wife and children went alone to fairs and festivals.

'Today the police in India are exploited by the politicians, bureaucrats, press and members of the general public, who use them for their own benefit yet do not hesitate to attack them as corrupt. There the police are losing their image day by day. It is unfortunate that the sacrifices made are not recognized by the government and the public. There is much less corruption in the police than in other government departments such as Excise, Forestry, Public Works, Revenue, Commercial Tax, etc. In these departments there is an understanding of giving and taking but in the police, there is only taking and as a result, there is more howling against them.

'Now that I am out of the police I silently observe that inefficiency among officers is rapidly increasing. Most of them lack the ability to investigate and consequently the percentage of acquittals in the criminal courts is very high. The police are used by the ruling party to safeguard their interests and protect their followers. They have now become incapable of protecting the life and property of the general public and, at times, they cannot even protect themselves. Many police officers have lost their lives because of the political tension. Politics has ruined the police administration and political touts are responsible for making police officers corrupt. There is "groupism" among high ranking police officers. They run after the government ministers and especially the Chief Minister for their promotions and posting. The MLAs and ministers are now instructing the officers in charge of the police stations to support their men and save them from criminal charges. It is openly discussed in public that they are protecting dacoits, murderers, smugglers and anti-social elements. The Chief Minister is also not free from such allegations. Some of the police officers are more loyal to the MLAs and ministers than to their police authorities. The district superintendents of police feel helpless. They cannot take disciplinary action against an officer or transfer him to some other place. Many police officers have been politically victimized and there is no appreciation for honesty and efficiency. It is rumoured that some MLAs are getting a share of the bribes collected by the officers in charge of police stations. This is the present state of affairs in the Police Department.

'After my retirement I stayed at Cuttack, where we have a small house. I found that my pension was not sufficient for city life. I decided to stay in my village, where we have a family house and a few acres of land. After shifting to the village I could not bear to see the poverty of the villagers. For a long time I felt helpless, as I could not help them financially. Then I thought of doing some welfare work to help the villagers.

'I was born and brought up in Nanpur, therefore I have a deep attachment to it. Most of the villagers are farmers and poor. The majority of the Harijans are landless and extremely poor. There has been no visible improvement in their condition and many of them do not get one square meal in a day. Many women, with their emaciated bodies, look almost naked in their torn saris. After forty years of Independence the government has failed to raise the living standard of the rural poor. The schemes provided to help them have proved to be failures. The officials responsible for the execution of such schemes are indulging in corruption and as a result the money sanctioned is not properly utilized. The supervisory staff are also not free from the allegation of corruption. Bank officials head the list and are believed to be number one in the country.

'When the villagers asked me to be president of the committee, I readily agreed on the understanding that no politics would be discussed. With our limited resources, and funds collected by local subscriptions, we have already been able to render help to some poor people. Through our endeavours we have settled many long-standing disputes which would have ultimately ended in serious violence and prolonged litigation. But due to political interference there has recently been an unfortunate incident in the village, resulting in a clash between two Harijan communities, one from Nanpur and the other from the adjoining village of Krishnadaspur. In the clash, people from both sides were injured. Bows and arrows were used and several villagers were hurt. A man from Nanpur was taken to the hospital at Cuttack in a critical condition. But fortunately, he survived.

'The incident relates to the cutting of paddy from the government land by the side of the road. A lot of land was compulsorily purchased by the government for the construction of the national expressway in the Nanpur area, but not used. It was auctioned every year to landless Harijans. For many years, the fishermen of Nanpur have been acquiring the land on auction and cultivating it. As the plots are not properly marked, part of their land was illegally used by the Harijans of Krishnadaspur. This year also, the fishermen of Nanpur got the land at the auction, and for the first time they obtained receipts giving the size of the plots. This was on the advice of our committee. The Harijans of Krishnadaspur realized that this year they would not be allowed to cultivate the land as the Harijans of Nanpur had the support of the committee. Some of the Krisnadaspur Harijans, with the help of the *sarpanchr*, of Balichandrapur, who was opposed to our committee, approached the local Congress M L A. He does not like the villagers of Nanpur because, in the last election, most of them did not vote for him. The Harijans of Krishnadaspur forcibly cultivated

about two acres of the land taken on auction by the fishermen of Nanpur, so a dispute arose over the harvesting of the
paddy.

'The fishermen of Nanpur came to the village committee
for help. We discussed the issue in the working committee
and decided to settle the dispute amicably. Some of the
Harijans of Krishnadaspur were called and after long discussions, a compromise was reached. It was agreed that the
Harijans of Krishnadaspur would give one bag of paddy and
fifty rupees to the fishermen of Nanpur and give up the land
before the cultivation of the winter crops. But this was not
accepted by a minority of the Nanpur fishermen and without
the knowledge of the committee, they opposed the claims of
Krishnadaspur. Consequently there was a clash between both
parties in the paddy fields.

'As a result, two criminal cases were registered. Forty-five
persons from Nanpur, including myself, the vice-president,
the secretary, and some members of the committee, were
accused. Fifteen persons from both sides were arrested and
kept in custody. Now all of them are on bail and the cases
are under investigation. The local police, under political
pressure, are supporting the Harijans of Krishnadaspur and
have not followed the proper procedures for collecting evidence in the cases filed against them. No steps have been
taken to search the houses of the accused persons and to
seize the weapons used. The station officer has caused the
disappearance of vital evidence. Proceedings have also been
started against members of both the groups to maintain
peace and tranquillity during the enquiries. The paddy on
the disputed plots has been harvested in the presence of the
police and kept in the custody of the local revenue inspector.
The cases have been registered at Jajpur, about thirty miles
away.

'An additional superintendent of police, Cuttack, took up
the investigation and visited Balichandrapur. After having
discussions with members from both parties and consulting
local opinion, including myself, he directed an engineer to

measure and identify the disputed land. During the measurement, it was found that the Harijans of Krishnadaspur had
unlawfully cultivated about two acres of land taken on
auction by the fishermen of Nanpur. The additional superintendent of police said that the Harijans of Krishnadaspur
should give a portion of the produce and the auction money
to the fishermen of Nanpur, and this should be amicably
decided. But this could not materialize because of the interference by the local M L A.

'I called on the additional superintendent of police in his
office at Cuttack and he told me that the local M L A was
frequently telephoning him. He openly admitted that there
is a lot of political pressure on the police and M L As are
always interfering. That morning he had cancelled an official
meeting in order to meet an M P who had asked to see him.
The M P did not turn up but in the afternoon a man arrived,
saying he had been sent by him to arrange police help in
protecting his fishing tank. I was surprised when he said he
was unable to take action against some of his officers, as they
were supported by politicians. Although he wanted to give
justice to the case concerning our village he could not, due
to political pressure.

'The local M L A and the *sarpanch*, who belong to the
Congress party, do not like our committee because we are
non-political and our aim is to help the villagers impartially.

'This incident has given opportunity to people with vested
interests to criticize the office-bearers of the committee. But
most of the villagers support the stand taken by us. I very
much regret the incident and am still trying for a peaceful
settlement.

'The members of the different political parties, and particularly the party in power, are trying to take advantage of
the incident. But the committee will remain free from
politics. We will continue our efforts to carry out positive
welfare work for the village.'

It is the morning of 26 January. The village committee has

organized a meeting to celebrate Republic Day. The sun is shining, the sky is blue and a cool breeze is blowing from the river. The villagers have gathered on common ground in a mango grove. The school children arrive, marching in line, led by a girl holding the national flag.

A temporary platform has been erected, covered with a canopy and decorated with leaves and flowers. A few chairs and a table have been placed on the platform for the important guests. I am invited to sit on the platform with members of the committee. We wait for the *sarpanch* to arrive but he doesn't come, so garlands are placed around our necks and the president of the committee opens the meeting:

'This is an auspicious day for us. Over forty years have passed since India became independent from the British Raj. Those were the days of darkness. Now, politicians and government officers come and tell us this is a time of light and they have done so much for us. But our children do not get enough to eat, most of our women have nothing to wear, there is little work in the village and many educated young are unemployed. All the government has done is to help the few people who support them. But the aim of our committee is to work outside party politics and carry out village development. This is the first time such a committee has been formed. All our members and workers have taken vows that no party politics will be discussed in our meetings. Our members have varied political beliefs – Congress, Janata, Communist – but we have never discussed party politics and never will. If our committee is successful, we will set an example for other villages to follow.

'Our aim is to create a village according to the philosophy of Rama Raj, based on honesty and justice. We will help to settle disputes among villagers and see that they do not run to police stations and courts, spending a lot of money and getting harassed. We have already settled several cases which could easily have ended in prolonged litigation. But people with vested interests are against us. They want our committee to fail.

'We must help the government whatever their party, because they have the mammoth task of developing India. We have a police station at Balichandrapur. If we co-operate, the police won't waste time dealing with small quarrels and will be free to work for the prevention of serious crimes.

'We have no money, but with your help that can be resolved. If each family donates one rupee a month we can build up a fund. Then we will be able to help poor students to continue their studies, and the sick to get medical treatment. In spite of repeated requests the school buildings are still not maintained by the government. They are overcrowded and the children don't have proper reading materials. We must help them too.

'Our village is divided into settlements and the road divides us further. We must have a sense of belonging to the village. This is our village and we must improve it. This is our Orissa, our India, our world. We must all work to live in peaceful co-existence.

'The educated young are leaving the village and only the old and the half-educated are staying. The others are traders, businessmen, farmers and craftsmen. But they do not attend our committee meetings regularly. We should all know about our responsibility to our village and take part in the work of the committee. Otherwise it will become like a government committee without any sense of involvement or participation.

'We should work together. The village is our mother and we are all her children. The rich, the poor, the old, the young, the Brahmins and the non-Brahmins – we are all brothers and sisters. We must feel and share the pain of our fellow-villagers and take action to remove it. If we do not help each other, if we do not help our poor brothers and sisters to stand on their feet, our committee will not be successful. We should respect each other and try to be good and honest. Only then can we help others through our example.'

Everybody claps. The national flag is hoisted and the children sing 'Bande Mataram'. In one voice, the villagers cry out, 'We want freedom from poverty, suffering and exploitation.'

POSTSCRIPT

Ten months later, Rajiv Gandhi called the general election. I was in London and the book was complete and under production. Although I could guess how the villagers were going to vote, I wanted to find out the real situation. I also wanted to cast my vote.

When I arrived at Nanpur ten days before the election everybody was discussing politics and corruption everywhere — in tea stalls, in paddy fields, under banyan trees. Television and radio were broadcasting propaganda for the government and the newspapers were full of different views. But the villagers had made their minds up, they wanted a change.

'A change is essential,' Kundera the farmer said. He compared India with his rice field and the politicians with rice plants. 'I change these every year so that I can recognize the hybrids and remove them, otherwise they will destroy my entire field. Similarly, our country is full of corrupt politicians. We must remove them, otherwise they will ruin our country.'

'I will vote for the Opposition, not Congress,' said a nineteen year old college student. 'Soon after the voting age was reduced to eighteen our college union election was held on party lines and the Congress candidate lost. It is an indication of what is going to happen in Orissa.'

'There is an Opposition breeze blowing from the north,' said his friend.

'No, it is definitely a cyclone,' said another young man.

'We don't expect anything from the Opposition but we want to teach the Congress politicians a lesson,' they all said together.

I was told by the president of the village committee that as soon as the election was announced the unemployed young men shouted, 'We shall definitely oust the corrupt government.' They went from door to door asking people to vote for Janata Dal, a major Opposition party with the wheel as its symbol.

The price rise became the major issue. 'We can't afford to buy sugar, the only source of energy for the poor,' said Sidhia the Harijan. 'Our evenings are dark, we can't afford to buy kerosene for our oil lamps. Even the price of salt has doubled in one year. Still there is no place for the poor in this country.'

The president of the village committee gave me his assessment. 'The villagers are now politically very conscious. When television and radio announced development plans in the names of Nehru and Indira Gandhi, the villagers were sarcastic. "Empty promises," they said. A labourer on fifteen rupees a day finds it difficult to manage his family. He sees how during the last ten years the others have prospered and the politician elected to power has only looked after his own interest. He is a citizen like any other citizen. He has a vote like everybody else. Why should he go on suffering while others prosper? You go to the public meeting Rajiv Gandhi is going to address at a place near here. You will see for yourself how he and his government are really alienated from the people.'

I arrived at the meeting ground at one in the afternoon and the Indian sun was unbearably strong. A crowd of about ten thousand people had gathered on the site which was rocky and barren. There were men, women, young, old – some women with children in their arms – and the majority suffered from malnutrition.

I was talking to a farmer from a nearby village when there was excitement among the crowd. A helicopter had appeared on the horizon. Soon, three Indian Air Force helicopters landed in the middle of the crowd, producing a cloud of dust. Rajiv Gandhi descended with a number of well-fed, well-clad Orissa politicians, including the Chief Minister, and walked up to the covered stage. But as soon as he started to speak the crowd began to leave. 'It is a sign of rejection. They had only come to see the helicopters,' one of my friends commented.

'People don't want a corrupt prime minister. If he had resigned on the Bofors issue and sought re-election, people would have trusted him and voted for him,' said a farmer.

'We don't like wearing the same dhoti every day. When it gets dirty we get it cleaned,' said another farmer.

Soon that symbol became a reality. On the day of the election the villagers of Nanpur came out in large numbers to vote.

'People don't get enough to eat and some come with empty stomachs to vote because they still have hope for a better life,' said the president of the village committee.

The Opposition candidate won. The Congress party lost in Orissa.

The villagers were worried that Opposition members would fight among themselves over the prime ministership and were relieved when the President of India invited Mr V. P. Singh, the Opposition leader, to form a government.

The young people of Nanpur danced with joy.

GLOSSARY

abadhan: astrologer, teacher
Adivasis: tribal people
amarpoi: a herb
annaprasanna: ceremony of feeding cooked rice to a baby
when it is nine months old
apsara: beautiful nymph, singing and dancing in the heav-
enly courts
ascharjya: wonderment
atma: soul
Ayurveda: ancient system of medical treatment based on
natural cure
Ayurvedic modak: herbal preparation used as a tonic, in
solid round form
ayusmana hua: a blessing meaning 'May you live long'
bael: fruit from the bael tree used for curing stomach ail-
ments. The leaves are considered sacred and offered to
Lord Shiva, the God of Creation
baidya: herbal practitioner
Baisakh: lunar month of April/May
baman: dwarf
Bande Mataram: Indian national song meaning 'We greet
you, Mother', that is Mother India
Bhagabat toongi: hut where *Bhagabat* (sacred scripture) is
kept and read
Bhagavadgita: part of the *Mahabharata* containing the
sacred teachings of Krishna

Bhagwan: God
bhai: brother
bhang: hashish leaves
bibhuti: holy ash
bidi: rolled tobacco in kendu leaves. An inexpensive country cigarette
bilati: British
bohu: daughter-in-law
burkah: covering of the body and face worn by Muslim women
chaddar: shawl worn by both men and women
chapati: circular bread, similar to pancake
chappals: sandals
chatashali: nursery school where children are taught to read and write
chor: thief
crore: ten million
dacoit: member of a gang of robbers
dakshina: payment given to a Brahmin for his religious services
dali bhat: dal and rice
danta: tooth
dasa: servant
dasa melak: the ten ways of matching horoscopes for weddings
dhaba: simple roadside eating place
Dipahara: afternoon
diwan: administrator of a feudal state
dowry: property brought by a wife at marriage, now illegal
Dusserah: autumn festival to worship Durga, Goddess of Energy
fakir: Muslim holy man
fakir charan: feet of a fakir
420: section of the Indian penal code dealing with fraud
gamcha: thin cotton towel
ganjod: someone addicted to smoking hashish

gauni: container made of cane for measuring grain, holding eight pounds

grama panchayat: village council, derived from the ancient system of settling disputes by five elders chosen by the villagers

handia: fermented rice wine

harida: a herb used in Ayurvedic medicine

Harijan: People of God, formerly known as 'Untouchables'

havildar: sergeant

Holi: spring festival to worship Krishna

isabgol: herb used as a laxative

jatak: horoscope, usually engraved on a palm leaf

jezman: client

jogi: wandering singer

jyoti: light

Kama Sutra: ancient Hindu manual of love-making

Katki: person born and brought up in the city of Cuttack

khadi: handspun and handwoven material

Kiristani: Christian

kirtan: devotional singing accompanied by special drums and cymbals, performed by the worshippers of Vishnu

Krushnapakshya: period from the day after the full moon to the new moon day

ladu: dry sweet made of gram flour

lakh: one hundred thousand

lathi: stick

Leela: Divine Play

LP: Lower Primary school

Mahabharata: religious epic

makhan: butter

makhan chor: butter thief. A reference to baby Krishna stealing butter

mantra: sacred words and sounds for rhythmic chanting

MLA: Member of the Legislative Assembly (state government)

mlecha: unclean, polluted

MSC: Middle School Certificate

naga nadi: like two cobras. A reference to matching horoscopes for selecting marriage partners
namaskar: main Hindu greeting with folded hands
napunsak: impotent
Nasik: town in Maharastra
nazar: evil look, believed to cast an evil influence
nisapo: hearing of a dispute by the village council
oja: grandfather
paddy: rice with husk
paisa: Indian coin; there are now 100 paisa in a rupee
pakhal bhata: water rice
pan: betel leaves with nuts, spices and sometimes tobacco,
chewed as a digestive making the mouth and lips red
pana: basket weaver, a Harijan
panjika: almanac
Parvati: consort of Shiva, God of Creation
peon: office attendant
piada: messenger
Prabhu: God
Pravati: morning star
puja: worship
Puranas: ancient mythological tales
puri: unleavened wheat flour fried in a circular shape,
puffed when freshly cooked
raj jotak: union of kings in the matching of horoscopes for
marriages
Rama Raj: rule of Rama, symbolizing fairness and justice
Ramayana: religious epic
Rati: night
roti: unleavened bread
rupee: Indian coin; there are now approximately 30 rupees
in a pound
Sakala: morning
Sani: Saturn
Sani sapta: in astrology: time when Saturn is angry
Sanja: evening
Saraswati: Goddess of Learning

sari: thin garment worn by women, fifty inches wide and five to six yards long

sarpanch: head of the grama panchayat

sashughara: house of the mother-in-law

seer: measurement of weight, approximately equivalent to two pounds

seva: service

shakti: female energy

shanti: peace

shastra: religious text

shiva lingam: phallic symbol of Lord Shiva, God of Creation

swaraj: self-rule

terrycot: terylene and cotton synthetic fabric

thakura ghara: room or house where gods are kept

tilak: chalky earth used for decorating the body

tulashi: sacred basil, having many medicinal properties, offered to Lord Vishnu, the Preserver

UP: Upper Primary school

urid dal: split black chickpeas

Varuna: God of the Sky. Rare tree named after the deity

Vasudha: Mother Earth

vedas: ancient Hindu scriptures